Praise for Gail Godwin

"Gail Godwin is one of the best writers we have today."

—*Atlanta Journal-Constitution*

"Godwin's plots are compelling; her atmospheres and imagery are bewitching."

—*The Christian Science Monitor*

"Godwin moves us, not by high-voltage language, but by a generous-spirited chronicling of the aches and illusions that flesh is heir to."

—*Chicago Sun-Times Book Week*

"Gail Godwin is a wonderful writer."

—*The Boston Globe*

DREAM
CHILDREN

DREAM CHILDREN

Stories by
GAIL GODWIN

Ballantine Books · New York

http://www.randomhouse.com

This edition published by arrangement with Alfred A. Knopf, Inc.

The following stories have been published previously: "False Lights" and "A Sorrowful Woman," in *Esquire*; "Some Side Effects of Time Travel" and "Why Does a Great Man Love?," in *Paris Review*; "My Lover, His Summer Vacation" and "The Woman Who Kept Her Poet," in *Cosmopolitan*; "Interstices" and "Nobody's Home," in *Harper's Magazine* and in *Bitches and Sad Ladies*; "The Legacy of the Motes," in *Iowa Review*; "Death in Puerto Vallarta," in *The Lamp in the Spine*; "An Intermediate Stop," in *North American Review*.

Library of Congress Catalog Card Number: 96-96059

ISBN: 0-345-38992-1

Cover design by Dreu Pennington-McNeil
Cover illustration © Prudence See 1995

Manufactured in the United States of America
First Ballantine Books Edition: August 1996
10 9 8 7 6 5 4 3 2 1

to WILLIAM I. GODWIN
and to the memory of
MOSE W. GODWIN

CONTENTS

DREAM
CHILDREN

DREAM CHILDREN

*The worst thing. Such a terrible thing to happen to a
young woman. It's a wonder she didn't go mad.*

As she went about her errands, a cheerful, neat young
woman, a wife, wearing pants with permanent creases and
safari jackets and high-necked sweaters that folded chastely
just below the line of the small gold hoops she wore in
her ears, she imagined people saying this, or thinking it to
themselves. But nobody knew. Nobody knew anything,
other than that she and her husband had moved here a
year ago, as so many couples were moving farther away
from the city, the husband commuting, or staying in town
during the week—as hers did. There was nobody here, in
this quaint, unspoiled village, nestled in the foothills of
the mountains, who could have looked at her and guessed
that anything out of the ordinary, predictable, auspicious
spectrum of things that happen to bright, attractive young
women had happened to her. She always returned her
books to the local library on time; she bought liquor at the
local liquor store only on Friday, before she went to meet
her husband's bus from the city. He was something in
television, a producer? So many ambitious young couples
moving to this Dutch farming village, founded in 1690, to
restore ruined fieldstone houses and plant herb gardens
and keep their own horses and discover the relief of finding
oneself insignificant in Nature for the first time!

*A terrible thing. So freakish. If you read it in a story
or saw it on TV, you'd say no, this sort of thing could never
happen in an American hospital.*

DePuy, who owned the old Patroon farm adjacent to her land, frequently glimpsed her racing her horse in the early morning, when the mists still lay on the fields, sometimes just before the sun came up and there was a frost on everything. "One woodchuck hole and she and that stallion will both have to be put out of their misery," he told his wife. "She's too reckless. I'll bet you her old man doesn't know she goes streaking to hell across the fields like that." Mrs. DePuy nodded, silent, and went about her business. She, too, watched that other woman ride, a woman not much younger than herself, but with an aura of romance—of tragedy, perhaps. The way she looked: like those heroines in English novels who ride off their bad tempers and un-requited love affairs, clenching their thighs against the flanks of spirited horses with murderous red eyes. Mrs. DePuy, who had ridden since the age of three, recognized something beyond recklessness in that elegant young woman, in her crisp checked shirts and her dove-gray jodhpurs. *She has nothing to fear anymore,* thought the farmer's wife, with sure feminine instinct; she both envied and pitied her. "What she needs is children," remarked DePuy.

"A Dry Sack, a Remy Martin, and . . . let's see, a half-gallon of the Chablis, and I think I'd better take a Scotch . . . and the Mouton-Cadet . . . and maybe a dry vermouth." Mrs. Frye, another farmer's wife, who runs the liquor store, asks if her husband is bringing company for the weekend. "He sure is; we couldn't drink all that by our-selves," and the young woman laughs, her lovely teeth exposed, her small gold earrings quivering in the light. "You know, I saw his name—on the television the other night," says Mrs. Frye. "It was at the beginning of that new comedy show, the one with the woman who used to be on another show with her husband and little girl, only they divorced, you know the one?" "Of course I do. It's one of my husband's shows. I'll tell him you watched it." Mrs. Frye puts the bottles in an empty box, carefully inserting wedges of cardboard between them. Through the window of her store she sees her customer's pert bottle-green car, some sort of little foreign car with the engine running, filled with groceries and weekend parcels, and that big silver-blue dog sitting up in the front seat just like a human being. "I think that kind of thing is so sad," says Mrs. Frye; "families breaking up, poor little children having to divide their loyalties." "I couldn't agree more," replies the young woman, nodding gravely. Such a personable, polite girl! "Are you sure you can carry that, dear? I can get Earl from the back. . . ." But the girl has it hoisted on her shoulder in a flash, is airily maneuvering between unopened cartons stacked in the aisle, in her pretty boots. Her perfume lingers in Mrs. Frye's store for a half-hour after she has driven away.

After dinner, her husband and his friends drank brandy. She lay in front of the fire, stroking the dog, and listening to Victoria Darrow, the news commentator, in person. A few minutes ago, they had all watched Victoria on TV. "That's right; thirty-nine!" Victoria now whispered to her. "What? That's kind of you. I'm photogenic, thank God, or I'd have been put out to pasture long before. . . . I look five, maybe seven years younger on the screen . . . but the point I'm getting at is, I went to this doctor and he said, 'If you want to do this thing, you'd better go home today and get started.' He told me—did you know this? Did you know that a woman is born with all the eggs she'll ever have, and when she gets to my age, the ones that are left have been rattling around so long they're a little shopworn; then every time you fly you get an extra dose of radioactivity, so those poor eggs. He told me when a woman over forty comes into his office pregnant, his heart sinks; that's why he quit practicing obstetrics, he said; he could still remember the screams of a woman whose baby he delivered . . . she was having natural childbirth and she kept saying, 'Why won't you let me see it, I insist on seeing it,' and so he had to, and he says he can still hear her screaming."

"Oh, what was—what was wrong with it?"

But she never got the answer. Her husband, white around the lips, was standing over Victoria ominously, offering the Remy Martin bottle. "Vicky, let me pour you some more," he said. And to his wife, "I think Blue Boy needs to go out."

"Yes, yes, of course. Please excuse me, Victoria. I'll just be . . ."

Her husband followed her to the kitchen, his hand on the back of her neck. "Are you okay? That stupid yammering bitch. She and her twenty-six-year-old lover! I wish I'd never brought them, but she's been hinting around the studio for weeks."

"But I like them, I like having them. I'm fine. Please go back. I'll take the dog out and come back. Please . . ."

"All right. If you're sure you're okay." He backed away, hands dangling at his sides. A handsome man, wearing a pink shirt with Guatemalan embroidery. Thick black hair and a face rather boyish, but cunning. Last weekend she had sat beside him, alone in this house, just the two of them, and watched him on television: a documentary, in several parts, in which TV "examines itself." There was his double, sitting in an armchair in his executive office, coolly replying to the questions of Victoria Darrow. "*Do you personally watch all the programs you produce, Mr. Mc-Nair?*" She watched the man on the screen, how he moved his lips when he spoke, but kept the rest of his face, his body perfectly still. Funny, she had never noticed this before. He managed to say that he did and did not watch all the programs he produced.

Now, in the kitchen, she looked at him backing away, a

little like a renegade in one of his own shows—a desperate man, perhaps, who has just killed somebody and is backing away, hands dangling loosely at his sides, Mr. McNair, her husband. That man on the screen. Once a lover above her in bed. That friend who held her hand in the hospital. One hand in hers, the other holding the stopwatch. For a brief instant, all the images coalesce and she feels something again. But once outside, under the galaxies of autumn-sharp stars, the intelligent dog at her heels like some smart gray ghost, she is glad to be free of all that. She walks quickly over the damp grass to the barn, to look in on her horse. She understands something: her husband, Victoria Darrow lead double lives that seem perfectly normal to them. But if she told her husband that she, too, is in two lives, he would become alarmed; he would sell this house and make her move back to the city where he could keep an eye on her welfare.

She is discovering people like herself, down through the centuries, all over the world. She scours books with titles like *The Timeless Moment, The Sleeping Prophet, Between Two Worlds, Silent Union: A Record of Unwilled Communication;* collecting evidence, weaving a sort of underworld net of colleagues around her.

A rainy fall day. Too wet to ride. The silver dog asleep beside her in her special alcove, a padded window seat filled with pillows and books. She is looking down on the fields of dried lithrium, and the fir trees beyond, and the mountains gauzy with fog and rain, thinking, in a kind of terror and ecstasy, about all these connections. A book lies face down on her lap. She has just read the following:

Theodore Dreiser and his friend John Cowper Powys had been dining at Dreiser's place on West Fifty Seventh Street. As Powys made ready to leave and catch his train to the little town up the Hudson, where he was then living, he told Dreiser, "I'll appear before you here, later in the evening."

Dreiser laughed. "Are you going to turn yourself into a ghost, or have you a spare key?" he asked. Powys said he would return "in some form," he didn't know exactly what kind.

After his friend left, Dreiser sat up and read for two hours. Then he looked up and saw Powys standing in the doorway to the living room. It was Powys' features, his tall stature, even the loose tweed garments which he wore. Dreiser rose at once and strode towards the figure, saying, "Well, John, you kept your word. Come on in and tell me how you did it." But the figure vanished when Dreiser came within three feet of it.

Dreiser then went to the telephone and called Powys' house in the country. Powys answered. Dreiser told him what had happened and Powys said, "I told you I'd be there and you oughtn't to be surprised." But he refused to discuss how he had done it, if, indeed, he knew how.

"But don't you get frightened, up here all by yourself, alone with all these creaky sounds?" asked Victoria the next morning.

"No, I guess I'm used to them," she replied, breaking eggs into a bowl. "I know what each one means. The wood expanding and contracting . . . the wind getting caught between the shutter and the latch . . . Sometimes small animals get lost in the stone walls and scratch around till they find their way out . . . or die."

"Ugh. But don't you imagine things? I would, in a house like this. How old? That's almost three hundred years of lived lives, people suffering and shouting and making love and giving birth, under this roof. . . . You'd think there'd be a few ghosts around."

"I don't know," said her hostess blandly. "I haven't

heard any. But of course, I have Blue Boy, so I don't get scared." She whisked the eggs, unable to face Victoria. She and her husband had lain awake last night, embarrassed at the sounds coming from the next room. No ghostly moans, those. "Why can't that bitch control herself, or at least lower her voice," he said angrily. He stroked his wife's arm, both of them pretending not to remember. She had bled for an entire year afterward, until the doctor said they would have to remove everything. "I'm empty," she had said when her husband had tried again, after she was healed. "I'm sorry, I just don't feel anything." Now they lay tenderly together on these weekends, like childhood friends, like effigies on a lovers' tomb, their mutual sorrow like a sword between them. She assumed he had another life, or lives, in town. As she had here. Nobody is just one person, she had learned.

"I'm sure I would imagine things," said Victoria. "I would see things and hear things inside my head much worse than an ordinary murderer or rapist."

The wind caught in the shutter latch . . . a small animal dislodging pieces of fieldstone in its terror, sending them tumbling down the inner walls, from attic to cellar . . . a sound like a child rattling a jar full of marbles, or small stones . . .

"I have so little imagination," she said humbly, warming the butter in the omelet pan. She could feel Victoria Darrow's professional curiosity waning from her dull country life, focusing elsewhere.

Cunning!

As a child of nine, she had gone through a phase of walking in her sleep. One summer night, they found her bed empty, and after an hour's hysterical search they had found her in her nightgown, curled up on the flagstones beside the fishpond. She woke, baffled, in her father's tense clutch, the stars all over the sky, her mother repeating over and over again to the night at large, "Oh, my God, she could have drowned!" They took her to a child psychiatrist, a pretty Austrian woman who spoke to her with the same vocabulary she used on grownups, putting the child instantly at ease. "It is not at all uncommon what you did. I have known so many children who take little night journeys from their beds, and then they awaken and don't know what all the fuss is about! Usually these journeys are quite harmless, because children are surrounded by a magical reality that keeps them safe. Yes, the race of children possesses magically sagacious powers! But the grownups, they tend to forget how it once was for them. They worry, they are afraid of so many things. You do not want your mother and father, who love you so anxiously, to live in fear of you going to live with the fishes." She had giggled at the thought. The woman's steady gray-green eyes were trained on her carefully, suspending her in a kind of bubble. Then she had rejoined her parents, a dutiful "child" again, holding a hand up to each of them. The night journeys had stopped.

A thunderstorm one night last spring. Blue Boy whining in his insulated house below the garage. She had lain there, strangely elated by the nearness of the thunderclaps that tore at the sky, followed by instantaneous flashes of jagged light. Wondering shouldn't she go down and let the dog in; he hated storms. Then dozing off again . . .

She woke. The storm had stopped. The dark air was quiet. Something had changed, some small thing—what? She had to think hard before she found it: the hall light, which she kept burning during the week-nights when she was there alone, had gone out. She reached over and switched the button on her bedside lamp. Nothing. A tree must have fallen and hit a wire, causing the power to go off. This often happened here. No problem. The dog had stopped crying. She felt herself sinking into a delicious, deep reverie, the kind that sometimes came just before morning, as if her being broke slowly into tiny pieces and spread itself over the world. It was a feeling she had not known until she had lived by herself in this house: this weightless though conscious state in which she lay, as if in a warm bath, and yet was able to send her thoughts anywhere, as if her mind contained the entire world.

And as she floated in this silent world, transparent and buoyed upon the dream layers of the mind, she heard a small rattling sound, like pebbles being shaken in a jar. The sound came distinctly from the guest room, a room so chosen by her husband and herself because it was the farthest room from their bedroom on this floor. It lay above what had been the old side of the house, built seventy-five years before the new side, which was completed in 1753. There was a bed in it, and a chair, and some plants in the window. Sometimes on weekends when she could not sleep, she went and read there, or meditated, to keep from waking her husband. It was the room where Victoria Darrow and her young lover would not sleep the following fall, because she would say quietly to her husband, "No . . . not that room. I—I've made up the bed in the other room." "What?" he would want to know. "The one next to ours? Right under our noses?"

She did not lie long listening to this sound before she understood it was one she had never heard in the house before. It had a peculiar regularity to its rhythm; there was nothing accidental about it, nothing influenced by the wind, or the nerves of some lost animal. *K-chunk, k-chunk, k-chunk*, it went. At intervals of exactly a half-minute apart. She still remembered how to time such things, such intervals. She was as good as any stopwatch when it came to timing certain intervals.

K-chunk, k-chunk, k-chunk. That determined regularity. Something willed, something poignantly repeated, as though the repetition was a means of consoling someone in the dark. Her skin began to prickle. Often, lying in such states of weightless reverie, she had practiced the trick of sending herself abroad, into rooms of the house, out into the night to check on Blue Boy, over to the barn to look in on her horse, who slept standing up. Once she had heard a rather frightening noise, as if someone in the basement had turned on a faucet, and so she forced herself to "go down," floating down two sets of stairs into the darkness, only to discover what she had known all the time: the hookup system between the hot-water tank and the pump, which sounded like someone turning on the water.

Now she went through the palpable, prickly darkness, without lights, down the chilly hall in her sleeveless gown, into the guest room. Although there was no light, not even a moon shining through the window, she could make out the shape of the bed and then the chair, the spider plants on the window, and a small dark shape in one corner, on the floor, which she and her husband had painted a light yellow.

K-chunk, k-chunk, k-chunk. The shape moved with the noise.

Now she knew what they meant, that "someone's hair stood on end." It was true. As she forced herself across the borders of a place she had never been, she felt, distinctly, every single hair on her head raise itself a millimeter or so from her scalp.

She knelt down and discovered him. He was kneeling, a little cold and scared, shaking a small jar filled with some kind of pebbles. (She later found out, in a subsequent visit, that they were small colored shells, of a triangular shape, called coquinas: she found them in a picture in a child's nature book at the library.) He was wearing pajamas a little too big for him, obviously hand-me-downs, and he was exactly two years older than the only time she had ever held him in her arms.

The two of them knelt in the corner of the room, taking each other in. His large eyes were the same as before: dark and unblinking. He held the small jar close to him, watching her. He was not afraid, but she knew better than to move too close.

She knelt, the tears streaming down her cheeks, but she made no sound, her eyes fastened on that small form. And then the hall light came on silently, as well as the lamp beside her bed, and with wet cheeks and pounding heart she could not be sure whether or not she had actually been out of the room.

But what did it matter, on the level where they had met? He traveled so much farther than she to reach that room. (*"Yes, the race of children possesses magically sagacious powers!"*)

She and her husband sat together on the flowered chintz sofa, watching the last of the series in which TV purportedly examined itself. She said, "Did you ever think that the whole thing is really a miracle? I mean, here we sit, eighty miles away from your studios, and we turn on a little machine and there is Victoria, speaking to us as clearly as she did last weekend when she was in this very room. Why, it's magic, it's time travel and space travel right in front of our eyes, but because it's been 'discovered,' because the world understands that it's only little dots that transmit Victoria electrically to us, it's *all right.* We can bear it. Don't you sometimes wonder about all the miracles that haven't been officially approved yet? I mean, who knows, maybe in a hundred years everybody will take it for granted that they can send an image of themselves around in space by some perfectly natural means available to us now. I mean, when you think about it, what *is* space? What *is* time? Where do the so-called boundaries of each of us begin and end? Can anyone explain it?"

He was drinking Scotch and thinking how they had decided not to renew Victoria Darrow's contract. Somewhere on the edges of his mind hovered an anxious, growing certainty about his wife. At the local grocery store this morning, when he went to pick up a carton of milk and the paper, he had stopped to chat with DePuy. "I don't mean to interfere, but she doesn't know those fields," said the farmer. "Last year we had to shoot a mare, stumbled into one of those holes. . . . It's madness, the way she rides."

And look at her now, her face so pale and shining, speaking of miracles and space travel, almost on the verge of tears. . . .

And last night, his first night up from the city, he had wandered through the house, trying to drink himself into this slower weekend pace, and he had come across a pile of her books, stacked in the alcove where, it was obvious, she lay for hours, escaping into science fiction, and the occult.

Now his own face appeared on the screen. "I want to be fair," he was telling Victoria Darrow. "I want to be objective. . . . Violence has always been part of the human makeup. I don't like it anymore than you do, but there it is. I think it's more a question of whether we want to face things as they are or escape into fantasies of how we would like them to be."

Beside him, his wife uttered a sudden bell-like laugh. (". . . *It's madness, the way she rides.*")

He did want to be fair, objective. She had told him again and again that she liked her life here. And he—well, he had to admit he liked his own present setup.

"I am a pragmatist," he was telling Virginia Darrow on the screen. He decided to speak to his wife about her riding and leave her alone about the books. She had the right to some escape, if anyone did. But the titles: *Marvelous Manifestations, The Mind Travellers, A Doctor Looks at Spiritualism, The Other Side* . . . Something revolted in him, he couldn't help it; he felt an actual physical revulsion at this kind of thinking. Still it was better than some other escapes. His friend Barnett, the actor, who said at night he went from room to room, after his wife was asleep, collecting empty glasses. ("Once I found one by the Water Pik, a second on the ledge beside the tub, a third on the back of the john, and a fourth on the floor beside the john. . . .")

He looked sideways at his wife, who was absorbed, it seemed, in watching him on the screen. Her face was tense, alert, animated. She did not look mad. She wore slim gray pants and a loose-knit pullover made of some silvery material, like a knight's chain mail. The lines of her profile were clear and silvery themselves, somehow sexless and pure, like a child's profile. He no longer felt lust when he looked at her, only a sad determination to protect her. He had a mistress in town, whom he loved, but he had explained, right from the beginning, that he considered himself married for the rest of his life. He told this woman the whole story. "And I am implicated in it. I could never leave her." An intelligent, sensitive woman, she had actually wept and said, "Of course not."

He always wore the same pajamas, a shade too big, but always clean. Obviously washed again and again in a machine that went through its cycles frequently. She imagined his "other mother," a harassed woman with several children, short on money, on time, on dreams— all the things she herself had too much of. The family lived, she believed, somewhere in Florida, probably on the west coast. She had worked that out from the little coquina shells: their bright colors, even in moonlight shining through a small window with spider plants in it. His face and arms had been suntanned early in the spring and late into the autumn. They never spoke or touched. She was not sure how much of this he understood. She tried and failed to remember where she herself had gone, in those little night journeys to the fishpond. Perhaps he never remembered afterward, when he woke up, clutching his jar, in a roomful of brothers and sisters. Or with a worried mother or father come to collect him, asleep by the sea. Once she had a very clear dream of the whole family, living in a trailer, with palm trees. But that was a dream; she recognized its difference in quality from those truly magic times when, through his own childish powers, he somehow found a will strong enough, or innocent enough, to project himself upon her still-floating consciousness, as clearly and as believably as her own husband's image on the screen.

There had been six of those times in six months. She dared to look forward to more. So unafraid he was. The last time was the day after Victoria Darrow and her young lover and her own good husband had returned to the city. She had gone farther with the child than ever before. On a starry-clear, cold September Monday, she had coaxed him down the stairs and out of the house with her. He held to the banisters, a child unused to stairs, and yet she knew there was no danger; he floated in his own dream with her. She took him to see Blue Boy. Who disappointed her by whining and backing away in fear. And then to the barn to see the horse. Who perked up his ears and looked interested. There was no touching, of course, no touching or speaking. Later she wondered if horses, then, were more magical than dogs. If dogs were more "realistic." She was glad the family was poor, the mother harassed. They could not afford any expensive child psychiatrist who would hypnotize him out of his night journeys.

He loved her. She knew that. Even if he never remembered her in his other life.

"At last I was beginning to understand what Teilhard de Chardin meant when he said that man's true home is the mind. I understood that when the mystics tell us that the mind is a place, they *don't mean it as a metaphor*. I found these new powers developed with practice. I had to detach myself from my ordinary physical personality. The intelligent part of me had to remain wide awake, and move down into this world of thoughts, dreams and memories. After several such journeyings I understood something else: dream and reality aren't competitors, but reciprocal sources of consciousness." This she read in a "respectable book," by a "respectable man," a scientist, alive and living in England, only a few years older than herself. She looked down at the dog, sleeping on the rug. His lean silvery body actually ran as he slept! Suddenly his muzzle lifted, the savage teeth snapped. Where was he "really" now? Did the dream rabbit in his jaws know it was a dream? There was much to think about, between her trips to the nursery.

Would the boy grow, would she see his body slowly emerging from its child's shape, the arms and legs lengthening, the face thinning out into a man's—like a certain advertisement for bread she had seen on TV where a child grows up, in less than a half-minute of sponsor time, right before the viewer's eyes. Would he grow into a man, grow a beard . . . outgrow the nursery region of his mind where they had been able to meet?

And yet, some daylight part of his mind must have retained an image of her from that single daylight time they had looked into each other's eyes.

The worst thing, such an awful thing to happen to a young woman . . . She was having this natural childbirth, you see, her husband in the delivery room with her, and the pains were coming a half-minute apart, and the doctor had just said, "This is going to be a breeze, Mrs. McNair," and they never knew exactly what went wrong, but all of a sudden the pains stopped and they had to go in after the baby without even time to give her a saddle block or any sort of anesthetic. . . . They must have practically had to tear it out of her . . . the husband fainted. The baby was born dead, and they gave her a heavy sedative to put her out all night.

When she woke the next morning, before she had time to remember what had happened, a nurse suddenly entered the room and laid a baby in her arms. "Here's your little boy," she said cheerfully, and the woman thought, with a profound, religious relief, *So that other nightmare was a dream,* and she had the child at her breast feeding him before the nurse realized her mistake and rushed back into the room, but they had to knock the poor woman out with more sedatives before she would let the child go. She was screaming and so was the little baby and they clung to each other till she passed out.

They would have let the nurse go, only it wasn't entirely her fault. The hospital was having a strike at the time; some of the nurses were outside picketing and this nurse had been working straight through for forty-eight hours, and when she was questioned afterward she said she had just mixed up the rooms, and yet, she said, when she had seen the woman and the baby clinging to each other like that, she had undergone a sort of revelation in her almost hallucinatory exhaustion: the nurse said she saw that all children and mothers were interchangeable, that nobody could own anybody or anything, anymore than you could own an idea that happened to be passing through the air and caught on your mind, or anymore than you owned the rosebush that grew in your back yard. There were only mothers and children, she realized; though, afterward, the realization faded.

It was the kind of freakish thing that happens once in a million times, and it's a wonder the poor woman kept her sanity.

In the intervals, longer than those measured by any stopwatch, she waited for him. In what the world accepted as "time," she shopped for groceries, for clothes; she read; she waved from her bottle-green car to Mrs. Frye, trimming the hedge in front of the liquor store, to Mrs. DePuy, hanging out her children's pajamas in the back yard of the old Patroon farm. She rode her horse through the fields of the waning season, letting him have his head; she rode like the wind, a happy, happy woman. She rode faster than fear because she was a woman in a dream, a woman anxiously awaiting her child's sleep. The stallion's hoofs pounded the earth. Oiling his tractor, DePuy resented the foolish woman and almost wished for a woodchuck hole to break that arrogant ride. Wished deep in a violent level of himself he never knew he had. For he was a kind, distracted father and husband, a practical, hard-working man who would never descend deeply into himself. Her body, skimming through time, felt weightless to the horse.

Was she a woman riding a horse and dreaming she was a mother who anxiously awaited her child's sleep; or was she a mother dreaming of herself as a free spirit who could ride her horse like the wind because she had nothing to fear?

I am a happy woman, that's all I know. Who can explain such things?

FALSE
LIGHTS

Then reckon your course on shadows

Mrs. Karl Bandema
Box 59
Ocracoke, N.C. 27960   June 16

Dear Violet,

Please forgive the familiar address when I don't even know you, but the more formal would still feel strange. I hope you'll understand. Along with this note, there should arrive a small parcel containing Karl's pills. I don't know if you have a doctor on the island, so I took the liberty of having Karl's old prescription refilled. The moment his weight goes over 185, he should take one of these every morning *after breakfast*. Also, no fat or salt in food preparation, less beef, more chicken and fish, more vegetables and salads, but no dressing on the salad, unless a little lemon. (Starting the meal with the salad helps cut the appetite.) And no cheese, except cottage cheese, and no alcohol.

                                   Sincerely,
                                   Annette Bandema

Mrs. Karl Bandema
231 E. 48th St.
New York, N.Y. 10017   June 18

Dear Annette,

The parcel arrived today, with your note. I will do as you say. K. is in pretty good shape at the moment. He goes for a long swim before breakfast, takes several walks by himself during the course of his working day, and then we swim and walk in the evenings. The vegetables are easy because I planted a garden. (Peas, beans, squash, cucumber, spinach, tomatoes, carrots, radishes, and three kinds of lettuce.) As for fish, no shortage of that here. I do bluefish stuffed with spinach sometimes three nights a week. There is a local doctor, but so far only I have had to go to him. I tend to get ear infections. There is no liquor store on the island. I appreciated your note and wish you all the best.

Violet

June 18—maybe June 19 by now

Dear Annette, dear Annette Bandema,

The most natural way for me to think of you is dear Mrs. Bandema, but how can there be two of us? And yet here we both are. I feel I cheated myself by mailing that letter off so quickly. I couldn't wait to write it, to hurry back to the post office and mail it, even though the mail had already gone out for the day. It said nothing, absolutely nothing. Spinach and beans, walks and swims, all wrapped up in a cautious parcel of triumphant politeness. "I will do as you say," etc. And yet I told you more about me than you told about yourself. You know, or will know when you get my letter, that I get ear infections and that I have a garden, and—if you read between the lines—that I am alone a good deal of the day. I have no knowledge about you, except what I manage to compile from my husband's novels, steering uncertainly between fiction and fact. I shouldn't probably say *my husband*. It hurts and bewilders you. It would me. It's all so strange. I think it would feel less so to me if we could meet, just the two of us, in some neutral place, the way generals of opposing sides meet to sign a truce. Not that we need sign a truce, exactly. We are not on opposite sides.

I'm going to tell you something very peculiar: I feel close to you. I think about you all the time. When I am walking around the island, or sitting on the beach by myself, or even—I hope you won't think this perverse—when I am lying in his arms. I hold imaginary dialogues with you (somewhat similar to the tone of our brief exchange, all about food and recipes and such), and sometimes I ask your advice about things I'm sure you know better than I. I often imagine you watching me, us, as I used to imagine God watching me when I was a child, and sometimes when I am swimming I find myself showing off to you in the sea, taking extra care with my strokes, or persisting a little longer than I ordinarily would if nobody were watching. And often I see little things I'd like to send to you. A tiny painting in oil, done by a local artist, of fishing boats or the lighthouse. I watch this artist work down on the beach. He is a strange, bitter sort of fellow who has lived here many years. He told me about the land pirates who used to work this stretch of shore. At night, they hung lanterns around the necks of mules and walked the animals back and forth across the sand, until some unfortunate ship captain, mistaking the swaying lanterns for lights at sea, would crash upon the shoals and spill his cargo right into their hands.

This artist has his easel rigged so he can paint six small pictures at once. He does all six seas, then all six lighthouses, or all six boats. He says there will always be pirates wherever there are fools. He sells his work to a gallery in Nags Head, which hangs one at a time till that one is sold then puts up another in its place, and so on. . . . I have often had the urge to send you one, just as I had to restrain myself the other day from buying you a shipwreck map from the Visitor's Center when I bought myself one, a map of the Ghost Fleet, all the ships that have gone down on the Outer Banks (more than five hundred ships, all along this treacherous coast): they call this "the Graveyard of the Atlantic," and I thought you would be touched and haunted, as I was, for the whole thing is rather mysterious and puts one in the frame of mind where individual lives and who is whose wife in a particular segment of time seem suddenly so fleeting and insignificant, mere events in an infinite process of events that will all be washed away, as the sea has washed away the faces of all those drowned men. I don't understand time. The more I think about it, the less I understand it. Sometimes I am quite certain it is only a way to console ourselves about the inevitability of change, merely a word containing no real thing, anymore than the shipwreck map can contain bodies or salt water—or "Mrs. Bandema" can be anything more than a legal and social convenience. There is no real Mrs. Bandema.

On such a level, I think we could meet.

On such a level, I think you could be with us now, on this island. I have so much time to myself. I would enjoy your company.

It occurs to me that as recently as a hundred years ago this letter would have been considered highly irregular, perhaps impossible. And what of a hundred years from now? Karl says the novel of 2075 would be unrecognizable to us today, that it will be a pure and better thing, tuned in to more important signals, no longer obsessed with gossip and personal petty detail. If we had lived in 2075, would marriage also be a new thing, where we could all survive together, nobody's happiness depleting anybody else's, all of us sailing through change as effortlessly as gulls through air, time no more enemy than water as seen from above? Will there be marriage, will there be wives, in 2075?

That young woman crawling through the mud, carrying medical supplies in her teeth, through two miles of mud in enemy territory: I don't know how many times I have reread that passage in Karl's book. That was you. What love, what danger, what a love story! I am sure there will be nothing in my life to compare to that. No such challenge, no such heroism. I did not have to crawl, or even walk outside my father's house, to get Karl. Karl entered my father's house, and I went straight from my father's love to Karl's, no alien land, no great test, between. I earned nothing. Heroics are not easily had for the young in our times. Perhaps that is why they go to such extremes to create their own dangers. Karl says he will never put me in a book; he says he wants me to stay where I am, on this island with him. He says that you only put people into books to improve their lives, or when they are gone, or when you are no longer able to see them. It is a kind of memorial, he says—as the shipwreck map is a memorial, I guess, and a keepsake for tourists who can never know what it is like to feel oneself dashed to pieces on rocks. And yet, though he has put you away so memorably in his books (I weep every time I read of your death, so young, at only nineteen, completed as a heroine at nineteen, before you ever had a chance to live, to marry, to have that little boy who died, but who in Karl's books has been allowed to grow up and live), you are very present to me. The real you, a woman in her fifties, goes on existing for me.

I imagine your days, tracking them alongside my own. I sometimes feel we are interchangeable, except for the accident of time. It might have been the other way around, me first, then you, a woman's face that changes through one long event of a man's, an artist's, life. It could have been me on all fours with the medicine that saved his life, and you, young and untried, years later, placing a pink tablet beside his breakfast plate with no danger to yourself, completing the journey, all danger over, all the interesting wars and legendary shipwrecks over. (". . . *With swift communications, advances in safety-at-sea techniques, and sophistication of tools for rescue, tragic incidents along the coast occur only rarely now.*") Perhaps I will send you one of these maps, after all.

I hear the ocean pounding. What are you hearing now? This is the time of night, or morning, when everything rushes through my brain. I can't stop or even control its course, so I just ride the torrent. Sometimes I don't fall asleep until I hear the birds singing. Not that I mind, it's just that insomnia seems such a waste on me. He would make so much better use of it. He salvages from everything—his anger, his disappointments, his mistakes, his boredom. He makes it all reappear in meaningful, lasting shapes. At the moment I am seeing my garden, the sea breeze ruffling the Bibb lettuces that glow faintly in the dark, delicate and phosphorescent-looking, and the weighted curves of the tomato plants, their first fruit emerging through the bluish, fringy foliage, and the straight dirt spaces between, glinting with diamond flakes of sand.

It appalled me at first when I had to "thin out." I knelt above those inch-high plants, thinking, Who am I to do this, what right have I to choose? But the book said you had to be ruthless, you weren't doing any of them a favor if you allowed them to steal from and stunt one another. So I taught myself to pull things up by the roots. Choosing between the weak and the strong, and sometimes between the strong and the stronger, is supposed to make you philosophical.

I remember a famous philosopher who once came to my father's house for dinner. He told us how, after the war, he had been taken on a tour of a concentration camp, and how he went back to his hotel seething with such impotent anger that he got a violent headache and could not eat or sleep. While still in this state, he picked up a book on Einstein and suddenly understood for the first time the world-shaking boldness of "Energy equals Mass multiplied by the square of the Velocity of Light," and was filled with a great tranquility and acceptance, could now view the thousands of charred and tortured bodies with the same meditative, detached eye one would view the death of stars or the decay of huge primeval forests into coal. As a small girl, I thought him a very cold, strange man, for whom $E = MC^2$ could balance the shredding and burning of people. Yet, in my garden, my fingers hover, choose, pluck. I hear the old killer sea behind me murmuring in my ear, and I accept the history of doomed sailors, the inexorability of evolution, and you, crawling through enemy mud, risking your life, in a Europe of thirty-three years ago, so that I could have a husband on Ocracoke today.

Something is always plucking, thinning out. The philosopher lost his headache and went down and had a huge meal. And I, in my garden, feel less guilty about you.

Yesterday I was walking on the beach, looking for unusual shells, along that particular stretch where the *Charmer*, the *Lizzie James*, the *Lydia Willis* went down. I was thinking about the women after whom these ships were named, wondering what kind of women they had been, and what they had meant to the men who honored their names—and of course I thought then of Karl's novel, the one he calls *Yolande* (which is you) and, though he has assured me I'll never be in any book, I couldn't help wondering what he would call me, the name he would think fittest to memorialize me.

I was walking along with my head down, not paying much attention to where I was going, and walked right into the fishing line of an elderly woman standing near the surf, wearing a pair of men's trousers cut off at the knees, her skin burned crisp as a potato chip. She said not to worry, she had caught nothing but two crabs all morning and was getting ready to quit anyway. She had sharp eyes and kept staring at my face, my legs, my wedding ring, and before I knew what was happening, I had told her all about myself. She hadn't heard of Karl, but she said she didn't read much since her husband died, she was too busy traveling, making up for lost time. She and another widow had bought a camper together and had so far camped, she said, in thirty-nine states, not counting Canada and Mexico. She asked me Karl's age, and my age, and then laughed dryly and said, "Well, dear, you'd better start making your list." I asked what list and she said, "The list of all the things you want to do, only he won't let you do, but you can do after he's gone." When I said there was nothing I wanted to do without Karl, she narrowed her old eyes and asked how long we had been married. "Oh, no wonder," she said when I told her. "You wait a couple of years."

I went back to the cottage and made lunch. Gazpacho, tuna-fish salad with only enough mayonnaise to hold it together, even though your letter had not yet arrived. I watch his calories where they provide the least enjoyment, but I doubt I will ever interfere with his lunchtime wine and soda, which he refills frequently if his morning has been especially good or bad. Yesterday it was bad. Over his second glass, he told me that he had been tricked by the dream of Art into throwing away his life, as my pirates had tricked all those captains. Nothing he had written was of any value to the future, he said; he had wasted his past producing quaint relics, and he was missing his present, imprisoning himself in a roomful of ghosts, while Life, and me in it, flowed by outside. He refilled his glass again, saying he hadn't even looked at the garden this week, and appeared to be on the verge of tears. I cleared the table and came and stood behind him and folded my hands upon his breast. I suggested we take a nap. He said I was the first person in many years to cause him to suspect real life was as interesting as fiction, but it was too late for him to change. I did something selfish: poured him more wine and we had the nap.

Was it you, many years ago, who also interested him in real life?

Today his work went so splendidly that at lunch he announced if the wind stayed behind him like this, he'd have "all those ghosts" out of his head by summer's end. He ate too fast and sloshed innumerable refills of Chablis to the brim of his glass. His eyes looked through me toward, I suppose, ecstatic horizons.

"But what will you do then?" I asked.

"I will write about whatever lies on the other side of deaths and births and ego, whatever lies on the other side of settling scores and erecting monuments." His face was angrily spiritual as he explained how the artists of the future would be impersonal receivers and transmitters of the messages of the universe. It was neither the time for mentioning your letter nor for uttering dietetic precautions. He had abandoned us for 2075.

I sat across from him, nostalgic for yesterday's nap, and imagining you and me, years from now, traveling together in our camper, both of us burned a deep earthly brown, each of us wearing an old pair of his trousers, cut off at the knees, bumping sagely up and down the roads of America's scenic landscapes, taking equal turns at the wheel, comparing our experiences as the wives of Karl Bandema.

Last Saturday, Karl and I went to a party in Nags Head. We had gone over on the ferry to buy supplies, and Karl ran into a newspaper columnist he knew while we were (I'm sorry to report) in the liquor store.

"You have got to come to this party, Karl. They'll be flattered to have you, and you wouldn't believe these people. They'll furnish you with material enough to last the winter," the columnist said.

Karl frowned. "Poor old Violet here would probably like it," he said at last. "She's stuck on the island with only my boring company all week."

And I said it might be fun—because I saw that he wanted to go.

The house, large and rambling in a Victorian style of architecture, was set high on stilts, and two cabin cruisers were docked underneath. A freshly painted sign over the garage said: "HAPPY SHACK, The Hon. Terence Mulvaney, Dunn, N.C."

The columnist introduced us to the host, Judge Mulvaney, a fastidious man in his sixties, with a birdlike profile and elegant manners.

"I have the greatest respect for literature," he said, shaking Karl's hand warmly. "It ranks second only to my admiration of youth and beauty," he said, shaking my hand.

"The judge is also a new bridegroom," the columnist told Karl, sending him a secret look that said, "See? I told you!"

"I don't normally wear shirts full of white ruffles," explained Mulvaney to me, "but my bride made me buy this on our honeymoon in Mexico, and her wish is my law."

Everyone around him laughed. Mulvaney looked delighted with himself. Karl took a long, deep sip of his julep, and I made my first public début as Mrs. Karl Bandema.

I looked around the gracious stretches of the room, with its comfortable faded furniture, its nautical touches. "I love your house," I said.

"Thank you, it's been in the family for a long time," the judge said. "Nancy Jean will show you the rest of it." He reached an arm sideways and fluttered his suntanned fingers, and within seconds a very pretty dark-haired girl ducked up at us from under his armpit. "Nancy, honey, show Mrs. Bandema the cottage. You girls run along and have a good time," he said.

Nancy put her arm around my waist. "I think you and I have got a lot in common," she whispered. Off we went, children, Karl and the judge watching us benevolently.

She led me upstairs to an enormous old bedroom. "All in white, that's me, the all-in-white girl!" She laughed and flung herself down in a swoosh of white silk trousers on a king-size bed covered in white organdy, with at least a dozen white lace and organdy pillows. The old casement windows were open, and you could see the ocean, peaceful and pink with sunset.

Nancy patted the collection of pillows. "Come lie down and let's talk! You don't want to be dragged around somebody else's old house. I'll tell you the interesting things about it later. I haven't talked to a soul my age in months. Did he divorce his old wife for you? So did mine! Does she bother you-all constantly? No? You're lucky, let me tell you! It's gotten to where I simply will not put a soufflé in the oven anymore, because as sure as I do the phone rings just as I'm taking it out and it's her, with one of her ladylike suicide threats. And then at the most *inopportune* times—I'm sure you know what I mean—she calls to say she's sure a burglar has broken into their old house, or the water pipes have frozen and she can't do a thing by herself, so I have to call up the plumbers or the police—the whole thing upsets Terence so—and then I have to deal with his bad mood and his guilt. . . . Oh, the *guilt*, I get so sick of the guilt—they hadn't slept in the same room for centuries and she was the one who wanted out first. . . . Listen, make yourself comfortable, let me pour you a little more. I keep a pitcher up here for myself when I get bored with the company downstairs. Don't you love this room! It was *meant* to be all in white. When his daughter—she's just a year older than me—saw the wallpaper samples and swatches of fabric I had when we were still engaged, she said, 'But Nancy Jean, you can't be meaning to put that in my father's bedroom; that's the kind of thing that's more suitable for a virgin's bower.' 'But that's just what I am, honey,' I told her. And I was, you know. The judge is a nut on chastity. You wait, when he gets into high gear tonight, he'll tell you how chastity and ambition are the lost virtues of today's young. What does your husband start preaching when he gets high?"

"How artists won't be obsessed with personal things in the future, how they will have left their egos behind in order to be transmitters for the universe."

"Honey, men will always have egos. You take my word for it."

It was dark when we went downstairs, laughing. I was tipsy. "You have got to come visit me this winter in Dunn," Nancy said. Then she got serious and muttered off a grave recitation. "The Mulvaneys were the third family to build . . . house built over the water so sailing boats could unload luggage and parties on the porch . . ." etc., etc.

Downstairs, Judge Mulvaney was saying, "The girls have lost their maidenhood and the boys their desire to succeed. That's why this country has gone to hell. I had a reputable gynecologist sign an affidavit that Nancy Jean was chaste before I married her. . . ."

"See," whispered Nancy happily, pinching me.

Later, sitting in the circle of Karl's arm, I listened to him tell his audience how, for the artist, personal concerns will be obsolete in 2075, no more hunger for fame or recognition, no preoccupation with pettiness. "We will only be interested in our anonymous role as messengers for the universe."

I caught Nancy's eye and winked.

On the last ferry back to Ocracoke, Karl put his head down into my hair. He stood behind me at the rail. The wind was cold, but he said it cleared his head. "God, what terrible people, what a wasted evening," he moaned. He had to hold on to me to keep his balance. "Why did we go? I wish we had just gone back to our own little island and had a quiet evening. I'm going to give up drinking. I'm going to give up people—all except you. I feel set back a hundred years! As if I didn't have enough people swarming around in my head, waiting to be disposed of, waiting to be explained! Why were you gone so long? What could you have possibly found to talk about with a girl like that? An *affidavit* for chastity, for Christ's sake! What on earth could have happened in that man's life to make him do a ridiculous thing like that? Listen, do you know what I'm thinking? We could stay on the island all winter. The hell with hurricanes! Are you afraid of hurricanes? Will you stay with me, Violet? Will you stay on with me while I endure my everlasting penance? What are you thinking? Tell me the exact flow of your thoughts, everything, leaving nothing out."

I was thinking of you, Annette, wondering if you were lying in the dark imagining burglars. I did not think so. When the thing you dreaded most has already come true, what further dangers are there to imagine? I was also thinking of pirates, and ripening tomato plants, and whether Karl would mind if I visited Nancy on the mainland if we stayed for the winter in Ocracoke. And whether I should even want such a thing in the first months of married life. And I was thinking about that night at my father's. Everybody was dancing, people of all ages, my father with the student who later became his wife—all these young brides—everybody was dancing except the famous novelist who had come to speak at our college's spring symposium ("What Are Our Next Frontiers?"). Earlier that evening, he and a famous biologist had agreed onstage that a new dawn was on its way, and our next evolutionary assignment would be to carry information around the universe. "All the old concerns will be sloughed off like dead cells," the novelist had exclaimed excitedly, "all those personal, selfish concerns we believe have to be the stuff of novels." He kept wiping the perspiration from his forehead, nervous and elated; he looked like an ill man inspired by a vision of perfect health. "Then will you stop writing novels?" demanded a student in the audience. "I would hope . . . yes . . . I would hope to have the courage and intelligence to do just that," the novelist replied quickly, his voice harsh. "I mean, if I could not get a clear reception, if I couldn't hear my assignment, yes, I would certainly stop writing novels." Then Karl laughed. "Luckily, I probably won't be around long enough to greet the new world. I can indulge myself in the fancies of the old one a while longer."

Then he was watching the dancers and I was watching him. He gulped his drink in compulsive sips, his tired, slightly wild eyes skimming us from beneath bristling eyebrows. I believed I could see him rapidly picking up, sometimes putting down in the same instant, our potential mysteries. Then his gaze came to rest on me, and I asked him if he would like to dance. "I have a piece of metal in my leg," he said, "but please stay and talk to me. I am lucky to be alive." Touching his damp forehead to mine, he shouted over the music, "A very courageous French girl saved my life—just about your age."

"I wish you wouldn't abandon the old world just yet," I said to him later that night. I was just beginning to discover that world, and so far he had been the best thing in it, the most compelling figure.

And you were part of it.

"What are you thinking?" this man asked now, my husband now, in a world fast growing extinct but not yet dead. Oh, no, not quite. For weren't we on a ferry crossing to an island that was ours alone?

"Perhaps we'll see a shipwreck if we stay the winter. They are rare these days, but not entirely impossible," I replied.

Now he is asleep, dreaming onward the mysteries of all those people who keep him from becoming a perfect messenger, who keep him here with me. You, in an infinite number of forms, but never older than nineteen, and that little boy who has led so many interesting lives, and maybe now the judge and Nancy Jean. I wonder what this man will make of them. Perhaps one night, in spite of himself, he'll experiment with a better form of me, and then I will join you. We will meet at last. That is a chance I made up my mind I would take. Do you think, for yourself, it's been worth it?

I am here for the time being near the dark cool of my garden, helplessly thinking of so many things, drowned captains in their watery slumbers, Nancy deep in white organdy with her judge, a million other things, all in the space of a single wink. I could no more transfer it to paper than I could have told him everything I was thinking. I do not understand time. I do not understand marriage. If they prove, like the sentimental demands of the ego, to be out-dated fancies, is it that you, Annette, drowned in the same archaic sea in whose dangers I furtively rejoice?

Affectionately,
Violet

Mrs. Karl Bandema
Box 59
Ocracoke, N.C. 27960   June 25

Dear Violet,

   Since there is a doctor on your island, he should be able to prescribe Karl's pills when needed from now on.

   I am afraid I cannot abet you in your extensive fancies concerning other centuries. The future I leave to those who must live in it; the past, insofar as it involves my own life, is my own affair. It is very much this year and this century for me. I assure you, time is more than just a word for me.

   Nor can I encourage you in your hopes for a meeting. Outside your imagination, we have nothing to offer each other. I prefer to remain

Sincerely,
Annette Bandema

(or Mrs. Bandema, if you like, but not a defeated general, not a shipwrecked or drowned swimmer, and certainly not a potential camping companion).

SOME
SIDE EFFECTS
OF TIME
TRAVEL

"Hwaer cwom mearg? Hwaer cwom mago?" asked Professor MacFarlane and he meant it.

He had a right to that poem. Gretchen had been waiting all during summer school to hear him eulogize that, his, our, her lost world. *Where is the horse? Where is the horse rider? Where is the giver of rings? Alas, that space of time has gone, become dark under cover of night, as though it had never been.* MacFarlane said, "In those days nobody cared about signatures. So 'The Wanderer' is anonymous." Gretchen raised her hand and said, "Do you think 'wanderer' adequately translates *anhaga*?" (Already knowing what he would answer, having read his thoughts on the subject in his own translation of Old English poetry, but wanting him to say it to *her*.) "No," he said, "some people," and named a professor of a rival edition, "say 'lone-goer.' I myself like to translate it as 'he who is solitarily situated.'"

Yes.

Professor MacFarlane is a bachelor. He lives alone in a big house in this Midwestern town and walks to the university puffing his pipe and swinging his Harvard bag. (*And storms beat against the stone cliffs. . . .*) His toes turn a little outward as he walks. He's sixty-two. The town he comes from in North Carolina is gone. His great-grandfather, a leader of men in the Revolutionary War, founded it. When the oldest of MacFarlane's nine sisters and brothers got ready for college, the mother decided to move them all to the state university. When the MacFarlanes left Mac-Farlane, so did everybody else, and now the town is wilderness again.

Gretchen loves MacFarlane next to Borges. The day Borges came to town, she cried for all the lost hours she could not spend with him. She went to Woolworth's and bought a gaudy yellow jersey (the same color as the old STOP signs) to wear to his colloquium because she had read in a *Paris Review* interview that yellow was the only color Borges could now see. At the colloquium he sat polished and bemused by a world outside of time. He was infinitely loving to everyone and said the reason his stories were so short was because he liked to carry all of them around in his head and there was just so much room. He signed Gretchen's copy of *Dreamtigers* with a shaky "JB," and she carried away his delight at still being able to see the tiger ("A very *Chinese* tiger, isn't he?") when he pressed her book practically against his eyes. She left her own pen in his hands and tiptoed away, wanting him to carry a part of her back into his timeless world.

When it lightnings and thunders, Professor MacFarlane takes a taxi to the English Building and sits out the storm (day or night) in the faculty lounge. Graduate students tell tales of how they find him sleeping erect with his spine ramrod straight against one chair and his impeccably polished shoes just grazing another. Sometimes, he wakes at their entrance and they invite him down to their offices for coffee. Being polite, he wrenches himself from the mead-hall dream, from the lost song of the *scop*, and travels down on the elevator to one or another of the basement offices to sit beneath posters of Paul McCartney or Che Guevara and sip freeze-dried coffee ("I'm terribly sorry, there's no cream") from a mug.

Some say he was frightened of mountain thunderstorms as a child. Others, including the campus policeman who guards the fortress of literature from 11 P.M. till 6 A.M., the Dark Ages, say that when MacFarlane was in the war, he was trapped for days in a trench and went temporarily mad trying to distinguish between the sound of machine-gun fire and the sound of thunder. Nobody has bothered to ask MacFarlane. The little mystery makes them revere him more.

Borges, who is older than MacFarlane, recently married his childhood sweetheart. Gretchen will soon be thirty-one, outliving Keats by five years and Shelley by one. She will be two years younger than Jesus of Nazareth and Alexander of Macedonia when they died. She'll still be younger than Virginia Woolf and Iris Murdoch when they published their first novels. All Gretchen's childhood friends have children in the second grade. She likes to tell herself that loving men like MacFarlane and Borges is just one more trick time is playing on her. (*Assuredly no man can acquire wisdom until he has been many years in the world.*) All she has to do is get outside of time, her mother keeps telling her. Her mother has made it. Her mother reads only medieval literature and science fiction. She refuses to truck with the present. She makes her doctor write her age in a code that only the two of them can decipher. She is an insomniac and married to a villain, which suits her fine, since he is in present time. While he sleeps, she lies next to him and reads St. Theresa's *Interior Castle* in the original. "God lives outside of time," she wrote to Gretchen at graduate school. "When are you going to get that through your head?" Borges told Gretchen and others who crowded into the same faculty lounge where MacFarlane sleeps erectly through his storms that Kipling had never understood what time was all about as long as he lived in that ancient country of India. But once back in England, he happened to dig up an old Roman coin in his own back yard and the past flowed over Kipling as a real presence for the first time.

"*Was your first lipstick Fire and Ice?*" A full-page color ad addresses itself to a reluctant Gretchen from the pages of *The New Yorker*.

Yes, what about it?

She looks critically at the stylish group of matrons waiting for their husbands at the Westchester depot. *"Then* you
are ready for Eterna 27," the ad soberly reminds Gretchen.
She runs to the mirror. Is it true? Does she need hormones
to stir up blood in an aging face? Did Virginia Woolf use
hormone cream? No, but her bones were better. Gretchen
will not ever be found waiting in a Westchester depot. She
is too old to be a hippie, but she reads about them and
secretly fears they might have the answer, like the Rosicru-
cians and the Scientologists and the little heretic band St.
Augustine went around with before he became a saint.
When she was an undergraduate ten years ago, everybody
was reading *On the Road* and she got along fine with the
Beats. They published one of her stories in their underground magazine. At the time she was flirting with prole-
tariat images, so her story was about a poor old newspaper
vendor who loved art. He saved for weeks to get his shoes
shined so he could go and see the Rembrandts but when he
got to the museum there was an admission fee of fifty cents
which he couldn't pay. Defeated, he returned to Joe's Diner
where Joe let him charge his dinner. He consoled himself
by walking into the scene of a Coca-Cola poster on the wall.
When the magazine came out (it was banned within hours
by the local postmaster and Gretchen always felt queasy
that the poem with the fucks that caused all the trouble
had been right across the page from the end of her story),
Gretchen went to a Beat party and necked with the editor
for a long time in the attic loft where a Negro lived with a
white girl, which was something in those days in that town,
which was the same university town in North Carolina that
MacFarlane's mother took her family to live in.

Gretchen Brown Wolf Finney Martin Brown. Maiden.
Adopted by villain stepfather. First marriage. Second. A
maid again. Social Security office going wild with her.
Martin is the only one licensed to drive. Finney may still
take books from a library in Copenhagen. Income-tax people still hunting her down south. A cache of confusing iden-

tities in her wallet. Husband No. 1: a stunt photographer on the big jazzy paper where she went to work after graduating from J-school. He flew upside down in planes and photographed cities devastated by earthquakes. Gretchen went out on the less spectacular assignments with him. When they were flying together into the eye of a hurricane, Gretchen suddenly felt reckless and proposed. He hit her in the face (after they were married, of course); Gretchen retaliated by locking him out of the house and making obscene gestures at him through the window. He came crashing through the glass and almost lost a hand. Gretchen's stepfather drove all night to come and get her. His favorite slogan from this day forward was: "She hates my guts, but who always has to come and pick up all the pieces?" The stepfather packed her books in the back of his station wagon, stopped by her psychiatrist's to get her a bottle of tranquilizers, and felt free to lecture her on the meaning and responsibilities of life as he drove her home to her mother.

She went to Europe on a Danish freighter called the *Oklahoma*, and sometime later stumbled upon her second husband in a creative writing class at the London City Literary Institute. He was a visionary, with side interests in astrology, ESP, magic, nudism, and Scientology. Together they joined the Scientologists, drove down on weekends to L. Ron Hubbard's castle in East Grinstead, donated by the Maharajah of Jaipur. They were Power-Processed, for a couple of thousand dollars, into more aware and potent human beings by being hooked up to an electropsychogalvanometer. They held tight to stripped V-8 juice cans that were attached to electrodes and answered questions, and they had to sign papers promising never to reveal them to anyone. (Ron said if the world got hold of these questions prematurely, it could blow itself up.) During Power-Processing, each processee was expected to have a certain number of visions. According to the Scientologist instructors, Gretchen was not having her quota. So, for another hundred bucks, they ran an S & D on her, which means Search and Discover, in order to find out just who or what was keeping her from "Making Gains," as they termed it. This onerous obstructer was called the Suppressive Person, a figure hated and feared by all Scientologists. Gretchen had to make a list of all the people in her life who had influenced her in any way. Then the auditor (the man on the other side of the meter) read these names aloud while Gretchen held tight to the V-8 cans and noted her electrical response on the dial. When he came to "God," she registered the worst needle-read of all, dubbed by Ron "the Rock-Slam," which is even more deadly than the agitating "Theta Bop." Gretchen was sent at once to Ethics, on the third floor of this drafty castle, where the Ethics Officer, a young woman with red lipstick from Austin, Texas, told her: "What you've got to do is take this yellow slip of paper and write a letter to your SP, disconnecting from him." "But listen," said Gretchen, trying to coerce the woman into a collusive smile, "don't you see who my Suppressive Person is?" "Honey," said the woman, "He's your SP, that's all that interests me. Do you want to disconnect or don't you? We'll have to separate you from your husband, otherwise. *He's* making good gains." So Gretchen took her slip of yellow paper and wrote under the probing eyes of the Ethics Officer: "Dear God. I am sorry, but I must disconnect from you."

She was awarded a Power Release pin, which cost twelve dollars, shortly afterward, and told never to take it off. She and her husband went back to London. "I think I am going to have a nervous breakdown," she said. "I think I'll go home for a while and see my mother. Okay?" She went and never returned. She told her mother what she had done. "Well, you go upstairs this very minute and write Him a letter saying you're reconnecting," said her mother. "Then you write a letter to the Scientologists telling them to go to hell." Gretchen obeyed. Soon they began the trip down, getting first in trouble with Parliament. Later, the murderers of several famous personages of our time were discovered to have been Scientologists and that didn't help, either. Gretchen followed the decline of this organization in the news media and felt avenged, but also strangely nostalgic for their perfect answers. Some of the secret questions had helped her.

Over the years, she has often waked and not known
what
where
who
she is. Once when it was really bad, she woke up and had to start from scratch as a one-celled creature and work up through fishhood, floundering on the shore until her gills had adapted to oxygen, and then struggling through evolution, not to mention generations. This was about the time when, having become confused by life, she decided to return to literature and get her breath in the ivory tower, picking up a few higher degrees while she gasped.

There was also the earlier time when she woke to the sound of a toilet flushing as if someone were choking it slowly to death. It took her at least five minutes to locate her identity and five more to ascertain her geographical position on the earth: a fifth-floor room in a third-class Barcelona hotel and her lover had left her, gotten noiselessly out of bed and fled on his Sollebus (Danish for sun bus) back to Denmark after having deposited some forty pale passengers in this February city. He was a bus driver named Sven. They had not been able to exchange a sentence in any mutual language, so she prattled English lovingly and he said short guttural things (some, she suspected, obscene) in Danish. The Spanish maid was flushing the communal toilet by pouring bucketfuls of water down it. Gretchen recalled nostalgically Sven's violent tattoos and realized she might indeed be pregnant and utterly alone with the wages of sin in a strange and chilly country. But real fears to her were never so bad as those *others*, the numinous, as Rudolph Otto calls it; God preserve her from the terrible sight of His face until she could see it without the side effects suffered by poor Brother Nicholas of Flüe, who prayed and prayed to see His face, so God let him see it, and his own became ever afterward paralyzed on one side; his heart, he after said, had burst into a million little pieces. Or, meshing with technocracy, you might paraphrase: Brother Nicholas had a stroke, and be less accurate. Gretchen could deal pretty well with real catastrophes; they seemed a necessary penance one paid to keep the others away. She went to Cook's and asked them didn't they have anything warmer than Barcelona. They sent her to a place off the coast of Africa, also Spanish, and on the plane she prayed for her period to come just this time and she would never be careless again. It came and she was careless again, with a young revolutionary who managed the hotel where she stayed. He hated Franco. They would go for walks on the beach. On the moonlit sand he would write with a stick: "FRANCO, sí! COMUNISMO TAMPOCO." Then he'd erase it quickly with his toes.

This morning she woke in Chicago and knew who she was but not where. It was a gigantic basement resembling a subway station. There were energetic cubist paintings everywhere. Outside, aboveground, someone was power-mowing and children were shouting. Also, men were working on a skyscraper. She heard their calls to one another between the thud of the pile driver. Then she remembered. "Ha, I'm improving." And rose and began writing on a rickety old Remington belonging to her hostess, who had gone to work. Last night she told the host and hostess, "I've finally hit upon a method of chronicling myself which won't bore me to death. I'll be me at my most entertaining with friends and wine after dinner. I'll tell it like the Icelanders told their sagas, just narrate, *This happened, Thor felt this*, and so on, before the dawn of the writer's self-consciousness. Forget H. James, God love him, and the rules, the expectations of the clever reader, and go searching for myself all over the printed page, like an old-country granny spieling her life, skipping around the years, sidetracking into the really choicy operations, the gall bladder, the hysterectomy, anecdotes about Ebenezer's drinking and how Maud was never the same since menopause, following her own infallible train of intuition like one does on long bus rides or just before falling asleep."

> Jung says: The word happens to us;
> we suffer it. . . .

Gretchen had this typed on a note card. Note cards are her way of tabulating and taping a madcap inner and outer world that shapeshifts and self-destructs by the second.

Whenever she gets bored with plotted, pared stories that restrict, leave out, scale down, distort, she shuffles through her vast collection of note cards, written over the heady years, which have no form, no system, no end and no beginning, no one subject or single style, no unifying principle.

These note cards are the nearest she has come to getting outside of time.

The first summer she went back to graduate school, she had one of her mysterious attacks in Burger Chef. She was sitting by herself eating a cheeseburger and reading *Sons and Lovers* (Mr. Morel had just hit Paul's mother in the face with the side of a drawer) and some boys behind her were tapping on their table with a pencil, when suddenly "it" happened. The world stopped. She forgot who she was. For a second—a half-second—eternity?—she was suspended egoless in a totally featureless nothing. "It," say the doctors, is a sort of vertigo. *They* don't know. One doctor had the nerve to call it *petit mal*. When she came to herself, she went out in the sunshine and felt her way along the street, touching the bark of old trees and saying aloud (an exercise left over from Scientology, actually): "Touch the tree. Thank you. Touch another tree. *Thank* you." She went to the English Building and sat at her desk in the basement and suddenly realized that the part she had taken for wood was only a clever plastic. She began to cry. Suddenly a vision materialized in the door: a tanned girl in white tennis clothes. "Gretchen, all you do is think and study," she said. "I'm taking you home to spend the night with us."

The girl and her husband, a law professor, lived in the country. They were also writers. That night they were very good to her, appreciated her, fed her, let her watch *The Magnificent Seven* on TV while the girl did her pregnancy exercises and the man dusted their golden retriever with flea powder, sent her to bed early like a cherished child where from her pillow she saw the moon climb across the sky and heard cows mooing in the night outside. She awoke temporarily cured and, after a big breakfast, was left alone with her Old English verbs at their dining-room table while they went upstairs to their separate studios to create fiction. Gretchen looked at the dining-room table and decided to anchor herself to her cure via a note card. So she wrote the contents of their table on a card. It preserves as long as ink will last a segment of time when life was good. Today in Chicago or tomorrow in who knows where, she can run to her suitcase (she always carries a bunch of the cards, revolving them like a wardrobe) and flip through and find that table, and a happy state of her psyche, as it will never exist quite that way again, containing:

Ann Page's Orange Marmalade
Pepper mill (wedding gift)
Port bottle in straw jacket
Matches
Silver stamp holder with the couple's
    initials engraved on it
An old 1966 appointment book containing
    grocery lists
A stack of postcards to be sent later that
    day and which did no good, saying:

"I am a housewife in your district
and a McCarthy supporter. When you
go to the Democratic convention I
hope you will take my preference
into consideration. . . ."
Yellow flannel dusting cloth
Paraffin lamp
Tin of Little Holland cigars
Record jacket: Toscanini conducts
   Mendelssohn's octet
Bill from Western Union, citing two
   telegrams sent, one to Saunderstown,
   one to Berkeley, with a reminder
   printed in telegram script below:
   THESE ARE A BIT OLD. PLEASE REMIT.
   THANK YOU.
Bill from McNulty's Tea and Coffee Co. in
   New York for 2 lbs. of French beans
Fourth page of a letter from somebody, which
   begins ". . . visit from Clare who is
   still seeing Jack who tells her she's
   intelligent and has gorgeous legs,
   then never calls again. She remembers
   everything he said. . . ."

"Do you see what I mean about this sort of chronicling?"
Gretchen asked her host in Chicago. "Sure," he said (he
made movies), "it's a matter of kinetics, kinetic art, where
the work of art is no longer the object but simply moves with
life along the path where the most relevant action is—"
"STOP!" said Gretchen. She ran to get a few blank note cards.

Now at this moment, her clever host is on the other side
of the city, editing his film, but she can have his wisdom
from last night as though he were sitting across from her.

Work of art is not the object but the
   path of the movement
Work of art does NOT have to objectify

the movement, sum it up, or give
shape to it; it simply charts,
like an encephalograph
The play of activity, life embraced BUT
NOT CAPTURED is the thing
There is no such thing as the finished
product

"I think the Middle Ages are coming back," Gretchen had said to her host and hostess, the Marvell Chapmans. "And so does Mother Maloney, that nun I was telling you about, and so does my mother and so does Roxanne and so do you, because Roxanne told me you said it last week, and I know MacFarlane will welcome it. But it will be the Middle Ages with a difference, all of us forming a cohesion but now allowed to keep our egos, which we developed so painstakingly during the Renaissance. We'll all be members of one body, like St. Paul's head and foot and arm in Corinthians 12, each doing our own thing; nothing can be interchangeable in this human multimedia performance, we all have our place, and we'll use one another, scrambling on shoulders if necessary, to reach de Chardin's God. It's all converging, I tell you. This afternoon your wife and I tried an experiment. Roxanne and I tried to pool ourselves and create a third person. Of course, Borges has already done this down in Buenos Aires with Bioy Casares. They get together every night (or did before Borges got married) after dinner and become a third person and write stories by him. The stories are different from the ones either of them write. Roxanne was trying to funnel through to me what it was like to be her, you know: 'trapped in reality,' as she describes her state. And I was trying to show her what it is like to be living permanently in a state of fiction. What do I mean? I'll give you an example and you must promise you'll believe it. During my bus ride here, I was engaged in a more or less constant story. I was writing myself from minute to minute. I mean I saw myself as being read by somebody else, a sort of omniscient audience. Gretchen was on the Greyhound bus going to Chicago, thinking about herself as usual. Gretchen looked at the man sitting across the aisle. He was reading a book. She could see part of the title, *How to*— How to what? She squinted at a page he was reading and she could have sworn it said 'Raising Scorpions.' Could that be possible? Then believe it or not, and you've promised to believe, this man took out another book whose title Gretchen could see. It was called *Becoming a Writer*. He began reading and smoking and making hypertensive notes on a coffee-stained piece of paper on top of his closed briefcase. She saw him write 'John Keats.' (Or was it 'John Knox'?) Now she was out of her mind with curiosity. She put on her glasses and read what he wrote out of the corner of her corrected eye. He wrote, 'In 1784 I went . . .' and turned the page, scribbled a bit more, blacked it out with his ballpoint, and went on writing: 'The word "late" may be used either as an adjective or an adverb.' The bus stopped and all the passengers fled through a driving rain to a fifteen-minute coffee break. The man never got back on the bus. Do you see what I mean, Marvell?"

"Sure," said Marvell. He and Roxanne always saw. That was why she valued their friendship more than most. The three of them got together five, six times a year and made a haptophorous consciousness, each increasing and enhancing the others. They did a psychic three-man balancing act. They brought new blood to one another's faces. It always exhausted them. Tonight, after they'd done it, Roxanne spat a few hissing remarks at Marvell about not putting up the bathroom shelves and Marvell slumped in a canvas chair and went away to troubled Israel via TV while Roxanne washed all the supper dishes and Gretchen excused herself and fell into bed underneath a frightening cubist painting. On the dark ceiling, she read the words "Gretchen Brown wrote herself to sleep. . . ." But she and Roxanne had failed at their synthesis. They were going to try again with a tape recorder. If Gretchen could release Roxanne from her prison of fact, then Roxanne could start dreaming at night and let herself live in a meaningful myth.

> Neurotics may be simply people
> who cannot tolerate the loss of myth.
> Had they lived in a former age . . .
>
> —C. G. Jung
> —a Gretchen Brown note card

"Did you dream last night?" Gretchen asked Roxanne this morning as Roxanne hung her heavy black tresses over the sink and splashed herself awake with cold water. "No." "I started to come in and shout you awake," Gretchen said. "I was going to scream, 'WAKE UP RIGHT NOW AND HOLD ON TO THAT DREAM!'" "God. You would have frightened me to death if you had done that," said Roxanne. "Well, keep trying," Gretchen said. "You're bound to have one soon, now I've put the suggestion in you."

If their experiment works, then Roxanne will have herself a myth and Gretchen will no longer live in terror of being swallowed up by one of her own fictions during the dark hours. "How can I keep the witches away?" she had once asked her second husband, the visionary. "It's easy," he replied. He had once gone mad himself. "All you have to do is turn the room gold." "How?" she said. "Simple. The same way you let the witches get in."

Gretchen is lucky. She has found several stabilization points around which she orients the flux that is herself against the worse flux of the world: the cards, hot baths (taken whenever she feels threatened), Roxanne (whom she has known for seven years, during which both of them have been in flux), a hometown, mostly mythical now, that contains a convent (which is in dire flux), and a library that contains the books she read as a child, and a mother (who lives outside of time with God), and finally there are Gretchen's marvelous dreams, which she has befriended (as all the existentialist analysts encourage us to do) and which progress nightly on their own time track, supplementing her days, providing her with clues to what she must do next, reminding her whom she really loves and really hates, forming hard gemlike little stories that read like fables and that reverberate with meanings overlapping the daylight world.

At the end of the Eisenhower era, Gretchen Brown graduated from journalism school. While she was perspiring away in her cap and gown at the entrance to the football stadium, her physics professor, a little German with bushy red hair, jumped out at her from behind a tree and said, "Hah! Made it in spite of me, didn't you?" (He had given her a D-minus, which wrecked her average forever, and told her to wake up to the world of truth.) She went to work in a gaudy tropical city for a newspaper that had the second largest advertising in the world. Her train had a five-hour layover in Georgia, where lives an aristocratic professor of English who once courted and lost Gretchen's mother. He lives alone in a big inherited house, his wife and sons having left him (taking all the silver and china: he had to eat off paper plates for months) because he was a villain. When Gretchen stopped for five hours in his city, he met her at the station and took her home and showed her all his books on Dante and gave her dinner and cried. He told her he might have been her father. Gretchen, who was still in the stage where she liked to make distinctions between truth and fiction, wanted to ask if he meant that literally or figuratively, but didn't. He took her back to the train, told her she looked like her mother, and gave her some money. She vowed to herself to write him a thank-you letter that would make up for all the suffering her mother had caused him, but somehow she never did. The professor called her mother later and said he really hadn't liked Gretchen very much. When Gretchen's mother told her this, Gretchen began having erotic dreams about the professor. Much later, she joined the MLA (Professor MacFarlane sponsored her) because her mother told her that the professor went to every MLA meeting in his private plane, regardless of where it was held. Gretchen had fantasies of meeting him at one of these conventions and afterward he would call her mother from a phone booth and say how delightful Gretchen had become, after all.

There was a convent on the hill in Gretchen's town. It had once been a very plush resort hotel. Edgar Allan Poe had slept on the fourth floor, which was now condemned. Only the nuns now slept on this floor, considering themselves nearer to heaven whether the building stood or fell.

Before Gretchen went to become a newspaper reporter, she returned to this convent to reaffirm her childhood moorings. There was a nun there, Mother Maloney, from County Galway. Gretchen at twelve had fallen in love with this woman who was then thirty-nine. It was a very helpful love for Gretchen, and *The Well of Loneliness* may flick through some people's minds but is anything so cut and dried? Several years ago Gretchen talked at some length to an Englishman in the Grenadier pub and he said there was no such thing as men and women. Under the rays of Mother Maloney's love, Gretchen learned Gaelic, read Thomas Aquinas and *The Seven Storey Mountain*, and got her saints in order. After supper, she would leave the unpleasant scene of her pregnant mother and villain stepfather and go to her room and lock the door. She would put on the Grieg piano concerto, get out her homemade journal (which she illustrated with little drawings and cutouts from magazines), and write down everything Mother Maloney had said personally to her that day. Mother Maloney used Cashmere Bouquet hand lotion, and so Gretchen bought a bottle and rubbed her whole body with it before bedtime. When Grieg was over, she put on Rachmaninoff and got out Tennyson's *Idylls of the King* and read aloud the part where Guinevere after disgracing herself with Lancelot enters the convent. The thought of becoming a nun sexually excited Gretchen, though she knew one was supposed to cancel out the other.

Then she would turn the light out and kneel down and look across row upon row of identical apartment houses (in those days the villain was poor) and pray to St. John the Beloved of Christ: "Please don't let the love of God die in me." She had a mortal fear of losing the feeling she had now. And she later did lose it. Then she would pray to St. Patrick, who was Irish, to let Mother Maloney go on loving her always. Gretchen walked back to the convent every Friday evening to go to the movie for the boarders. She and Mother Maloney arranged to sit together, and when the lights went out they held hands in one of the deep pockets of Mother Maloney's habit.

In bed, Gretchen would smell the Cashmere Bouquet she had rubbed all over herself. When she took a bath, she looked down at her growing breasts. Mother Maloney had small ones, hardly discernible beneath her habit. The heavy silver cross rested in a very slight depression between them. "Please, God," Gretchen would pray in the tub, "don't let them grow anymore."

Thank God He was paying attention to the farmers in Iowa who were praying for rain . . . or something.

At the convent that summer day before Gretchen went off to become a journalist, she and Mother Maloney sat on the porch of the old wooden hotel where E. A. Poe had slept. "Journalists can influence the world if anybody can," said Mother Maloney. Gretchen looked at the fine freckled skin of the nun and breathed in the smell of her habit (the smell of ironing and Cashmere Bouquet) and wanted very much to hold hands again. She felt that this convent containing this woman was a bastion of her own psyche which would remain stable when all else defected.

But the fire department condemned the third floor and then the second floor and finally the first floor and the old hotel was stripped and dismantled. The villain stepfather, who had by then become a successful builder in the town, came and took away all the old lumber. "They don't make wood like this anymore," he said. He saved a piece of banister railing for Gretchen, who was then in Europe. The nuns moved into his modern convent, which looked like a grasshopper about to jump. They named it Madonna Hall. Vatican II happened, the hippies happened, and the nuns were obviously not doing as good a job as Gretchen's mother in living with God outside of time. They shortened their skirts, they abbreviated their veils; they took them off altogether. The saintly principal, a beautiful nun of thirty-four who had gone in when she was seventeen, went to New York to visit her twin sister who was an actress. One morning the milkman came. The saintly nun was still in her dressing gown and he thought she was her sister. "Hi, gorgeous," he said, "you've cut your hair." She came back and taught another year at the convent and then she read a story in the *Atlantic Monthly* by Joyce Carol Oates about a nun who hid her coldness behind a habit and wouldn't hold the hand of a Jewish student at the hour he most needed to make contact with someone and afterward he went out and killed himself. The saintly nun went to Reverend Mother and begged to be excused from her vows. She went to New York and got a job on a magazine. A year later her "story" was published in a ladies' magazine. It was a rather sensational article including such sentences as "What did my first kiss feel like? I'll tell you. . . ." The town was emptied of this magazine in three days. Some said the Reverend Mother had ordered all copies bought and destroyed. Gretchen wondered, when she heard about it, if her stepfather hadn't cornered the market and sold the copies for ten dollars apiece up at Merrill Lynch, where he often sat all afternoon in his overalls, chuckling aloud at his own good fate on the boards.

Gretchen was profoundly affected by this world that wouldn't stop changing. She wrote note cards by the dozens. At the time, she was back home, recovering from her second husband and Scientology. Meanwhile the saintly nun up in New York married an ex-priest. Vows flung fast and fierce, like a spiritual squash court. Has McLuhan done this to us? Gretchen applied, was accepted, hurled herself back into the comparative calm of a university. She killed herself and got an M.A. in one year, then started on the Ph.D. in summer school. After completing MacFarlane's course in Old English and dropping a course entitled The Pursuit of Happiness, she was home again to get her bearings. Where were they? Certainly not at the convent. Mother Maloney was wearing a rust skirt and a round-collared blouse that had been in style when Gretchen was an undergraduate. The heavy cross was nowhere to be seen. Her hair she had tried to wrench into a couple of spit curls over the ears. It was gray and very thin from being cooped up under a veil for so many years. She and Gretchen walked on the grounds and made coffee in the nuns' kitchen. Gretchen kept feeling embarrassed. It was as if she were seeing her friend undressed for the first time. "The only thing I'm sure of anymore is that God is," said Mother Maloney, who was now really Sister Maloney, because the nuns had changed that, too. "*Are* you?" Gretchen asked. "Yes," she said, "and I accept Christ as the son of God by Revelation. Farther than this I cannot go at the moment."

Adjoining the convent property was a majestic antebellum home with stables, which Gretchen's stepfather would not have the pleasure of demolishing for some time yet. It was being repainted and refurbished by a rival contractor. It sat splendidly on the crest of the hill overlooking mountain ranges on three sides and a river called the French Broad on the fourth. A Catholic bishop lived there. A Dalmatian belonging to the bishop shot out from behind the stables and barked at the two women, but then he recognized Mother Maloney from her previous walks and slunk away, rather ashamed of himself. Mother Maloney and Gretchen sat down on the front steps of the house and looked pensively out at the French Broad. "Now when I go into stores, people don't pay special attention to me," Mother Maloney said, pleased. "I am not set apart or revered. I'm just an ordinary person. That's why I'm glad to be rid of the habit. Also, it was hot and you never could hear properly behind the veil." "God," said Gretchen, "the

habit was one of the reasons that attracted me most about
being a nun." "Then you obviously didn't have a vocation,"
replied Mother Maloney, flicking a fly off Gretchen's brown
leg. "I've just finished this marvelous book that everyone
else read years ago," she said. "For a long time we couldn't
read it because of the dirty words. But it's so wonderful.
The little boy is so honest, just like today's teen-agers. They
just won't accept a lot of the institutions we have always
put up with. Like at the Rejuvenation Meetings here last
month . . . all the nuns in our order coming together from
all parts of the world . . . The whole system's changing.
It used to be that Reverend Mother's word was law. Now
it's the word of the community. One young nun stood up
and said to the liturgist, 'What's so sacred about black? Or
brown? Or white? Why can't we be good women in polka
dots or stripes?' And, you know, I found myself agreeing
with her. Why not?" Gretchen said, "Those meetings sound
interesting. You don't happen to have a tape recording of
the Rejuvenation, do you?" "No," said Mother Maloney,
"it was a private thing, after all." "Oh," said Gretchen,
"well, what was the name of that book you were reading?"
"It was called *Catcher in the Rye*," said Mother Maloney.

Gretchen's mother and grandmother came to get her at
the convent. Gretchen's mother shielded her eyes from the
sun, the better to frown at Mother Maloney. She bit her
lip censoriously and shook her head. "I take it you don't
approve of my outfit," said Mother Maloney cheerfully.
"No, I don't," said Gretchen's mother, who taught American History her way and Medieval Literature to the seniors
at the convent. "Wait till school opens. I'm going to show
up in a long black dress and veil to compensate for you all."
"But this is much cooler," said Mother Maloney, smiling.
She and Gretchen's mother were affectionate with each
other in spite of their political and liturgical differences.
Gretchen's mother was High Episcopal and looked down on
the changing forms of the Catholic Church. Gretchen's
grandmother, whose father had managed to keep most of

his slaves after the war without paying them wages, called coolly from the car window: "How are you, Mother Maloney?"

After Gretchen kissed her friend goodbye for another year, and drove away in the back seat of her mother's station wagon, the grandmother said, "Her neck is wrinkled. She would have done better to stay behind that veil." Gretchen's mother ran her favorite red light, saying, "Now what they need is Theresa of Avila. Gretchen, remember how in the fourteenth century when the Carmelites were acting up and getting all vain about their clothes, she swooped down on them and put them in their place?" "I have often thought of trying to write a play about her relationship with St. John of the Cross," ventured Gretchen from the back seat. "Why don't you start it this afternoon? You've got a whole hour before dinner," said her mother, who pushed her. Gretchen's former psychiatrist had told Gretchen: "Your mother has been quarterbacking your entire life."

Now the three generations of women were driving swiftly over a bridge. To the right was a Negro housing development all in pinks and lavenders and greens. It stretched as far as the eye would want to see. This land had once belonged to Gretchen's grandmother's father, who married a hussy on his deathbed and left his land to this hussy, who sold it to the Negroes. My grandmother is going to say her piece, Gretchen thought, and sure enough, at precisely that moment Gretchen's grandmother, still a pale and beautiful woman at seventy-seven, turned her profile to the pastel houses on the right and said sadly, "If Fran hadn't been such a hussy, we wouldn't have to drive past those awful houses now." "I have to stop by the damn supermarket," Gretchen's mother said, "and you know, no matter what I fix he won't be satisfied." Her mother's library books were digging into Gretchen's rear so she restacked them, examining the titles: SF Nebula awards, a novel called *Other Orbits* with a dust jacket from one of Hieronymus Bosch's more gruesome panels, and a book on the medieval mind. Gretchen flipped through this last one and found an article by Professor MacFarlane. She began to read. "You're going to ruin your eyes," her grandmother said through the rear-view mirror. Gretchen thought of Borges and Joyce and Homer and Milton and wished she could fall in love with a really good man.

Eating with the Marvell Chapmans went on and on forever. Gretchen loved to visit them, busing to Chicago from her university, and talk and eat until she fell in bed hardly able to breathe for excitement over ideas. When Gretchen had first met Roxanne at the Ambassador's house in Copenhagen, Roxanne had been on a diet. That was seven years ago. Since then, Gretchen could more or less measure the state of her friend's soul by whether or not she was on a diet. When Roxanne had had enough of the world, she stuffed herself with starches and candy until she was unable to get into her clothes. That would force her to stay inside while she sorted herself out. Then when she felt strong again (usually she was twenty or thirty pounds fatter), she would surface slowly back into time via a diet. Now that Roxanne had acquired a husband (a rather thin one), she made him go on her diets with her. After Roxanne was asleep, Marvell secretly read cookbooks. Now, on this visit of Gretchen's, they were on the best diet of all. It was one where you ate and ate and became thin as a Dachau prisoner. Certain foods burned up other foods and you just sat and stuffed and left chemistry alone to rearrange your figure. Gretchen and the Chapmans had been sitting for three hours at table, like a trio of Roman degenerates, having consumed

Two cans of Alaska sockeye salmon
Eight tomatoes, seasoned
Two onions, finely chopped
Sliced green peppers

Sliced pimentos
Celery and mushrooms cooked in milk
Sliced cucumbers marinated in Sucaryl
  ("Don't you remember this from Denmark,
    they served it everywhere," said
    Roxanne.)
Fresca, with ice and glasses as an afterthought
  ("Marvell," said Roxanne, "just tell me
    this: is it too much trouble for you
    to get out the ice tray and the glasses?
    If it is, just please say, 'Roxanne,
    it's too much trouble for me to get out
    the glasses and the ice tray,' and I will
    do it myself." Marvell smiled and said,
    "Roxanne, it's too much trouble for me
    to get out the glasses and the ice tray.")

For dessert, Roxanne got out assorted spices, electric hand-beater, dried coffee, orange extract, Sucaryl, gelatin. She made a coffee jello, with unfattening topping made from condensed milk, cinnamon, nutmeg, and water. Gretchen said, "This is the best dessert I have ever eaten anywhere, ever." Later that night, she flung herself exhausted from talk into the bed under the cubist painting and heard Marvell say to Roxanne, "You know, she really meant it. It was the best dessert anywhere, ever." All marriages have their moments, thought Gretchen.

Roxanne came and lay down at the foot of Gretchen's bed. The Chapmans lived in a mammoth basement on West Bittersweet Avenue that had once been a famous Chicago cubist's studio. In return for leaving his huge canvases there, he let them have it for forty dollars a month. This had greatly helped them. Marvell could pay his root-canal bill and Roxanne was able to pay off her lawyer, who had gotten her off with monthly visits to a social worker after Roxanne had been apprehended for shoplifting a paperback book on women's rights from the bookstore of two queers.

"I'm exhausted, too," she said at the foot of the bed. "It's always fiercer when you're here. Although Marvell *will* verbalize everything. There are moments when I wish I was married to a bus driver."

"No, you don't," said Gretchen, and the two of them giggled. Gretchen had told Roxanne about Sven and Barcelona.

"Will you be able to sleep all right tonight?" said Roxanne.

"Oh, I always sleep perfectly here," said Gretchen, "I don't even need a light on. You two are near enough to keep the bogeys away."

"What actually do you see? Is it with your eyes closed or open?" Roxanne asked.

"Open, I'm afraid. Well, once in England I saw a huge Negro in a loincloth. He was sitting on the edge of my bed. I had dozed, then woke to feel this huge hand on my forehead. I knew it wasn't my husband's hand. 'Uh-oh,' I said to myself, 'when I open my eyes I'm going to see something awful.' But I opened them anyway and there he was. I decided I'd better talk to him, so I said (I'd been reading about archetypes): 'Are you the Great Father, then?' As soon as he answered, I knew I'd made a mistake. I had addressed him as though he were part of my own imagination and, as such, would of course know who the Great Father was. But he just giggled wildly and said in scarcely human English, 'Yep, Ise de gret fadder,' and then he started to lie down and I knew he was going to rape me. At first I fought it; then I said to myself, 'Well, he's going to do it anyway, so I might as well not struggle,' and I relaxed and then I realized I was actually looking forward to it. At that precise moment, he vanished."

"That must have been frustrating," said Roxanne.

Saturday was the last day of Gretchen's visit with her friends. After lunch, they set off in the sunshine to see 2001 again. As they waited for the A-train, Gretchen moaned, "I don't feel like going back there and teaching Renaissance poetry to two sections of undergraduates. I'm more in a medieval frame of mind. Back to miracle and mystery and all that."

"You'll get over it," said Roxanne. "I always favored the Jacobean era. So doomed, so violent, so extreme."

The train came. They had to split up and sit separately. They were hurtled screamingly through a tunnel that seemed to fling giant sheets of aluminum foil at the windows, making an unholy racket. Gretchen looked up at the Traveler's Times Message of the Week, next to the advertisement for Excedrin. Secretly she was a sucker for messages, although artistically she abhorred them. Damn, damn, damn, she thought as she read this message, I'm going to have to write this down and I didn't bring any note cards. So she wrote in her checkbook, to be copied over later on a note card:

> I refuse to accept the idea that
> man is so tragically bound to
> the starless midnight of racism
> and war that the bright daybreak
> of peace and brotherhood can never
> become a reality.
> —Martin Luther King, Jr.

She looked over and saw Roxanne tapping her foot to some private music of her own. Why can't I just live, Gretchen wished. What if, far worse than being called to be a nun, I have been called to be the note cards on which my time is written? (*"A wise man must perceive,"* MacFarlane *translated aloud, "how mysterious will be the time when the wealth of all this age will lay waste, just as now in diverse places throughout this earth walls are standing beaten by the wind and covered by rime. . . ."*) But it's so exhausting to be chronicling yourself every minute. I've got to have a breather. I've got to write myself purposely off the page for a while: "And Gretchen went to the movies with her friends and we will hear further from her when she comes out several hours later." Roxanne just lived. She got better-looking as the years went on. She seemed annually to be gathering herself up toward an overwhelming personality. Gretchen remembered the evening of their first meeting at the American Ambassador's house in Copenhagen. They were the only two single girls there. She and Roxanne were seated on either side of the prison warden of that city, whose name was Mr. Worm. Roxanne said, "I think Danish will become an extinct language pretty soon, don't you, Mr. Worm?" The poor man shook his head unhappily. "I don't hope so," he said. Oh, God, I'd better cheer him up, Gretchen thought. She swallowed her mouthful of frikadeller and asked with great charm, "What's the most prevalent crime in Copenhagen, Mr. Worm?" "Oh, stealing bicycles," he wailed, and looked more depressed than ever.

After 2001, Marvell, Roxanne, and Gretchen took a safari round the windows of Marshall Fields. "I want to get a pair of thigh boots," said Roxanne. "Then I will also need some very short boots to wear with the pants suits I'm going to get." Poor Marvell looked very pale. I'd better cheer him up, thought Gretchen. She said, "What do you think it meant? I still don't understand. What was the black slab? Why was Keir Dullea in that room at the end? If I could see it twice more, once with MacFarlane and once with Kurt Vonnegut, I think I could understand."

Roxanne slant-eyed another window of expensively dressed mannequins and said, "Man's eternal quest to get back where he started from: a space capsule, a Louis XIV bedroom, a womb."

Stop! Gretchen told herself. Here's a good place to switch off for the day. I am not going to let it record one more item on my poor quivering consciousness.

But then when they got back to West Bittersweet, where the pile driver on a new high-rise apartment site was throbbing its heart out, deafening the passers-by, they saw a large crowd gathered on the sidewalk. "What's happened? I wonder," Marvell said, and the three of them made their way into the crowd and saw a black girl at its center, dancing the Bugaloo all by herself to the beat of the pile driver. Before a minute had passed, Marvell, Roxanne, and Gretchen had joined the crowd in clapping time to the beat.

NOBODY'S
HOME

A married woman, Mrs. Wakeley, alone with her thoughts all day, watches a building rise out of the ground across the street from her house. She becomes involved with this building and its progress. It seems to be telling her something. At last it is finished. The plaque goes up, very tastefully, on the right side of the entrance.

NOW RENTING: ONE-, TWO-, AND THREE-BEDROOM
APARTMENTS. INQUIRE AT OFFICE INSIDE.

She can read the gold letters on the black background quite easily from her own bedroom window with the top part of the new bifocals she hates, and suddenly the building's message flashes out at her!

She is going to go and live there, make all the arrangements without telling her husband, then simply leave one day. When he comes home, she will not be there and he will not know why. She will be across the street, watching to see what happens without her.

Mrs. Wakeley dresses carefully to look like a responsible person (but she always dresses carefully; she always has been a responsible person) and leaves the house by the back door, walking quickly down the alley. She wears a fitted black coat with a fur collar, dark stockings, and plain black pumps with a sensible heel. She is a short woman, full-fleshed but compact. As a girl she was called petite. Within a few months of letting herself go, she would now be called plump. She has dreamy gray-green eyes and very white lustrous skin, exactly the same color all over, as she has been allergic to sun, even in small amounts, all her life. She wears her hair the way she has worn it for years: parted down the middle and fastened into a bun low on the back of her neck, where a few strands have already drifted down onto the fur collar. The hairs that have lost their pigment glisten brightly against the dark ones that haven't. I am on the borderline of everything, she thinks, her heart beating like a criminal's, this woman halfway between youth and age, holding her purse close to her, a woman not usually met with in alleyways.

And so by a circuitous route, she enters the new building and goes to the manager's office. He rises to greet her, recognizing respectability at once—probably a widow, he is already thinking—there is something about her face that shows she has lost a man; there is no doubt in his mind that she had one, for she is still an attractive woman, and there, of course, is the ring. This is all very lucky for "Mrs. Jones," now shaking hands with Mr. Frascati, as she has decided to pose as a widow. At first, she played with the idea of being a single woman, "Clara Jones," but upon testily removing her ring, Mrs. Wakeley saw that its twenty-eight years on her finger had left an indentation so deep it was suspicious. Mr. Frascati is a dapper gentleman to whom age has brought weight and substance and authority. He is not much taller than she. He wears a large diamond in his own wedding band, and his beautifully manicured nails sparkle with a very light pink varnish. Pictures of wife, children, grandchildren flank him on either side of his desk. I will have no children, decides Mrs. Wakeley, keeping it simple, as Mrs. Jones is asking whether she might be shown one of the one-bedroom apartments. Too late she remembers she should have specified one that faced the street, just as Mr. Frascati is accompanying her into a lovely sun-filled room with new wood floors whose beams rush toward the windows as toward the light. He points out with pride the small area below that will be a private garden, accessible to tenants only, and where, as soon as things are organized, there will be flowers and shrubs year round. "More privacy back here," he is saying. "The view of a garden in the city is a rare thing. And for the same price as the apartments on the front, with the noise and the ugly streets." Mrs. Wakeley, delicately repinning a runaway piece of hair back into the secure loop of her bun, takes courage and says, "But—if you don't mind—I think I'd rather face the street. I like noise. I like the . . . distraction, you see. . . ." And remembers to glance poignantly at her ring. The good man understands.

He shows her the apartment like it facing in the other direction. Mrs. Wakeley stands at the window into which no sun shines at this time of day and looks down at her own front door. It looks small and impersonal from this angle, not much different from the other doors on either side of it. She is eye-level with her bedroom and bathroom on that other second floor. Ah, "Clara Jones," the single woman, would have liked the bright apartment better, with her back turned to this street, with the sky streaming through, bringing an unpredictable succession of lights and moods; and below, the quiet garden of repose, where one could cultivate new thoughts and grow one knew not what. But "Mrs. Jones" has certain unfinished business, and as she asks the proper questions about rents and leases and fixtures and utilities, she is focusing on her own front door and imagining that first scene like the opening shot of a film. Her husband is coming down the street from his bus, carrying his briefcase. As he approaches the door, his pace . . . quickens? Lags? She has never seen her husband approaching the house in which she waits. Only, of course, now she will not be inside! But he doesn't know that yet. She is no longer an actress, sealed into her part, but an anonymous "audience" who watches calmly from a distance, waiting to see what happens next.

Mr. Frascati mistakes the flush of triumph on her face for an indication that he has rented another apartment. Having taken an interest in the predicament of this modest woman (the "if you don't mind" left its impression on his masculine soul), he is *somewhat* disappointed he couldn't persuade her away from this gloomy view of the kind he has been trying to escape all his life. He cannot understand people who can resist a garden; but then, women have their own reasons for things. He is happy to inform her that this apartment will be ready for occupancy within two weeks, as soon as the electricians finish some wiring. She asks may she let him know in a few days. Of course (giving her his card, Emilio Antonio Frascati, Manager), that will be fine; he would not want her to make such an important decision without first satisfying herself as to the optimum. . . . He is already feeling protective toward this little woman with the fragile white skin, and he stands behind the curtain of his office and watches her leave the building. Mrs. Wakeley, amazingly adept for one so new to subterfuge, walks away, down the street, giving her house not a glance, and spends the rest of the winter afternoon daylight browsing in a library. She reads how "all marriages are power games," in a new book called *The Integrity of Divorce*, "and when one partner becomes permanent winner or loser, then that marriage can be said to be over, even though the couple continue to live together." She is instructed how to "cut her meat costs to the bone" by preparing "Stuffed Mediterranean Veal Breast with Prune Dumplings, Korean Spareribs with Soy and Sesame Sauce" (at which point she snaps open her purse, takes out a silver pencil and a memo pad, then remembers something and puts them back at once). She reads a letter in the same magazine's Reader's Column from a woman who is angry because her husband has left her for a younger woman. ". . . and what do I have to show for it? Memories of years and years of housework? What do I have left of my *own*? It should be a law in this country that before any woman gets a marriage license she should be required to set up her own pension fund. A fixed amount would have to be put into this fund annually. But it must be the law, so that people won't feel guilty about doing it. It would be a relief to young housewives who don't dare mention such matters for fear of casting a shadow on things.

Then when she wears out and her husband trades her in for a new model, she will have her own pension fund which would support her till she trained herself to work. . . ." She reads that the new fashion trend is "romantic long dresses with designed-in nostalgia," and sits gazing at two full-color pages of young models in their early twenties wearing lawn-party dresses of their great-grandmothers' vintage. She still cannot get used to her new glasses. If she looks through the bottoms, she falls up the stairs; if she reads through the tops, everything blurs. What do all these untried wisps of girls in their quaint costumes have to do with her? How, for that matter, will belated knowledge of power games and pension plans change *her* life? Rather miffed at herself for wasting precious time escaping into magazines when she should have been planning her move, she puts on her coat and heads out into the dusk with a weary heart (stopping at a grocers to buy artichokes, which her husband likes, in order to make up for the canned corned beef she's going to dish up at the last minute), and it is at precisely this moment, alone on the dark cold street, that her courage begins to falter.

To begin with: the money. Mrs. Wakeley and her husband have a joint bank account, both in checking and savings. In the checking (she ought to know; she does all the household accounts) there is $560. In savings there is $5,030, plus whatever interest has been earned since the last quarterly payment. She could, she supposes, with impunity (remembering the angry letter from the woman in the magazine) go down to the bank and withdraw exactly half of both accounts, and then walk anonymously across town, a small woman with graying hair, wearing a forgettable black coat, and open another account under the name of Mrs. Jones. Mrs. Clara Jones? But do you need identification to open a bank account? She might get a driver's license for Clara Jones, except that she doesn't drive. A Social Security card! But how does one go about getting a Social Security card? At her age, she doesn't even know. Every one of those young models posing in old-fashioned dresses for a magazine has been carrying around her Social Security card for years! She imagines some bullying woman booming accusingly across the desk at the Social Security office (Where was it? At the post office, perhaps?): "Where have *you* been all these years? Why have you waited so long?" And even if Clara Jones obtains a Social Security card to prove she has the right to open a bank account in order to write Mr. Frascati a check for the first two months' rent— (Oh, God, and the security deposit . . . "Just a formality," he said, "but in these days . . . disregard for private property . . . Yours will certainly be refunded in its entirety when you leave.") But she hasn't even arrived yet! The rent on that little apartment (Oh, how is she going to furnish it? She will have to select the furniture and have it sent, waiting for it furtively upstairs, for what if her husband saw her down there on the sidewalk, waving her arms at moving men?) is $250. Two times $250 plus $200 more is $700—and that includes neither utilities nor the bare essentials of furniture. (Kitchen utensils, she suddenly remembers; would it be fair to take a few things from her own kitchen, packing them up secretly a few days before?) And, lost in calculations, Mrs. Wakeley uses her own front door by mistake, even if it is dark and Mr. Frascati is surely settling down in the bosom of his family in another part of town. She glances rapidly over her shoulder, heart starting to pound, but the ground floor of the building is innocently dark. On the upper floors are several lighted windows: early tenants already moving in . . . her future neighbors? But she will have to keep remote from neighbors, won't she, with her secret? She imagines herself being invited to supper by a young couple in the building (Why a young couple? Why not a lonely, middle-aged woman without a man, like herself?) and how, grown carelessly boastful with wine and abundant spaghetti, she will tell those two young, idealistic lovers, "You know, my husband lives just across the street. He has no idea where I am, no idea in the world, but I can see him brushing his teeth if I want!"

Boiling the water for the artichokes, she subtracts her initial payment to Mr. Frascati from her "account," and realizes that will leave her with eight more months' rent— without utilities, furnishings, or food. Well, she will have to get a job. Mrs. Clara Jones will have to get a job. Mrs. Wakeley imagines "jobs." She sees women's fingers galloping over the keyboards of huge electric machines; women in white uniforms; women in black dresses behind counters; the woman behind the desk in the library; the woman behind the desk in the Social Security office screaming, "Where have *you* been all these years?" And now she sees the bank manager in the bank where Mrs. Clara Jones will open her account. A kindly man with steel-rimmed glasses, pictures of family on desk like Mr. Frascati, he is asking her gently, in a tone of mild disbelief, "But, Mrs. Jones, do you mean to say that you have never had a previous account with any bank? But surely your husband, then . . . Could you perhaps give us the name of his bank?"

A terrible thought begins to form in her head: behind every real person in the real world there is a Social Security number and a bank account. Therefore what does that make her? She has no Social Security number and only half a bank account. That makes her exactly one-fourth of a person. Was it this one-fourth who made the plan of moving across the street? How could a fraction of a person live anywhere by herself? Was her plan just a fantasy, then, one of those daytime fantasies of a lonely wife? Suddenly she sees herself no longer worthy of her own life story, with a name of her own. She could accomplish the purposes of her fantasy within the confines of a small, impersonal fable, the message of which is vastly more significant than the nameless woman who inhabits it. In fables, no cash or job is required. In fantasies, you can fly now and never pay. One day there was a wife, thinks Mrs. Wakeley (opening a can of corned beef),

> One day there was a wife who absented herself from her home and, unbeknownst to her husband, went and lived across the street. The first thing he did was call the police. The second was to mourn her. The third was to find a replacement for her.
>
> The wife watched these things. When he called the police, she perspired with guilt. When he mourned her, she wept with him. When he replaced her, she burned from head to foot with the miserable triumph of self-vindication.

In the kitchen hang three small framed watercolors. Seascapes of Okracoke: primitive, rather depressing pictures, signed "T. Roscoe." An old uncle, now dead. But she remembers the old straw hat he wore in the sun and is sentimentally attached to the Okracoke that was a product of his eyes alone. When she and her husband purchased this house and were frantically trying to fill up so much space all at once by themselves, she said, laughing, "We could string out Uncle Roscoe's pictures on that long wall in the living room." "We *could* . . ." replied her husband, not meeting her eyes. When he came home soon after and found them hanging in the kitchen, he brightened at once and said, "This room will cheer him up a bit." Should her fable go on?

> The wife began watching her replacement. She saw her doing many of the things that she had done. And some she had not. She even saw her start making some of her old mistakes. One day, when she could bear it no longer, she sat down and wrote her replacement an anonymous letter explaining certain things.

When she hears the familiar turn of the key in the lock (the artichokes bubbling away, the corned beef simmering with two poached eggs on top), Mrs. Wakeley imagines that future evening when this house will be dark. (Or should she leave on a light?) No favorite smells or bubbling sounds will come from the kitchen. The cheerful walls will be somehow *different*, though it will take him a minute to figure out why. She has decided to take her uncle's pictures with her.

"Anybody home?" her husband calls, as he has called for years, coming home for years through the halls of different houses, when he always knew there would be someone home, then two people home, then three, then two again, then the one who'd been there all the time, right from the beginning, the one who always answered, just for a joke: "No, nobody's home."

"No, nobody's home," she calls.

In the split second before he enters the kitchen, she resolves to keep her distance, to remove herself from her own involvement in this familiar scene, and take the first step toward her move across the street. She will become an observer as she watches him now, coming through this door, the "husband" of a "wife," performing, as he has for almost three decades, the ritual of "coming home."

But soon she discovers more difficulties than she had ever anticipated.

In the first place, she finds that his presence works a subtle change in her. As she sits across the table from him, trying to surprise him in his own otherness, she is no longer *quite* the woman who watched that new apartment building rise before her eyes like a vision, growing taller every day. She is no longer exactly the woman who saw a way out of a dilemma and went so far as to cross the normal borders of her life to explore it further. She can't even articulate what it is that the flesh-and-blood reality of her husband— as he sits with his napkin flung across his lap, his toes pointed slightly outward beneath the table, dipping an artichoke leaf into a pool of lemon butter—does to her own flesh and spirit. All she knows is that a *verticalness* seems to go out of her, and that as she leans forward toward her husband across the table, the molecules of her body seem to rearrange themselves in smaller, rounder patterns, homing in on themselves, retreating from long and difficult flights.

The second thing is: she discovers that she cannot see the totality of her husband anymore, and thus cannot form a judgment of who he is in relation to her. She can't grasp him in quick totality, as she could Mr. Frascati, or even the kindly but disbelieving bank manager, or even the young couple who invited Mrs. Clara Jones to share their spaghetti supper. Yes, it was true what she told them (reckless from too much wine): she *can* see her husband brushing his teeth! She can count the gold crowns in his mouth without ever looking, and the root canals he's suffered through, and the secret bridge that mortified him for the first whole year, and the gum-bleeds he gets sometimes in the night, his touching vanity when he says, "Well, at least I've kept all my hair!" But what she can't see anymore is "Wakeley" . . . "that man" . . . that stranger as seen from behind, or across the street. She can imagine Frascati, the exact smile he would have for his grandchild, his mistress, his bank manager, but what has happened is that, somewhere along the way, she has lost the power to create her husband's life, intuitively, with the sure hand of intuition, when he walks out of this house and becomes "just himself," alone.

And she knows he has also lost this power with her. She has not felt for some time that priceless tug that signals to her in his absence that she is securely attached to the strings of his imagination, that he is imagining her, not merely remembering her. And when they are together, he does not "see" her. He, too, sees only details. (She wonders which details. Her new glasses which, even though she tried on every pair of frames in the shop, make her face look crooked and her eyes too critical? Her apron? Her gray hairs? *Her* teeth?)

Is that what marriage is, after all: details? The gradual

accumulation of details blocking up the person you once mysteriously loved, until that person can no longer be seen?

Her husband is relating various interactions between himself and somebody called "Tyson" and somebody else called "Wingate." It all sounds very innocuous, the kind of associations anybody might have with anybody during the course of a working day. But behind "Tyson," Mrs. Wakeley sees the poor shadow of a good-natured clown, habitually beset by mishaps, misunderstandings, who, by comparison, makes everyone else feel more sure of himself. ("Poor guy. You know, I really like Tyson.") Whereas the mere utterance of the name Wingate, like an east wind, bodes no good. It is a name linked to villainous conspiracies and unjust accusations, a figure sporting years of unearned praise. ("What I can't understand is, why can't intelligent people see *through* Wingate?") She sees through Wingate very clearly, she sees all around Tyson, she sees the other characters and the props on that stage. She has even wondered what part "Wakeley" plays in the dinner conversations between Tyson and his wife and Wingate and his wife. She would give anything to suddenly have Mrs. Tyson's easier view of Wakeley, Mrs. Wingate's nutshell character sketch of him.

She sees, sitting across the table from her, a man of forty-nine guiding the heart of an artichoke into his open mouth and lowering his eyes, which, having been nearsighted for years, are now restoring themselves annually toward perfect vision.

She sees a person with a real job in the real world; a man in a nice shirt she doesn't remember having seen before, who perhaps takes a pretty young woman with a job for a "business lunch."

Dear Replacement [the wife wrote],
　　You think you know him. You do. Enjoy this knowledge. It passes. Memorize him. Be memorable yourself.

"What did you do today?" he asks, one of those rare spouses who help clear the table without a fuss. He stacks the dishes beside the sink. He loads up his arms, like an agile waiter, with things to go back in the refrigerator.

"I went to the library. I bought these artichokes."

"What did you read, anything interesting?"

"A woman wrote in to a magazine that housewives ought to set up their own pension funds. The new fashions will have designed-in nostalgia. Do you think I ought to get a job?"

"Nostalgia is all over the place," he remarks with interest, making himself the customary glass of ice water. "It's the big supersell, nostalgia, everywhere you look. Why is that, I wonder? Maybe because we don't like where we are and don't want to know where we're going." She recognizes the exact moment when his voice shifts from speculation to assertion. He is a person who can hear through the sound of his own voice the answers to things he thought he didn't know. "A job? Why? What kind?"

"I'm not sure. But don't you think everyone ought to do some kind of work before they die?"

"*Die?*" He turns to touch her on the arm, astonished. "What kind of mood is that?" His ice cubes tinkle in his glass. "You have worked. You do work. If what you do isn't work, then who has worked? If you mean a *profession* . . . Would you like to go back to school? We can afford it. I've often thought . . . "

But she is thinking of the touch on her arm—"her arm," that detail on a totality he has not apprehended for so long a time. Does he still remember that her skin is exactly the same color all over? There are certain things people do not really want the answer to.

They watch television. The first year they were married, they could not stop watching each other long enough to go to the movies, which they both loved. Now Mrs. Wakeley watches as a hand lowers a fork into a pie and pulls out a string of pearls covered in blueberries, then slides the purplish mess into a glassful of effervescent denture cleaner. The pearls come out looking like new. She laughs so long and so hard that her husband turns to her, alarmed.

She goes to the window to adjust the blinds for the night, and gazes through a chink across the dark street and up at certain unlighted windows. She stares through the top part of her glasses, trying to flush out from obscurity the outline of that other woman who can reveal to her who she is. Oh: how to make that leap to that other, higher window from which, at last, unencumbered by the motes of habit and the beams of affection, she can assess her position by spying on her own absence from it!

Will she be missed? And how should her fable end, on a note of "built-in" nostalgia?

Memorize him [the wife wrote].

Or on a note of cynicism, based on one's scant knowledge of the unhappy present?

At first he trains his eyes on the shortsighted necessities of your mutual existence, leaving you free to focus mistily on your continuing happiness.

Then one day the visions shift. You find yourself looking at things more closely, just in time to see him looking away.

On a visionary note, perhaps?

One transcends this dilemma, of course, by . . .

But Mrs. Wakeley is no visionary. Ruminator, closet fabulist, fledgling fantasizer, yes. Now that the banks are safely closed and that terrible Social Security woman double-locked with her pet dog in unlovely rooms and Mr. Frascati settling down with a saucerful of grapes, wearing carpet slippers whose insteps shine in the dark, perhaps to watch this same channel on TV with his wife—now Mrs. Clara Jones waves the movers boldly on. In darkness they ascend the elevator in shifts, ghostly figures of men who do her bidding, bearing on their shoulders everything she will need to begin her new life. When they finish, she gives each of them a handsome tip that costs her nothing. Days pass . . . nights . . . and, stationed at her window, scarcely bothering to eat or sleep, she stares down and across at where her marriage no longer is, until she understands it. And then what? Will she turn her back on it forever and go to live in that other, bright apartment with the changing skies and the private progress of flowers watched by someone as self-sustaining as "Clara Jones"? Or is that another story, perhaps not belonging to her at all?

"What are you looking at?" asks her husband, who has been quietly watching her from behind.

MY LOVER, HIS SUMMER VACATION

FIRST DAY

7:15 a.m. He leaves town. He packed the car last evening before going to see his mistress. The luggage is neatly strapped down, beneath a canvas, on the new carrier rack. The ends were too long so he sawed them off himself. He is proud of the job. His son, thirteen, sits on the other bucket seat, blank and noncommunicative, picking at a hangnail. Between them, on the carpeted hump, is an AAA Trip-Tik. (Prepared Expressly for You, M——— L———. Have a Safe Trip! Jim.) Jim is a nice fellow, so agreeable. His competent blue marker leads this man and his boy out of their city and shows them exactly where to get on Interstate 74 going east. Jim might have ordered the weather as well. Clean blue skies, a few harmless clouds. He is tense as he enters his body and his son's into the right lane of the highway. So many cars, going so fast. As always, he wonders if he can ever accelerate enough to match their speeds. Fifty, fifty-five, sixty, seventy. Yes, he is one of them. He sits back a little. His face relaxes. He says to his son, "We couldn't have asked for a better day." His son grunts. He is dying to turn on the radio and his fingers twitch a couple of times, getting up nerve to flutter toward the dial, but no. His father never plays the radio while driving. His mother does. She says music insulates her, keeps her from being scared stiff of all those fools on the road, including herself. She has gone on ahead, to visit her mother.

The man thinks of last night. He took his mistress a

present. ("Here is a little going-away gift.") He stayed till half past three, two hours longer than usual. She said, "I am going to miss you more than you will miss me. You won't keep saying to yourself, 'I wonder what she is doing right this minute.'" He said, "It's true I don't have obsessive thoughts about people. I really don't think about people a lot, except when they are in trouble." He added, "I do the best I can."

They could have left at 7:00 a.m., but his son wanted to finish watching a cartoon. Did other people's sons watch as much TV as his did? When he was that age . . . what was he doing at that age? He remembers so little. His mistress is always asking him little things about his childhood. "Why do we want to drag up all that mess?" he says. Then later he had remembered that when he was nine he had flown. His mistress was delighted. Kept pressing for details. "Well, it's not too clear. It only happened once. I just lifted up my arms and jumped, and I flew for a minute. Then I wondered whether such things were possible and I hit the ground with a thud." "Ah, you shouldn't have thought," she said.

He passes a truck. Easily. Using his signal lights both times. The truck driver flashes his headlights "Thank you." Now they have achieved a steady seventy-five. He feels good.

10:03 a.m. His mistress's confidante comes by. Pilar. She is from Buenos Aires. Pili for short. She just walks in the screen door, calls out, "Anybody here?" His mistress comes out of the bathroom where she has been doing various things to her hair and face. The women embrace, Pili naturally, it is the custom of her country, the other woman shrinking slightly, because she would not want anyone to mistake her for a lesbian. "I'm glad to see you," says his mistress; "you have saved me from my mirror." The two women laugh. His mistress makes tea. They sit facing each other on the sofa, legs tucked under, and talk about men, men and women. "Do you think men are basically more remote than women?" his mistress asks. "Yes," says Pili, "they are, but it's not a physiologically caused thing; it's because they've been protected, they've been excused from all the efforts we make because we make them for them." Her voice trips piquantly over "physiologically," making the word lyrical and delicate and foreign, like Pili herself. "Do you think it might be a sign that the marriage is breaking up when the wife leaves ten days early to go and see her mother?" his mistress asks. "No, that is bourgeois to think like that," Pili says. "It simply means that they have lived together so long that each can go off and do what he likes. It is no small thing to have someone who lets you go when you please. The reason I stay with Ricardo is because he has learned not to bother me." "I'm so depressed," says his mistress. "That is because you are stuck midway in the water," says Pili solemnly. "You want to surface but cannot. Perhaps you should touch bottom and then start up. Go against your own tides. Make it difficult for him sometimes. You are an attractive woman. You are attractive even to me. I think it is important for a woman to be attractive to other women. I think you will find a man of your own. I like the way you move, the way you walk, the way you get excited about things. There is something sweet about you. I have often thought . . . well . . . that he is not enough for you. Whenever I see him at parties, there is like a glass tube around him. He looks interested in what you are saying but he is not really listening. Now have I hurt your feelings?" "No," says the other, "you have made me more cheerful." They laugh. Pili tells more anecdotes about the year, before her marriage to Ricardo, when she worked as a model at Elizabeth Arden's. "I would put on anything and walk around and all the fat ladies on their massage tables would want what I had on. They would look at me—I was exquisite in those days—and buy whatever I was wearing right off my back. Lace negligées, bathing suits, little-nothing bed jackets. They thought they could buy the way I looked by buying the garment. One day I sold two hundred dollars' worth of colored wooden beads. The manager said, 'Pili, we have got to get rid of these awful beads,' so I flung a few strands around myself and walked by this lady and she looked at me hard and said, 'How much are those beads?' I told her we had a whole tableful, but she said, 'No, I want those, the ones you have around your neck.' So I took them off and sold them to her and she put them around her neck where they didn't do a thing. By the end of the day, I had sold all of my beads."

He does not know his mistress has a confidante. It would annoy him intensely, after he recovered from the fright. She was so loyal at first, handling their secret like a blessed icon. Then one night he didn't call and Pili was there and . . . She has moments of terror and regret. She shouldn't have told. What if he finds out? ("I am disappointed in you. I thought you understood that I value my privacy more than anything.") Would he leave her? Then at other times, when she gets in a rage, she is glad Pili knows, she is glad she has sent her own secret spy into his precious privacy like a worm into his garden. She counts her betrayal of him as an evening of the score.

10:45 a.m. He takes the exit marked "GAS FOOD LODGING," drives round to the side of the Shell station, parks in front of the rest rooms. Unbuckles his seat belt and looks at his son. "I don't need to," says the son. The father frowns. "You'd better anyway. I don't want to stop again. We're having lunch at that place in Kentucky the man at the AAA recommended and we won't get there till after one." "I couldn't go if I tried," protests the son. The father sighs, uplifts his palms in that familiar gesture of resignation, and leaves the car. As soon as he disappears into the MEN's, the son grabs for the radio dial. Wonderful noise blares through the car: static, music, a confusion of excited voices. He finds a good song. His face goes beatific and slack as he loses himself in the song, its last bar synchronizing with his father's reappearance. Quickly, furtively, he snaps off the radio as his father reenters the air-conditioned silence. "Sure you won't change your mind?" says the father.

1:09 p.m. He takes the Berea exit off I-74 and drives through a shady college town. All the young people on the street look cheerful. That is because they are working their way through college, he thinks. He will have to send his own son; otherwise he might refuse to go. They find a parking place right in front of the Boone Tavern Hotel, lock up the car. He puts a dime in the meter. The dining room is pleasantly uncrowded. "If we'd come at noon, no telling how long we'd have had to wait," he tells his son, pleased with their good timing. Several people look up as they are shown to their table: a tall, shy-looking man in his forties and a tall, rosy-faced son who walks just like the father. They have a fine meal with many courses, breads, choice of desserts. Cooked by the students, served by the students, even the chairs they are sitting on have been made by students. Different students come by, offering and describing various breads and cakes they have made. There is one young man, rather pale and plump, peddling a spoon bread. He speaks with a very precise diction, moving his soft, pale hands as he describes this bread. "Yes, we'll try it, thank you," says the father, annoyed because his son is giggling behind his hand. The plump young man looks hurt, serves the two of them quickly and leaves. "What was that all about?" he asks his son. "He's a fem," says the boy. "Well, this bread is certainly very tasty," says the father. "There's this guy in our class who's a fem," the son continues, animated for the first time during the trip. "What has he done to earn your endearing label?" "Oh, it's not just me, all the guys call him fem." The son stuffs spoon bread into his mouth. The father waits. "He has this funny way of talking, see, he uses this huge vocabulary nobody can understand, and he hates sports; he would rather talk to girls, or the teacher. We had this creative-writing project; everybody had to make a box, decorate this shoebox and put things in it that would represent this imaginary person, this imaginary person whose box it was supposed to be. He covered his box with flowered paper! His imaginary person was a girl! He was the only person in the whole class that did a girl. Even the girls chose men. He had feathers in the box and an old valentine with lace and all sorts of stupid things." "Who was your imaginary person?" asks the father, glancing covertly at his watch; he does not want to get a ticket. "It was a sports hero. A football hero. Only he dies tragically, you see, he has a heart attack, right on the field after he makes this touchdown that wins the game." The father calls for their check.

3:45 p.m. His mistress shops. She buys a week's worth of porterhouse steaks, a large carton of nonfat cottage cheese, assorted fresh vegetables, a dozen grapefruits. She has decided to lose ten pounds during the two weeks. Where is she going to find them to lose? Nevertheless, going on a diet is bound to change something. She needs the discipline. She wants to be changed. She wants him to come back and say, "You look different." She buys *Jane Eyre*, a book she has always loved, and drives her dusty car home, feeling hopeful about these purchases. This is the first day of her vacation as well.

8:10 p.m. The man and the boy are in bed watching TV. They are staying at the Holiday Inn—Central. There are three Holiday Inns in Knoxville. Jim at the AAA called ahead and made reservations for one double room tonight, and a double and a single tomorrow night. This room is enormous. It is decorated in a Spanish style: heavy furniture of dark pine, bedspreads in dark gold and black and turquoise, a sort of Moorish design. There is one lamp on (the son wanted them to turn all the lamps off, but the father explained it was bad for the eyes), and the room is full of distances and shadows. They had steaks for supper and baked potatoes with sour cream, butter, and little bits of chives and bacon. Each has a king-sized bed to himself. During a commercial, the son says, "You know why you always win everything? It's because you won't get involved." "Did your mother say that?" he asks. "No," says the boy, "I figured it out myself."

SECOND DAY

8:45 a.m. Humid. It wasn't supposed to get humid in the mountains. There is an implacable white film over the entire sky, edging down into I-40. They will miss all the views Jim marked for them to see between Knoxville and Asheville. His mistress wanted to know everywhere he was going so she could follow along in her imagination. "To tell the truth, I'm kind of dreading it," he said. "It's so laced through with duty." Then he had added prudently, "I'm not complaining, since I chose it, but I'm saying it's less than ideal." His wife will be on the early-afternoon plane from New York, where she has been visiting her mother. He and Carl will pick her up at the Raleigh-Durham Airport, they will spend the night at the Holiday Inn in Goldsboro and drive to Ocracoke the next day. The trip is expertly planned by Jim.

10:30 a.m. His mistress and her confidante go swimming at the YMCA's new health club. Women can swim from 9:30 till 11:30, but must be cleared out by noon. The two women use Ricardo's locker, since women are not allowed to rent lockers. Pili tells her friend that she really ought to wear a cap in that chlorine, and put protein conditioner on her split ends before she puts on the cap. But his mistress cannot wear a cap, because even while she is swimming laps, she imagines that he is watching her. Pili has a specific number of laps to exercise different sections of her petite, trim figure. So many for crawl, so many for breaststroke, so many for the kickboard. She wears a pink cap with a pointed tip that makes her look like an imp. Her face bobs up and down in the water, serious with Exercise. Afterward, in the shower, she smacks and slaps herself to encourage circulation and break down fatty tissue, Muzak leaks out of the walls, surrounding them with platitudes of melody. "Really," says Pili, rubbing cream into her elbows and kneecaps, "when we get to my house, we are going to sit down and each write a postcard protesting that music. It won't take two minutes. I keep a stack of stamped postcards for just such occasions." "Oh, they would never turn it off for just the two of us," says the other. "Two is also a group," says Pili.

2:22 p.m. Raleigh-Durham Airport. They had cheeseburgers, French fries, and a waxy apple pie for dessert. He sits at the table by the window, watching planes taxi in and out, land, take off. He wishes for a 747, but his wish is not granted. His son is slouched over the magazine rack, reading a comic book, his face devoid of any intellectual struggle. Do other people's sons read comic books all the time? A dark speck materializes upon the whitish surface of sky. At 2:30 precisely, his wife's plane, an ordinary DC-4, touches the runway. He has already paid the check. He parts Carl reluctantly from his comic. They go through the terminal, which is being enlarged, he leading a polite trail between soldiers and families with too much luggage or too many children to handle both successfully. A power saw grates against his eardrum. In the waiting room for Gate 4, they can look through the window and watch the passengers disembark. Where is his wife? Once she missed a plane. What if she missed it today? They would have to wait here for hours, maybe even spend the night in Raleigh, where they don't have reservations. Jim's schedule ruined. He feels annoyance, then hears his son say, "There's Mom." She looks apprehensive descending the metal steps, her eyes cast down as though she is terrified she might fall down and make a fool of herself. She smiles too gratefully at the airline official who stands at the bottom of the steps handing people down. It's his job, after all.

8:17 p.m. Blue dusk fills the town he has abandoned. It gets darker earlier every evening now. His mistress drives by his house, a routine she has often indulged in. But tonight she cruises slowly, blatantly by. Even if she did have a blowout right in front of his house, no curtains would part, no startled face peer out, recognizing the guilty Mustang. The house is dark, a mere silhouette, a mere sketch of a house. No life there tonight. No having to guess who is in what room, doing what. No one weeps, cooks, watches TV, increases the ties that bind in that house tonight. Good. Apples are falling off the tree, rotting in his yard by the dozens. Good. Pili went to a party in his house last spring. She made frequent trips to the bathroom in order to investigate the upstairs for her friend. "What I want to know is, how many bedrooms," said his mistress when Pili came by afterward to report. "Well," replied the secret agent, "one has football players pasted all over the walls. I do not think that room is his. Then the other—I am sorry, my dear, but I could only find two—has a double bed in it. It is a very low bed, with a madras spread. It is practically on the floor. I don't know how people can sleep in those low beds." "How long was it? You know he is very tall," persisted his mistress. "Well," said Pili, reconsidering, "now I think of it, it was a very *short* double bed. . . ." "I knew it," said the mistress. "You know, he told me he has a darkroom in the attic. . . ." "Ha!" cried Pili. "Our mystery is solved. He has a bed in his darkroom. Even Ricardo has a daybed in his study for when we have fights."

9:15 p.m. Holiday Inn, Goldsboro. Carl has a room all to himself. He is in bed watching TV. The room is in total blackness except for the TV screen. There is a great show on. It is a weekly show about a doctor and all the different cases this doctor has. Tonight it is about this basketball player who has to have this dangerous operation on his knee, which may mean that he cannot go on to be a star. The first time Carl saw this particular show he could hardly watch it he was so nervous. Would the operation succeed or fail? This time he can really enjoy the show, because he knows what is coming next. Now it is that scene where the doctor is explaining to the boy that he will be able to lead a perfectly normal life, etc., etc., even if he can't fulfill his dream of being a great basketball star. He wishes he could get this boy on the TV to himself after the doctor leaves the room and say, "Don't worry! I know how it is going to end. You are still going to win that game and get the championship for your team!" The light from the TV screen dances upon his face. His eyes narrow, his lips grow slack, revealing healthy young teeth. At this moment, his face is an exact youthful replica of his father's at the moment of orgasm.

THIRD DAY

9:30 a.m. A whole hour behind Jim's schedule. She was in the bathroom for thirty-five minutes. Now she is in the bucket seat, wearing both kinds of safety belts, and Carl is in the back, looking out the window at nothing. They will reach Cape Lookout by early afternoon if they don't dawdle over lunch. They are renting a beach house with Bob and Mildred Taylor. Bob, a linguist, has written many articles on the Hatteras dialect. Mildred weaves rugs of gorgeous design and sells them for hundreds of dollars.

11:43 a.m. His mistress sketches Pili's garden with felt-tip drawing pens. It is a late-summer garden whose colors are bright and sharp. She uses carmine, magenta, burnt orange, clear yellow. Pili has told her the names of the flowers, but she keeps forgetting. She has not sketched in years. The pens, bought this morning, are a joy. They move easily and make the garden look brighter than it is already. Pili is snipping dill from her herb garden. "You could still go to Mexico for your vacation," she scolds from beneath her garden hat. "Tomorrow afternoon you could be strutting up and down the beach in your bikini, attracting men like flies." "It's better I stay here," says his mistress. "I owe hundreds on my charge accounts." "Oh, yes, I know. You have bought too many clothes. You are so far gone that you would curl up and die for him under a palm tree instead of enjoying yourself," says Pili. "I was like that with Alistair." "Who was Alistair?" "Oh, some ridiculous creature I suffered over before I met Ricardo."

3:10 p.m. "I got the carrier rack home from Sears," he is saying as they wait in their car for the ferry to Ocracoke, "and the ends were too long for the car. I borrowed a metal saw from Jack Atkinson and trimmed them down to fit."

"That's wonderful," she says.

10:00 p.m. His mistress opens *Jane Eyre*. The beginning seems to have changed. Didn't the story open in an orphanage? Or was that the movie? Did she read this book before, or did she only imagine she had? Oh, well, it is going to be a wonderful book, she knows. But she can't concentrate. Her eyelids have sandbags attached and she keeps replaying dialogues from two nights ago in this bed.

FOURTH DAY

8:00 p.m. Too much sun. His face is hot. Mildred's good supper. Oyster stew and what was the extra green in the salad, sort of bitter? He praised it, so his wife will find out and put it in their salads. She and Mildred in the kitchen. He just heard his wife say, ". . . I wish I had some talent, something of my own. . . ." Bob has lit his pipe. "I am going to the Hebrides this fall," he says. "I got that grant." "Mmm," replies his friend appreciatively, "good." Bob says, "Would you like to go over to this tiny island with me tomorrow? It's marvelously peaceful. Just gulls and egrets and wild birds." "That sounds fine," says the other. Carl is happy, too. He sits by himself on the dark screened-in porch, impervious to the sound of the sea, watching his regular programs on TV.

8:00 p.m. Dinner at Pili and Ricardo's. Pili has the knack of making the simplest fare elegant. They are having a spicy hamburger casserole baked inside pastry, marinated cucumbers with the dill she snipped yesterday, carrots cooked with baby onions, fresh pineapple flavored with Benedictine, and plenty of decanted Valpolicella. The table is set with one of her great-grandmother's hand-embroidered tablecloths, and each piece of cutlery (sent from Tiffany's to Buenos Aires in the nineteenth century) has a wild animal carved on it. His mistress's knife has a rabbit peeping out from behind some graceful leaves. Ricardo is courteous but distant. He has a way of treating each woman. He teases Pili a little, compliments her, makes demands. With their guest he is more gentle, but more impersonal. He is an architect, a small man who looks larger. He has a mustache like Marlon Brando's in *Viva Zapata!* and wears smoked, gold-rimmed glasses and impeccable white cotton shirts with tucks in them. During the pineapple, the phone rings. It is one of Ricardo's clients. "Americans eat so early and expect everyone else to do likewise," he says, going out of the room. He calls back to Pili for her to hang up when he takes it in his study and to please bring him coffee.

The women clear the dishes. The guest loiters in a corner of the pretty kitchen while Pili whisks about, an efficient sprite. How she yearns for an order comparable to Pili's life: spices on their little spinning racks, home-grown herbs in their airproof glass jars. . . . Ricardo's voice drones above, explaining building specifications. Safe in his own house, planning the houses of others. "Let's take our coffee to my study," says Pili. "I want you to read what I have done on the new chapter." Pili is writing a book about the beauty secrets of her family: her great-aunt Isabel, who is now ninety and has the skin of a young girl, her mother's facial that any woman can make from the ingredients in her own kitchen. . . . "When I finish the book, Ricardo's secretary will type it on the Selectric. Then I shall get out my good clothes and go to New York and visit the publishers." "You will be a walking advertisement for your book," says her friend, thinking: *Ah, married, passion over with (except for the 'cariñitos'), able to devote your days to snipping dill in your garden, dispatching angry postcards to encroachers on your freedom, writing a leisurely, humorous book about women putting mayonnaise and vinegar on their faces to make themselves irresistible to men. . . .*

FIFTH DAY

11:00 a.m. The two men row out to Bob's island, which turns out to be less than one hundred yards long. They tie their boat to a tree and tramp around, serious as scouts. Wild cries of birds. No human sounds other than their own feet in the grassy sand. Suddenly Bob breaks the beautiful peace. "I might as well tell you. Mildred and I are splitting at the end of this summer." His friend does not answer. "I'm going to the Hebrides alone. No, that's not true. Someone is going with me. We're terribly in love. She's so young, I could almost be her father. But it's not like *that*, she's no little empty-head, Susan isn't. Do you know, she has made a movie? A feature-length film! Shot the thing herself with a sixteen-millimeter. Why, she's not even beautiful." He shakes his head, dazed by his luck. Then, embarrassed by his friend's silence, he fills his pipe and puffs it vigorously. The other man watches an egret tuck his ungainly feet under him and float heroically up the warm sky. Finally he says, "There will probably be lots of material for a film-maker in a place like the Hebrides." Bob explodes with laughter. "Oh, Matthew, you'll never change!" Bob has grown a droopy mustache this past year, and when he laughs he resembles a sad old walrus trying to be young and gay.

SIXTH DAY

Anytime.

Lands of the Outer Banks are constantly under-going changes caused by wind and wave action. Some believe the landmass is moving a minute dis-tance toward the mainland each year and will con-tinue to do so as long as the ocean remains at its present level or until the mainland is reached. Inlets connecting the ocean and sounds sometimes have had a lifetime of less than 100 years. They appear or disappear as the result of storms. . . .
—*AAA Tour Book, Southeastern Region.*

She paid $26 to join, just so she could get the maps and books to follow him.

11:30 p.m. Jane Eyre locked in the red room without a candle because she stood up for her rights.

SEVENTH DAY

In one week he comes home.

What are *cariñitos*? They are what has replaced passion in the twelve-year-old marriage of Pili and Ricardo. *Cariño* means affection, kindness. When Pili, or sometimes it is Ricardo, has had a horrible day, she, or sometimes it is he, falls face down on the bed and implores the other: *"Cari-*

ñitos, por favor." Then the stronger of the two at that moment (i.e., the one implored) gives the other a back rub.

EIGHTH DAY

Sometime. The four adults have dragged Carl to Kill Devil Hill. It is so historical. In the year ———, Wilbur and Orville Wright flew the first airplane, blah, blah, blah. Mr. Taylor: "Oh, you don't know how it killed me to see that bridge go up, that pure Elizabethan dialect gone forever. . . ." Carl's mother in her shy, uncertain voice: "Sometimes I think progress is awful." If progress is awful, why have they dragged him all the way up here to see this useless monument?

NINTH DAY

In five days he comes home.

She will have to make herself small again, move over and share this city with him. He won't have missed her. He'll smile and say, "Gee, I'm glad to see you. Let's go to bed." Perhaps she should buy an animal of some kind.

TENTH DAY

Around noon.

His Wife: How are my shoulders?

Mildred: They're okay. You were careful the first week. I'm not really too depressed about it. After all, the girls are grown, there will be enough money because this Susan's father is in sausages or something, and I have my rugs and can go back to being a vegetarian. Bob told Matthew, you know.

His Wife: No, I didn't. What did Matthew say?

MILDRED: He said there would be lots of things to film in the Hebrides.

HIS WIFE (*laughing*): Poor Matthew!

11:59

Dear Charlotte Brontë:

I am writing to you from the late-twentieth century. I just this minute finished your novel and felt like chatting. The novel has done extraordinarily well since your early death in 1855. You were taking a risk. Even today when we can do heart transplants and good-looking young poets no longer die from TB, it is incautious to have a first baby at 39. I am 32 myself next birthday, and for two years have been doing something Jane refused to do. Yes, I am mistress to the man I love. His wife is still living, and, unfortunately, not confined to the attic. I don't think he is capable of loving me as much as Mr. Rochester loves Jane, for, you see, he has never known solitude. If you were writing your novel today, you could have saved yourself the trouble of that last 132 pages in the Signet paperback* edition. You could have saved yourself that whole episode with that prick** St. John, marking time till Rochester's wife could burn up. Today it is accepted that sometimes even nice girls sleep with (when they can) men they are unable to marry.

A Mistress
(circa 1970)

P.S. It must be gratifying to know that one's art product will live longer than some land masses.

P.P.S. * A paperback is a book printed on cheap paper with an illustrated cardboard cover that usually misrepresents the story.

** Prick (noun) is a modern pejorative term usually applied to a selfish man, a sexually inconsiderate man, or a man one happens to be furious with.

ELEVENTH DAY

Tomorrow he starts home.

Swimming and lunch with Pili. In the afternoon paper, his mistress sees an ad for six-week-old seal-point Siamese kittens, already litter-trained. Calls the woman. "They really are darling, we have only two left. A little boy and a little girl. They really are inseparable. I'd probably sell them both for the price of one just so they could stay together." She has plenty of room, a fenced-in back yard, a perfect place for the litter bin. Winter nights with a fire in the fireplace, two elegant, independent creatures leaping and cuffing each other on her green-and-turquoise Danish rug. But what if he is allergic to cats?

In the evening she goes to see *Blow-Up* again with Pili and Ricardo. Afterward they have a terrible fight in the parking lot. He says the movie was meaningless, it had no value system. "Oh, your values! Your systems!" screams Pili. It gets so bad they have to switch to Spanish. She stands a discreet distance away, burrowing the toes of her sandals in the gravel. She thinks how she will offer him this scene as a humorous anecdote.

TWELFTH DAY

Jim gets them almost clear across North Carolina via 70 and 85, then it's into Winston-Salem on 40, overnight at the Blue Bird Motel. (Rating, Good, but giving them a head start on 52 next morning.) The good thing about Jim is that he's dependable but keeps the journey from becoming monotonous.

THIRTEENTH DAY

Morning. She gets up, dresses in anything. So much to get done! Forces self to make coffee so won't faint downtown.

Paces while it perks, checking herself nervously in mirrors. Dirty hair! Legs and underarms unshaved for fourteen days! Gulps coffee, backs down driveway, drives halfway to town before releasing hand brake. First stop: Bronson's Department Store. Can't wait for elevator. Escalator to fourth, Household Goods. August White Sale. She needs towels, thick towels. He told her once he could not stand drying on a thin towel. How thick does a towel have to be for him to consider it thick? She imagines miraculous towels in his own bathroom, weighing five or six pounds, discovered by his wife at some incredible bargain in some store she would be denied admission to. Goes around feeling the edges of towels. Finds some. They are not on sale. She buys four, sucking in her breath and strolling about nonchalantly while the saleslady calls up to Credit to check her charge card. The thing is, she has already gone over her $300 limit with that green crêpe dress she bought for the night before he left. She gets away with it. Bronson's probably wants her to, probably flourishes on fools like her. Passing through Shoes, she sees these sandals, dark blue with red stitching, an arrogant little heel. The summer's almost over. She needs boots, not sandals. Once he said, "You have such nice, slim feet." Charges the sandals, feeling positively hubristic. Bronson's wouldn't dare stop her now. Bronson's doesn't. Liquor store. He likes good Scotch, sometimes imported beer, depending on his mood and where he's supposed to have been. She buys a fifth of Johnnie Walker Black Label and a six-pack of Tuborg dark, sucking in her breath as she writes the check. Now she has $9.17 left in her account. To supermarket. More cottage cheese, more grapefruit, more milk. Must make it till next payday without meat. Driving home, decides to have her car washed. Free if she buys gas. But her tank is full; she has gone nowhere in two weeks. Charges the car wash on credit card. As she drives the left front tire onto the rack, she sees a sign advertising hot or cold wax. "What is the difference between hot and cold wax?" she asks the black man who is pushing down her aerial. "Hot is fifty cents more." "I'll have the hot," she says. Goes into a little waiting alley where she can watch her car being cleaned for his homecoming. An enormous green sponge, cut in strips, undulates across the hood like a fat hula dancer. When time comes for the wax, red and yellow lights flash, bells ring, and a sign saying "YOUR CAR IS NOW GETTING HOT WAX" flicks on and off, on and off. She drives home sparkling, euphoric, to clean her house.

Evening. Columbus, Ohio. Jim really understands the rhythm of a vacation. He understands that, going away, one wants to spread out, wants more luxury, more views. Coming home, it doesn't matter so much; one's thoughts return to the convenient, the economical. Only the average-sized double bed in this room. His wife goes first in the bathroom, because she knows he takes his bath in the evening. She splashes water quickly on her face; he will not know the difference. Actually she is too tired, but this is one of those Institutional Times. Thanksgiving, Christmas, Anniversaries, Last Night of Vacation. A sort of test. She slips her gown over her head. It smells of suntan oil. She runs a brush through her hair.

He is sitting in his undershirt and shorts on the side of their bed, his reading glasses on, studying the map. She puts her hand on his neck, leans her hip against the side of his head, and looks down with him at all those confusing, possible routes. She says, "Poor Mildred and Bob." "Yes, it's complicated," he says.

She savors her solitude in bed. Cool sheets. Hears him splashing in the bathroom, but she is already at home, back in her house, going from room to room checking the damage. What lights did they leave on? Did they remember to empty the garbage? What will be rotted in the refrigerator? She cruises the aisles of the A & P, filling her basket with the staples they have forgotten to replace. The apple tree. All those apples will be ripe, rotting. Baked apples, apple pies, apple turnovers, apple chutney . . .

He comes out, releasing a gust of steamy air into the dark room. She has switched off the lamp and he feels his way cautiously till his eyes adjust, till he can make out her hair like dark feathers on the pillow. "Boy, am I beat," he says, getting in on his side. "Yes, I know you are," she says. They lie in the dark, not touching. He puts his hand on her arm. "How are you?" "I'm fine, Matthew, I'm always fine." "Yes, I know," he says. He raises up on his elbow, looks for her mouth, then bends to kiss her, his lips puckering like a child. She wraps her arms about him. She really is tired, but he's aroused and it seems a sort of tribute to her, when he has been driving since morning. Would she be happier if she could weave rugs or make speeches on the floor of the Senate? How many times over the years she has cried herself dry. But now she no longer expects miracles, even wants them. How unsettling a miracle would be.

After he is asleep, she lies there planning meals for the rest of their week.

FOURTEENTH DAY

9:10 a.m. "Do you want me to trim it, or what?"

"Yes, please. No, don't. Wait, could you just snip off these dead ends?"

Under the dryer, she opens the map and traces her finger along 70, just this side of Dayton.

Afternoon. Waiting. Mirror. Lie down on bed. No, ruin hair. This beautiful sunshine. Her last day of vacation. Should call up Pili and go for a stimulating walk. Back to mirror. *What is that?*

Regards with fatalistic horror the Thing growing on her left jaw. Oh, no, oh, damn!

Backs down driveway, forgets hand brake all the way to town. Parks outside Bronson's. Rushes in. Cosmetics. Where, what? Scans the cases: Ultimate, Intimate . . . Urgent!

"May I help you, honey?"

"Oh, yes, I don't know. . . . Listen, do you see this thing on my face, this bump? Well, I've got to get rid of it before tonight. Tonight is the most important night of my life. It's my—it's my wedding rehearsal. Tomorrow is my wedding!"

"Donna, will you come over here a minute? This young lady's wedding day is tomorrow. What do you think?" The two women scrutinize the spoiler on their customer's face.

"Disaster Cream," prescribes Donna.

That much money for this little tube? Charge it. Sucks in breath and strolls nonchalantly. Gets away with it again. Perhaps Bronson's is seeing how far a fool will go before clapping her into jail. Perhaps they are televising her with secret cameras, using her as an example.

There is a yellow ticket on her windshield. She gets in the car, rips open the slim cardboard box, unswivels the tube, applies the white, gritty potion.

Evening.

7:30 p.m.—Bathes, shaves legs and underarms, applies skin lotion liberally to entire body. Disaster spot under control and camouflage.

8:00 p.m.—Sits on sofa, fully dressed, wearing new sandals.

8:30 p.m.—Calls a number. "You park free while banking in First National, your full-service bank. Time: 8:28."

9:00 p.m.—Opens the Johnnie Walker.

9:30 p.m.—This is degrading.

9:40 p.m.—An accident. State Highway Police picking through debris. What and whose debris? All three? Mother and son? Father and husband? How much damage? Seriously? Critically? Abrasions and contusions, released from ———— Hospital? DOA? The two women meet in the waiting room. In the mortuary. "I've decided to keep the coffin closed." "You can't do that to me! I loved him, too!"

9:50 p.m.—Jane was right to leave Thornfield till she could have all or nothing.

10:10 p.m.—Prick.

10:17 p.m.—Drives furtively by his house, her Mustang absolutely exploding in his face with shining HOT WAX! All their lights are on.

10:33 p.m.—Calls up Pili. "Did I wake you? Did I disturb the two of you?" (Murderously.) "Oh, no, we were just watching an old Greta Garbo movie," says Pili. "Well, I just wanted to tell you it's all over. I've given him up. I wanted you to be the first to know." "Sweetie! How marvelous!" cries Pili. "Let's go swimming at ten and have a long lunch, okay? You can tell me all about it." "I can't. I have to go back to work tomorrow." "Oh, *pobrecita*, I forgot. I know! Come for dinner Tuesday night. That is Ricardo's squash night. We can have a good long chat." "Okay. Fine. I'd love to, Pili. See you Tuesday." Goes to bathroom, scrubs face till bump shines, combs hair flat for bed, kicks sandals behind toilet. Uses one of the Sacred Towels. More Johnnie Walker. So long, Prick.

11:15 p.m.—Phone rings. Awakens her out of dream in which the wife is saying, "Yes, I know it's hard, but do you know, he really loves you. What he loves most, he told me, was the way you appreciate our house. He is always begging me to ask you over."

"This is Matthew. I'm down at the office. I thought I'd give you a call. Were you asleep?"

"No. Yes. I don't know."

She hears him laugh softly. His voice sounds younger than she remembered it.

"How are you?" he says, going slowly, risking nothing.

"I'm great. How was your vacation?"

"Oh, you know how vacations go. It rained quite a bit. Carl got a pretty bad bee sting. Now I come back and see these piles of letters waiting for me. I was hoping we could see each other perhaps tomorrow evening—"

"Well, we could!"

"But I hadn't bargained on these dozens and dozens of letters. I was thinking maybe Tuesday evening, but even that's not certain. We could make tentative plans, unless you already have something. . . ."

Rain! Bee stings! Will she ever be able to know everything about him? There is always one more fact she hadn't counted on. And dozens and dozens of letters! She will be kept busy from now until Tuesday trying to imagine the contents of those letters. And how he will answer them. And what he will be doing in between. And what if he can't make it Tuesday? And how is she going to get through now until Tuesday?

"I'll save Tuesday," she hears herself say.

"And now tell me," he says (she can see him smiling attentively in his dark office as he speaks softly into the receiver), "what have you been up to these past two weeks?"

Someone left the freezer door ajar and the Princes' hoard is melting. Frost weeps down the orange-juice cans to the wrapped cuts of meat below, then drools through the crack in the door and streams across the basement floor. It passes beneath Lucy Prince's washing machine, her dryer, the rockers of Mark's cast-off hobby-horse, then veers at a depression in the floor. It snakes beneath a table on which are stacked dozens of Lucy's canvases, paintings from the years after Paris, before the hospital. Now it passes through an open door into the TV room, where Esther and Sidney make love, shortly after having been introduced. They knock the eiderdown off Sidney's bed. When they fish it up, Esther says, "How did this thing get wet?" And Sidney says, "It must be the storm." "The heirs to half a million," says Esther, "and they have a leaky basement." Sidney laughs. He hugs her to him. In this moment of sharing their poverty, they are closer than in their lovemaking. "Nothing to worry about," Sidney says. "It's a genuine eiderdown."

Outside a rainstorm tears the yellow leaves from their limbs and flings them against houses, piles them up on lawns. The windows of the Princes' house shake with wind. The storm begins suddenly, just as the party is breaking up. Taylor Prince and wild Marsha, both drunk, put on matching rubber mackintoshes (one belongs to Lucy) and walk through the rain to Marsha's house.

Esther thinks of seasons. She can't get back to sleep since Sidney half killed her that second time, so she lies with her back against the sleeping man, and tries to make autumnal metaphors to fit her life. Her personality, she decides, has always had the sorrowful colors of autumn. Even as a child, she was never spring or summer. As for winter, she sees herself descending again and again toward stillness and snow, but never touching bottom. My most successful poems, she thinks, arrest the reader at the still-point of this eternal sinking and leave him enchanted but never bruised by the fall.

The TV room is pitch dark, but Esther can imagine where everything is. As a friend of the Princes', Esther has been down here many times before. Once she and Lucy had been down here together, exchanging woman talk while Lucy ironed her sons' clothes. Esther had been sitting on this very hide-a-bed. She had been thinking, Lucy looks like an angel since she chopped off her gold hair short as a boy's and left the shorn tresses on the dining-room table for Taylor to find when he came back from class. Esther had been thinking, Was Taylor really serious when he said his wife was going mad? Esther had been thinking these things when Lucy put down her steam iron and said: "I can't stand my first born. I wonder if all mothers feel that way. I don't mean I hate him. I mean there's too much pressure, just containing his existence. Today when I was giving him his bath, I suddenly had this urge to push him under. I got as far as pressing him down by the shoulders. Then I noticed his penis, how it actually floated. . . ."

And later, Esther had been down here watching TV with Taylor. Lucy was in the hospital then and Esther had come over to watch a documentary on "The Royal Family at Home." During a commercial, Taylor said: "Do you want to see how Lucy looks when she's having her shock treatment?" And he gripped the arms of his chair and went rigid, like the electrocution scenes in films; his head snapped back and his mouth went slack. "How horrible, Taylor," Esther said. Later she wrote a poem about it.

Sidney turns toward her in his sleep. He breathes into her hair. She was surprised at the size of him, for such a small and wiry man. He hurt her with his lovemaking. "Do you have anything against Southerners?" Taylor had asked Esther over the phone. "I think you'll like Sidney. We taught at the same prep school. He's a hard guy to know, but in many ways you two are much the same." So Esther went to the trouble of washing her hair, even though she had washed it the day before.

In what ways are the two of them much the same?

Sidney breathes into her hair. Esther imagines herself married to him. She knows he has just finished another degree. She knows that Taylor trusted him to drive Lucy back from her convalescence in Boca Raton. She knows he is thirty-three, with the soft voice of Virginia. He is probably not as smart as she is. Esther pictures herself the poetess-wife of a headmaster, circumscribed by tweeds and autumn leaves fluttering down through eternal falls and tea hours of courteous voices that skim the abysses lightly. Each night he would subdue her anew with his powerful, insensitive weapon. There would be poems she could no longer write. She resists and yet longs for a life with this man. In a sudden perverse flash, she sees the good in shock treatments.

About the eiderdown: there are two of them in this house. Lucy brought them both back from Europe. She had not finished with studying art and being a handsome girl on her own in Paris. She had not even had a French lover yet when Taylor flew over at Thanksgiving and knocked her up and flew back to his university. "PLEASE SEND MONEY GET RID OF RESULTS OF YOUR VISIT LOVE L.," she cabled. "DELIGHTED RESULTS WILL YOU MARRY ME," he cabled back.

She got on the train and went to Hamburg. College friends of hers and Taylor's were in the diplomatic service there—they would lend her the money. But Taylor called them first and told them everything. So Lucy arrived in Hamburg to her host's transmittal of Taylor's promise of happiness if only she would let things be. The host took her to his home and his wife worked on Lucy. Lucy loved Taylor, didn't she? Lucy did. But she didn't want to draw the line just yet and put an end to possibilities. Where, persisted the wife, would Lucy ever find another person so intelligent, so exuberant, and, let's face it, so rich? Probably nowhere, said Lucy, but nevertheless she would like to have a look around first and see what other qualities there were. The wife went sober, mystical: some things, she warned, arrive in their own mysterious hour, on their own terms and not yours, to be seized or relinquished forever. Lucy listened and drank gallons and imagined the thing in her womb moving. The wife played on this: perhaps Lucy was further along than she realized. It would endanger her health, her youth; besides, how could she bear not to see how he would turn out, with the two of them being so gifted, so beautiful? Lucy knew exactly how far along she was and she knew the child would probably be beautiful. At the end of the week she wired Taylor: "LAUNDRESS ARRIVING NEW YEAR WITH CHILD CONGRATULATIONS." Taylor splurged on a ninety-six-minute call. What fun they would have next year! In June he'd have his degree and a teaching job at his old prep school. She would love the place; there was skiing. "Listen, baby, buy two of the biggest eiderdowns you can find. They're fabulous to sleep under. We'll have one for us and one for him."

Five winters later, Esther and Sidney sleep under one. Upstairs in the children's room, little Davie sleeps under the other. Mark, who cut short his mother's career in art and freedom, is allergic to goose feathers.

· · ·

Esther, who is she? He thinks of mysterious, costly oils and those grave and suffering women whose names give fragrance to the Old Testament, a queen who saves her people from slaughter. His nose buried in her hair, he is only pretending to sleep, wondering about the waywardness of his body that can ravish suffering Jewesses and good-time girls but goes limp at the sight of the woman he wants. Sitting beside him at the festive table, candlelit with Lucy's homecoming, Esther touched him repeatedly in the course of conversation. She was aware of him, playing to him, he knew that, even if Taylor had not taken him aside and said Sidney, she wants you. "She wants you, old man. She said you were inscrutable." While Lucy was doing the crêpes suzette—even better, Taylor said, than before her shock treatments—and the guests milled around in swirls of marijuana and rock, Taylor took Sidney aside and said, "You could make that scene if you wanted, man. She wants you if she says you're inscrutable." Sidney smiled inscrutably and said nothing. Taylor hooked his arm about Sidney's neck joyfully. "You are, you are!" he said. "I've known you five years, but do I know you? Does anyone?" "What is there to know?" Sidney grinned and went back to sit beside the Jewess he was going to seduce. He sits modeling the candlelight on the planes of his face, knowing he is watched. And he thinks of his father, who never finished grammar school. He calls up images of his boyhood, hidden now behind scholarship and inscrutability. Esther flutters her hands, and he sees how the nails are ragged. He feels himself grow big as a giant inside his pants.

The sherbets are melting now. Orange, raspberry, and lime slush drips down on the cuts of meat. Taylor is the one who eats sherbet in this household. He likes the brittle sparkle against the backs of his front teeth. He likes to say, "It's eating snow year round." He buys gallons of it at a time, now that Lucy cannot shop. Taylor loves to shop. Taylor and the boys do the shopping. They make a game of it. Taylor will say to Mark, "Let's see how many things we can buy with a bird on the front today," and off they'll go, Davie shrieking glee, to pile the cart with turkey stuffing, wild rice, birdseed, room freshener, anything with a bird on the front. Once, horseplaying at economy, they bought one of everything on sale. "This is fun!" screams Mark. Then, cagily assessing his father, adds: "Why didn't Mommy like doing this?" "She felt all the labels were getting back at her," explains Taylor, picking up a box of Arm & Hammer soda and running after the squealing child, gnashing his teeth, pretending to be a label in pursuit of Lucy.

Two floors above the TV room where Esther and Sidney pretend to sleep, Lucy pushes up through light sedation to meet the wild storm. In the next room her children sleep. Taylor is not back from walking Marsha home. Lucy thinks of herself locked away in the remotest chamber of the tallest tower of the most unreachable castle on the highest peak. The storm tears through the trees and accosts the castle. But nothing can get in here, nothing and no one. A million hardships lie in wait for the foolish climber: the treacherous rocks, the howling storm, the rain like blades in his eyes, the steep, hopeless, unrewarding distance.

In the dark, Lucy hugs her knees. Often, before the breakdown, she would dream of days in some foreign city. Her dreams would build on one another. She knew the streets of this city, she sat in its private gardens, she swore she would never leave. Then she would wake sobbing.

Now she thinks of the city. She thinks of her poor ruined Sidney. But she no longer sobs. It all seems remote. She is an angel. She is clear and clean. Whatever is, radiates through her, colors her. She can be gold with the sun and gray with the storm. She can live in a house with other people and yet live as one alone. She can manage the shopping now. She understands the labels. But Taylor prefers she need him. It no longer touches her, changes her. She is free.

Driving back from Boca Raton, she and Sidney stayed every night in the same motel room. She had to suggest it. It would save money, she told him. He lay awake watching her from his own bed. He kept the lamp on so he could watch her. She did not take her sleeping pill because it was so good to doze and wake, hoping each time to catch him gone to sleep, to find herself unabandoned. Under the light his ordinary brown hair was gold, like hers. She climbed into his bed and told him it truly did not matter. She said that she had seen his love for her under the lamplight and they could be angels together, mingling from head to foot.

Taylor is drunk. Rubber mackintoshes flapping, he and wild Marsha leaf down the rainswept street. Illuminations! Coming fast and hard, visions: headlights through raindrops. Marsha clutches Taylor's arm and pirouettes beside him through the graveyard. She tells him how the big stones scare her, why can't people be buried under little markers? Taylor lets her be a child. The truth is, she runs a very successful dancing school. She is a shrewd businesswoman; there can be very little child left in her. At night, she puts away the tap shoes and the metronome and goes to parties when she's invited, or lets the fathers of her students drop by and entertains them in her private quarters above the school. She has cultivated an ironic singsong. She pours the fathers drinks and listens to them tell what is graceless in their lives, and sometimes she falls into bed with them. They call her a good listener and encourage her to be a child. Taylor's boy Mark goes to Marsha's school. During the months when Lucy was sick in the hospital, and later in Boca Raton, Marsha had been a good listener. On the other side of the graveyard, they will turn into

Marsha's street and she will expect him to come in. He is willing. But at the moment he's distracted by thoughts of Esther and Sidney in his basement together. How many times have they done it? Sidney is good with women, they've often discussed it. Relentless, inscrutable Sidney. Taylor is pretty sure he can get Esther to tell him about it. Maybe not at first. She will be loyal and silent for a couple of weeks, but then, Taylor knows Esther. She'll break down and feed the whole thing into her creative meat grinder and what comes out she'll ask him to read.

"Will you come in for a drink?" says Marsha. "How strange you look. All that rain on your face."

"I am in tiers," Taylor replies. "There's enough for everyone. A huge birthday cake, that's me." He's back there in that basement, with Esther and Sidney. Oh, how he wishes they could all be like children holding hands in a circle, telling and sharing everything, sleeping and hugging one another. He has so much, so much to give.

"I'll come in," says Taylor. Oh, the rain pouring down my cheeks could be tears, he thinks.

"Good boy," sings Marsha.

Now the meat is beginning to go. Already gone, in this order, are: sherbets, frozen orange juices, Lucy's raspberries and strawberries put up from last summer before she went under, all the frozen vegetables in their cardboard boxes, unbaked bread in foil, and Taylor's stock of pizzas. Now a shank of lamb loosens itself from the bandage of freezer paper, the whole side of a cow in her separate white packages, the chicken breasts, the side of pork . . . .

Lying in the dark, her back to Sidney, Esther reviews the critical words and actions. Marsha had wanted Sidney, too. There had been a moment of rivalry between the two women during dessert when Marsha said, "Sidney, will you put some Triple Sec in my coffee?" So Esther had pulled all emergency stops, left the table mysteriously, and wandered into Taylor's study where she lay down in the dark on the sofa and covered herself with the skin of some animal. She willed him to come to her and there he was. "I thought you'd given up on me," he said in a voice that indicated nothing of the kind. His lean face came down hard on hers and he kissed her till her jaws ached. "Come downstairs to the TV room," he said. "That's where I sleep."

Is she sleeping? Sidney wonders. He has not heard Taylor come back from walking Marsha home. The storm is subsiding. Daylight will come: it always does. He could slip out now, softly, pretending to be going to the bathroom upstairs, and go to Lucy instead. Pressed against the buttocks of the Jewess, he feels it might be possible to rise and carry it, quick, like a candle to Lucy's room.

Oh, no, thinks Esther, feeling the sex in him wake. She moves carefully away but his hand arrests her. He makes space for himself somehow. He covers her face with kisses. "Angel . . . angel . . . angel," he mutters, like a man in love.

The storm is over. Taylor drops his party clothes to the floor and climbs beneath the covers of the bed next to Lucy's. A table separates them, piled high with magazines, journals, and whatever paperback on communication or schizophrenia or experimental literature Taylor is reading. Once he told Lucy when she asked about his future that he would not be ashamed to be a student forever.

"Baby, you asleep?" he whispers across the space. Lucy does not answer. Neither does she pretend to breathe as one asleep. After a while, she hears him breathing deeply, so she gets up, wraps her robe around her, and goes barefoot downstairs to clean up the party.

When, Esther wonders, will it be polite to get up? He is holding her so intricately, can she move without waking him? She hears Lucy at the sink, the clatter of dishes, soft bare feet with their Florida tan padding back and forth above her head. Esther wants some coffee, but she does not want to begin the day. Once she gets up, it will be never to lie beside this man again. Although she has not loved him, the itinerancy of their night makes her sad. "I'll be back," she murmurs, in case he is able to hear, and gets up, searches the floor for her clothes. Her blouse has been touched by the puddle of water beside the bed. She is so sore she can hardly put on her stockings. As she tiptoes toward the stairs to the kitchen, she has an urge to rush back, throw herself across his body, kiss him goodbye. She hears him saying, "That was a test. If you hadn't come back, you would never have known. I love you, Esther."

The two women sit across the kitchen table from each other, drinking coffee, leafing through different magazines. Davie makes patterns of wet breakfast food on his tray. Lucy says in her bell-clear voice, "I didn't know people still got leprosy." Esther looks across and reads upside down: "YOUR GIFTS CAN HELP SRI LAI FIGHT LEPROSY." "Yes, it's depressing, isn't it?" she feels obliged to say. Lucy does not answer. What does she think of me, spending the night in the basement with their houseguest? wonders Esther. Lucy shows nothing. Those shocks have lowered her IQ, thinks Esther. She turns the page of her magazine and her stomach lurches, for there is a poem by a rival of hers. The poem is called "Afterwards." It is about the resuming of boundaries after lovemaking.

"Would you like to stay for lunch and go with us to take Sidney to the airport? He leaves at two," says Lucy tonelessly. Her eyes are so clear, so blue.

"Oh, God, no," cries Esther. Then: "I didn't mean it the way it sounded. It's just that I want to get home and do some work."

They hear Sidney's steps ascending from the basement. Esther lowers her head into her magazine. Lucy pads to the stove to heat the coffee.

Sidney enters. He says, "Hey, Lucy, someone left your freezer open and everything is ruined." Esther looks up. Why does he look so smug? she thinks.

God, she's made him sore. He puts on his socks, his pants, his T-shirt, and the V-necked cinnamon sweater that Lucy bought him. Then he sees the stream trickling across the cement floor. It leads him into the adjoining room. He switches on the light, sees her washing machine, dryer, a stack of old paintings. He turns one over, dusty. Oh, my poor Lucy, let's get out of here. The stream stops at the corner of the freezer, the door ajar. Sidney looks inside and studies the mess. It was in progress, he thinks, while he and Esther opened their bodies. He is filled with a sudden energy and goes upstairs to tell the others.

They all three troop down to survey the disaster. Sidney has not yet looked at Esther. Dressed again in last night's clothes, he has reassumed the slouchy appeal that promised so much. Esther wishes the night were not over.

"You'll just have to have another party," says Sidney, touching Lucy lightly on her brown wrist. "Can't refreeze this stuff, you know. Have a party tonight to celebrate my departure." His laugh is strained. He doesn't want to leave, thinks Esther.

"Do you want us to help you get rid of this stuff?"

Lucy stands contemplating the ruin in the freezer. It does not seem to upset her. The eyes are blue and toneless, her skin clear. She shuts the freezer. "It will be all right," she says. "I will throw it all out later."

Taylor soaps himself and sings. He has left the shower curtain open so he can look out the window at the beautiful falling leaves. Why does Sidney have to leave today? "Stay another month, old man," he said. "Why go home and waste three months in Virginia?" "I've stayed too long," said Sidney, smiling inscrutably. "Well, you haven't, you know," persisted Taylor. "Why don't you go to Europe? That's what I'd do if I didn't have my classes." Sidney said, "I'd rather sit on the porch of my father's house and reread Virgil."

Taylor admires Sidney so much, is a little in love with Sidney.

They should all go out to lunch. Taylor will invite Esther, and then they will all go to the airport. Mark and Davie will love that. He will explain the planes to them again. What to wear? He selects a lime-green oxford-cloth shirt, dark green corduroy trousers, the alligator belt Lucy brought him from Boca Raton, and . . . this red and royal-blue paisley ascot. Tonight after supper (he will help Lucy put the dishes in the machine first, she tires so easily), he will take a six pack and drop by Esther's, ask her how she enjoyed the party, what her impressions of Sidney were. He might offer her his night with Marsha in return for her night with Sidney. As he comes spiraling downstairs, the morning fills Taylor.

Sidney drives Esther home in Taylor's car. The storm has blown the leaves from the trees. Esther asks Sidney what time his plane departs. Two, he says. "But there's a long

layover in New York. I won't get home until eight."
"Eight," repeats Esther. Then she adds, "Those in-betweens
are hell." They are silent. Sidney drives fast. Esther asks,
"Are you one of those Southerners who hates black people?" Sidney answers, "Are you one of those Northerners
who thinks Southerners hate black people?" They both
laugh. "There's my place," says Esther. "That's my cat looking through the curtains." "Oh, a *cat*," says Sidney, and
Esther doesn't like the assumptions in his voice. He stops
the car, keeps the motor running. She turns her face to
him, a quick goodbye prepared on it. He grins suddenly,
hooks her to him with his right arm, and mashes his mouth
and teeth into hers. She does not want it, but responds out
of politeness. Then he breaks away and says, "Well, good
luck." "Yes, same to you," she says. He has had it all his
way. She gets out of the car. "Goodbye," she says. "Hope to
see you again," he says, his courtesy topping hers. She
waves and goes up the leaf-strewn walk. By the time she
reaches her door, he has turned the car and is off. Esther
goes inside. Her cat comes and rubs up against her. She
goes to the kitchen and opens a tin of sardines and shakes
some hard food into the bowl. She changes his water. The
cat lowers himself on his haunches and begins to breakfast.
Esther is seized by an attack of diarrhea. She hurries to the
bathroom and sinks down, head lowered to her knees,
hands clasped. She gives herself up to her body. He was
not even a good lover, she thinks. She will write a poem
about the whole thing. The thought disgusts her.

Sidney is packed. They are going out to lunch, then to the
airport. It is almost over. He thinks of Esther saying, "Those
in-betweens are hell." As he passes the Princes' hall telephone, a thought presents itself to him and he leafs
clandestinely through the book. Taylor catches him. "Are
you looking up Esther? Go in my study. Her address and

phone number are on the first page of my memorandum book. You don't want to wade through all the Kleins."

Sidney obeys. All the Kleins. He sits down at Taylor's wide desk in the study. He picks up the red leather memorandum book. "Taylor Orton Prince," in gold letters. TOP. SAL. Sidney Arthur Lee. For the next three months, he will sit on his father's front porch in Roanoke because he has no money to go anywhere else. Each day he will read a bit of the *Aeneid* and mix himself a bourbon and water. He will begin again in a new place in January as Mr. Lee who reads Latin and Greek and is ever so inscrutable. New boys will come down with crushes on him, and the masters' wives will try to fix him up. He remembers Lucy's offer to be angels together. Lucy, my dear, get yourself ready. We're driving away together again, just as we came, your gold curls caught in your little kerchief. We will take the children, too.

Sidney gets up from Taylor's desk, forgetting Esther's address. Lucy is standing just outside the door. She burns him with her blank blue stare. "We are ready to go when you are," Lucy says. Sidney takes the stairs two at a time to fetch his bag. His heart is a stone. If only she had smiled.

Taylor is pleased with events in general. He will drop by Esther's place tonight, and maybe stop by and see Marsha, too. A drink at Marsha's just to show he's no hit-and-runner, then over to Esther's, popping an allergy pill on the way. Settle into her comfortable sofa and say, "Hey, guess who was beside himself to take down your address?"

"Can we stay and watch the planes, Mommy?" Mark asks from the back seat. The car radio is on, and a warm, lively melody fills the car. It has turned out to be a beautiful clear day.

"If you want to, honey," says Lucy, who sits beside Taylor, Davie curled into her lap. How serene she is, facing front! What a beatific smile! All those clouds gone now.

Taylor thinks she is ever prettier than before. What, he wonders, could she be thinking, to make such a smile?

Mark sits soldier-straight beside that man Sidney who is the reason they are going to the airport. He is very happy since his mother has come back to him. He clenches and unclenches his sticky hands, savoring his secret. It is between him and his mother. She tells it to him every day, like a story. He must never tell the others, not his daddy or Davie. It would hurt them, she said. The secret is: she loves him more than anything in the whole, whole world. So much that it made her sick. So much that she had to pretend not to, because it would make the others feel bad. That is why she used to act funny sometimes, pushed him that time beneath the water. But he knows better. She loves him, she said, more than life itself, which he does not understand exactly, but he feels the force of it. The day she came home from Boca Raton, she took him by the shoulders and her eyes were very blue. "You saved me from myself, coming when you did," she said. "I must try and look at it like that from now on." He tries to remember when he came, imagines himself like the knight in one of his storybooks, riding up to their house on a big black horse. I have come, Mommy. But how can there be two of her, one to save from the other? Mark squints into the sun and thinks. Then forgets the problem in his happiness. She has said they can watch the planes and Sidney the man is going and they can have their TV back again because he won't be down there in the bed.

"Can we stay and watch the planes, Mommy?" She knows Sidney is in the back seat, her son on one side, Sidney's suitcase on the other. He is sorry to leave. He is frightened of what he is going to. Taylor came smiling into the kitchen, just before they all left, and Taylor said, "Shh.

We'll have to wait a minute. He's in there getting Esther's address." Well, people did what they wanted and usually hated it after. She is willing to be done with all that. A smile brushes the corners of her mouth and wings its way up as she plans the dinner party she will give with all the rotten meat. Let it freeze again. Then, in a couple of days, she will lose herself in a flurry of roasting and baking and boiling. A gala affair, just for the family. The ruby cut glass and the Royal Worcester she'd made him give her for agreeing to be his laundress. She sees them gathered at that sumptuous last supper, little Davie, napkin tucked beneath his chin, serious Mark, happy Taylor. She herself will propose the toast. Lifting the red wineglass so that the candle-light splinters it, she will say, "Let us take these mammals into our bodies and, by so doing, shed their tendencies." Taylor will beam, that lover of mystery, and say how inscrutable she's become since the hospital. She herself will lift the first forkful to the baby's mouth.

After a couple of days—a week?—some neighbor will notice all those newspapers and magazines and milk cartons, and he will break in and confront the table from which angels have risen.

"If you want to, honey," Lucy says.

THE
LEGACY
OF THE
MOTES

*Pour new seas in mine eyes, that so I might
Drown my world with my weeping earnestly. . . .*
—Donne, Holy Sonnet 5.

London, 1961.

"Look up at the dome," Van Buren instructed the young scholar. "And roll your eyeball round to the left."

"I was going across to that pub for lunch," Eliott told the helpful attendant, "when I saw this thing like a bird flying sideways through the sky. At least I thought it was the sky. But then at lunch it kept wafting back and forth across my page and I realized it was inside my eye."

"One really shouldn't read in pubs," cautioned Van Buren. "The light is so poor." He gingerly pried back Eliott's eyelid with dry fingers and peered deep into the left eye. Good old Van Buren, he'd been able to flush the rarest of seventeenth-century obscurities out of forgotten stacks and was going to be remembered specifically in Eliott's acknowledgments. "Does it hurt?" he asked.

"Not a bit. That's the odd thing. Do you see a hair in there or anything? Though I'm sure I'd feel a hair."

"Hmm. Roll it up and around. Now over that way. Not a thing. Do you think perhaps you've been overtaxing your eyes? It's quite possible, you know. You've been going at those books rather devilishly these past three months. Why not give things a rest? Go to a park, enjoy our English spring. If your eye is still troubling you tomorrow, you might pop over to Moorfield's Eye Hospital."

Tomorrow. Wasn't that just like them? They took a week to launder a shirt. They were always going to parks. Van Buren spent half his lunch hour trudging back and forth to Lincoln's Inn Fields just so he could eat his sandwich in one. All the time in the world they had. That's what happened to their pound.

"Well, I've only got my index to go and I hate to stop so near the end," he told the older man, who stood balanced lightly on his crêpe soles, frowning earnestly and ready to be of service. "I want to finish it up, I want to be back in the States by the end of May so I can defend it, you see. I want to have it over and done with." He gave a queer, fractured little laugh. "After all," he said, because Van Buren still looked dubious, "it's not as though the eye were hurting. Whatever it is will probably work itself out of there."

"Very well," said Van Buren. "Let me know if you need anything." He pronounced it "annathing." Eliott watched him retreat to his own raised desk; a wisp of a man of indeterminate middle age: the only friend he'd made in England.

Eliott returned to space F5 beneath the circular blue dome of the British Museum Reading Room. He still could not get over being impressed that he was really here, where generations of the best scholars had polished these desk tops to a fine sheen with the rub of their elbows. Over the weeks, this round room had become the center of his universe. It drew him irresistibly into its vortex of scholarship until the world outside became a faded adjunct, a kind of anteroom where he must retreat at grudging intervals to eat and sleep.

Now, before beginning his afternoon's work, he leafed sensually through the heavyweight bond pages of his *Catalogue of Metaphysical Conceits*. He'd captured them once and for all, those canny little bastards. All day, every weekday since coming here, he'd sat oblivious to the slow unfolding of the English spring outside and culled them first from major writers (Crashaw, Donne, Vaughan) and then from increasingly minor ones (Benlowes, Godolphin, Habington, Sherburne) rooted out for him by the fortuitous Van Buren, who had early confided to Eliott his own less scholarly but abiding fascination for the metaphysical poets. By day, Eliott had explicated the complex, startling, ingenious analogies, scribbling furiously over hundreds of 4 x 6 cards, his pencil breaking, running out of lead, as it raced along, trying to keep pace with its owner's ambitious inspirations. By night and on weekends, he sat at the typewriter in his Bloomsbury bed-sitter and typed, ignorant of the deepening blue of the late northern twilight. He had pinned them down, one by one, the audacious hyperboles, the paradoxes, until all that remained was to lead each of these broken images into the alphabetical stalls of his index.

A Catalogue of Metaphysical Conceits: his eye swept gratified from left to right across the title page (home in May, Ph.D. with a job at a prestigious school at the age of twenty-five), but a pair of shadowy wings followed the movement of his eye. He brushed at the paper with his fingers, he brushed at the air. He looked up suddenly. The wings beat away to the left. He reread *A Catalogue of* . . . and they floated back, filigreed wings crossing and recrossing the purity of his title page. He tried them on the walls, the dome; they blended cleverly in the hound's tooth of a neighboring scholar's jacket only to reappear, like a mischievous doodle, on the scholar's fresh foolscap notepad. Eliott sat stiff-shouldered and obsessed, swiveling his eyes up, down, left, right, trying to shake the wings. But they sailed indomitably across his vision. They were haunting, rather beautiful in themselves, but then, so were cancer cells. If they kept on, he'd see about them; not today, not today. He clamped his hand over his left eye and began writing the note cards for his index: Ague, Alchemie,

Apparition, Anatomie . . . no: Anatomie, Apparition . . . but then he had to sneak a look and see if they were still there. They were.

He went up to Van Buren. "Look, how far is this Moorfield's?"

"Walking distance, actually." Van Buren gave directions.

"Okay if I leave my things here? It's two now. I should be back by three at the latest."

"Not to worry. I'll put them away with Reserved Books if you don't get back before closing."

"Closing!"

"There might be a bit of a wait," said Van Buren.

Eliott went out into the afternoon cursing. It was probably nothing; they could wash it out with something. But how perverse for it to happen now! While trying to flag a taxi on Great Russell Street, he tested the wings on the dingy stone of buildings, the patches of green grass, and then upon the glare of mottled spring sky where he'd first picked the damned things up. The wings soared at a ninety-degree-angle tilt, like little linked bubbles. Eliott noted with no pleasure that it was the smooth, light surfaces (pages, sky) where they most strongly made their presence felt.

Moorfield's smelled of alcohol. Its waiting room was jammed with people of all ages and occupations suffering from afflictions of the eye. One woman's bandage had a perfect circle of red in the middle, like a Japanese flag. What if he lost an eye, both eyes? A receptionist gave him a ticket stub with No. 143 on it. "There are quite a few ahead of you," she said, disappearing through a swinging door, carrying the other half of his stub.

Eliott paced the waiting room. He wished he'd brought along his note cards. No, that might diminish the urgency of his case if others saw him reading his own tiny writing on cards. He sat down at last and began playing the wings on the pale green walls. Agonie, Aire, Angells . . . no, Anagram of the Virgin Mary. Hell, he needed the cards. The receptionist returned and called No. 87.

His afternoon slipped away. A whole afternoon wasted! At half past four a Pakistani doctor about his own age came through the swinging door and spoke in meticulous English to an old man dabbing at his eyes and looking bewildered. "Can you tell me, Mr. Fiddler, when exactly did you begin having the blacknesses again?" He arranged for the old man to go to surgery early next morning and assisted him gently to his feet. At a quarter to five, a mother with her hair in rollers rushed in, carrying her little boy who had shot something into his eye, and this took precedence over all ticket stubs. Eliott felt sick. He was not accustomed to the sight of such sad, suffering people. What a dreary place this Moorfield's was!

Finally, around dinnertime, the young Pakistani asked tiredly if No. 143 would please come to the examining room. Eliott followed him through the swinging doors into a long room where people sat in a row of dentist-type chairs. The doctor motioned Eliott to one.

"What seems to be the trouble?"

"Well, there's something strange in my left eye," Eliott said.

"Strange? How do you mean strange?"

"Well, I mean it's in there, I can see it floating back and forth across everything, but it doesn't hurt. As a matter of fact, there it goes now." Excitedly, Eliott traced something swiftly through the air with his finger. The doctor's butterscotch-smooth countenance ignored the finger. He pondered Eliott's face instead.

"What does it look like?" he asked. "How does it feel?"

"That's the thing. It doesn't feel any way at all. I can't feel a thing. But I can tell you exactly what it looks like. It's made up of these bubbles, it's about the thickness of a hair, and it looks like a pair of wings flying sideways." Eliott felt pleased with the accuracy of his description. He felt suddenly everything would be all right.

The doctor, seemingly unimpressed, flipped his eyelid onto a square-edged wooden stick and rolled it back like a rug. Eliott's eyeball grew cold. To his right, another doctor said, "Now, Mrs. Murdoch, I am going to anesthetize your right eyeball." Eliott's nerves spun into an uneasy contemplation of his vile jellies: their vulnerability, their defenselessness. . . .

"I think I am going to pass out," he told the Pakistani doctor, who looked interested and unrolled his eyelid at once. He led Eliott into a private room and helped him to lie back on the examining table. A colored nurse appeared and wafted smelling salts gravely beneath his nostrils, as though trying to hypnotize him. Eliott had the sensation of being demonically overcome by these two brown, unsmiling faces floating over him. He fainted.

When they brought him round, he shouted at them, "What time is it? I've got to finish my index. Are you people going to be able to flush this eye out or not?"

"There is nothing in the eye," said the doctor. "I looked carefully while you were out." He spoke slowly, as to a foreigner or a small child. Eliott could not help but feel they had stolen something from him, he could not say what. Peering into the mirrors of his soul when he was out cold . . .

"You are a student?" the doctor inquired politely. He looked at his wristwatch.

"No. Yes," Eliott said, sitting up. His present position, in a limbo between student and professor, struck him as a precarious one, which he must change as quickly as possible. "There they went, they just floated through your white uniform," he announced to the nurse, who remained standing by with the salts.

"Perhaps you have been working too hard," said the doctor, helping Eliott to stand. "At times people see," he waved his slim brown fingers negligibly about, "things, small impurities, rather like dust in the air. Maybe you should take a little rest. Enjoy the nice weather—"

"Go to a park," supplied Eliott savagely. A whole afternoon wasted. "How much do I owe you?"

"We are under National Health." The doctor clapped a palm to Eliott's shoulder and steered him toward an exit. "A very good park I can suggest is the Regent's Park. They have an excellent zoo. . . ."

Eliott found himself wandering the adjacent streets, displaced in a strange interstice of early-evening sunlight. It was too late to get back in the museum, too early to go to bed. He felt very lonely and did not know which way to go. Perhaps he should have a beer, some supper. He walked on, the wings accompanying him languidly in the slow yellow light. A quaint-looking pub under the sign of a rose tree materialized on his side of the street. He went in and sat down at a table in the corner. He was the only customer. A publican in a clean white apron came over and took his order. Eliott sat in the soft timeless gloom, munching delicious sausages, coating his frayed nerve ends with a pint of soothing bitter. The publican brought him a second when he was ready for it, though he could not remember asking. He tried his eyes on the brown paneling of the walls, but the wings seemed to have retired for the night. Well, he would follow their example. Tomorrow he would begin fresh and early on the index.

Going out into the blue twilight, he noticed a little mews beside the pub. Its cobbled walk was lined with pots of bright red geraniums that glowed in the dusk. He had never seen such a quality of light as this dusk. Feeling mellow, he decided to explore. Van Buren had told him that London was a secret city that opened itself up to you slowly from within, revealing itself discreetly to those who had found their way inside.

At the end of this mews was a vast green park that seemed to stretch to the frontiers of the evening. He walked soundlessly over its sward. The air hummed around him. He suddenly wanted more than anything else to lie down, and did. Stretching luxuriously upon its cool turf, he suddenly remembered the two halves of his ticket No. 143 at Moorfield's. What did they do with those stubs at the end of the day? Where was his now? He tried to imagine, but a lassitude was stealing over him, the likes of which he'd never known. Everything seemed to be melting away, his overcrowded brain opened all its doors and windows and the contents spilled like books all over the grass. Canonizations, Compasses, Dirges, Epitaphs, Fevers, Fleas and Fools, Lectures and Legacies, Meditations, Nocturnals, Quiddities and Quips—all tumbled out and dissolved like tears into the thirsty green. Only his eyes remained. Eliott woke the wings and sent their soft specters up, over the ground, the trees, to see what they would find. They hovered above a pale spot burgeoning out of the dusk. It came closer, sprouting legs, an undulating tower of a neck, lolloping soundlessly toward him. It was an elegant white giraffe. It passed within a foot of him, never making a sound.

He woke next morning feeling something awful had happened. Why was this bright light pouring into his room so early in the morning? What was wrong? It was afternoon, that's what was wrong! He was in bed and not in the Reading Room. He remembered the preposterous events of yesterday and slammed his eyes shut. Dear God, he prayed for the first time in years, let those things not be there today and I'll finish my index in a week, hiding all night in the museum if necessary, and get the hell out of this slow-motion country. He tried to visualize his index in its finished form, but his mind felt soft and doughy, as though all the muscles had been removed. He tried to stick one, then another conceit on its surface, but they would not hold, they flaked away. For one mad moment, lying there with his eyes squeezed shut, it occurred to him that he had already finished the index, had pushed himself to the point of exhaustion, and was now back in the States suffering a breakdown in which his mind returned over and over again to England, to do it all again in a compulsive dream.

The eyes, the eyes would be his test. God, I'm going to open them now. Please let yesterday have been a dream.

He opened his eyes. Refreshed, triumphant, they wheeled back into his life, trailing several small progeny born during the night. He cried out in despair. The new ones were less winglike. They were ungainly and squatty, resembling jumbled commas. Oh, it was all true, then, even the giraffe? He put his hand over the left eye and blotted out the wings. But the squiggles wafted on across the right. Both eyes! Possibly he was going mad as well, but one thing was sure: something terrible was happening to his vision. Not that he was losing it violently, with blood, nor intermittently, in a series of recurring "blacknesses" like the old man at Moorfield's, nor under the slowly thickening mauve of cataracts. No, by some freak of fate, the prolific wings and squiggles were destined to block up his vision gradually, footnoting his eyes like ivy covering windows until there was no clean space left. He was to be relegated to darkness, untrained for anything, his brilliant future snuffed out at twenty-five.

He indulged in a brief orgy of self-pity, then rallied via his years of drive and dialed directory inquiries and asked for the number of the British Medical Association. The four alphabetical phone books were stacked beside his phone, but he felt he no longer had the right to small print.

"I want the name of your top eye doctor," he told the secretary. "Money is of no concern. I have this friend who thinks he may be going blind." She explained that there were MANY excellent physicians and the BMA really could not . . . He lectured her on the British nation's lack of drive, his voice rising to a shriek. "No spirit of competition! That's why your goddamned pound has shrunk to nothing." She hung up on him.

He closed his eyes and practiced touch-dialing GRO-9000, the number for any American in trouble. He asked the switchboard operator for a consul. A nervy east coast voice snapped onto the wire. Eliott told him that he was an American professor, doing important research in the British Museum and his eyes had begun to go bad on him. Who was the best eye man here? The consul without taking a breath named Derek Hunter-Hyde, the famous ophthal-mologist. He was booked for months, of course, but the consul had reason to believe he could get the professor in.

Late that afternoon, Derek Hunter-Hyde, R.C.B. Every-thing, quietly drew the heavy blue curtains, darkening his consulting room on the third floor of a Regency town house that overlooked a sweep of park. He murmured reassuringly in public-school English as he squeezed a clear and cooling drop of anodyne into each of Eliott's troubled eyes. He had him sit forward in a comfortable chair and look into a little black machine that rested on a highly polished Chippendale table. Hunter-Hyde looked into it from the opposite side and conducted a responsible and leisured search of Eliott's eyes. Then he invited him to sit at his own desk and sketch upon a little pad the things he saw in his eyes. Together they studied the drawings, joking at resemblances to melting airplanes, badly car-pentered crucifixes, and a little uroboros who couldn't quite make his tail. Finally, with a charming stutter that was worth every one of the ten guineas, he told Eliott he had something in his eyes called *muscae volitantes*, "Which is Latin, you see, for f-flying flies, or, to put it another way, f-flies in flight." Eliott began laughing and Hunter-Hyde added his own chuckle. Then Eliott inquired amiably if these flies in flight were serious. He was a scholar and depended on his eyes. A few flying flies were one thing, but what if they kept multiplying? *Would* they keep multiplying, did Hunter-Hyde think? Were they dangerous? Ought he . . . ought he to stop reading? He waited for the great man's answer fearfully. Yet what really awful news could anyone receive in this tasteful room?

With equanimity, the famous ophthalmologist replied that he really couldn't say. Nobody knew much about the *muscae*. They came and they went, rather much as they pleased. *Some* of them were dangerous, in that they prefigured retinal detachment: he did not think Eliott's were of that kind. There might be more; Eliott should be prepared for that. Close reading *had* been known to attract them. On the other hand, Eliott might read close-print dictionaries all day every day for the rest of his life and no more would come. *Or* he might wake one morning to find them gone. Hunter-Hyde's mother had one shaped like the spine of a leaf; she had grown rather fond of it, actually. The vitreous humor was a curious thing. "You know, that jellylike substance that f-fills your eyeball?" Well, this vitreous humor sometimes developed, inexplicably, little defects, which in turn cast shadows upon the retinal rods. It was impossible to prophesy: Eliott would have to leave it to nature or to God, if he was a believer. The doctor suggested his own favorite park, a small island off Greece. He made Eliott a present of some eye drops in a small shapely green bottle that looked like a faery decanter. "Use them," he advised, "whenever you feel particularly annoyed by the little fellows. And go and have yourself a walk."

Outside in Regent Square, the world impinged on Eliott. The purplish shadows of afternoon seemed to throb in tune with his eyeballs. The drops Hunter-Hyde had squeezed in seemed to have propitiated the *muscae* for the time being, and a languor similar to the one he had abandoned himself to the evening before now rapidly overtook him once more. What day was it? Wednesday? The Reading Room stayed open till 9 p.m. He should go back and start the index. But what he really felt like doing was finding that pub with the sign of the rose tree again, ordering more of those delicious sausages, and wandering afterward into that park, seeing how it looked the second time round. That was the test, wasn't it? He felt certain if he could repeat the evening up to the point where he had lain stretched out on the grass, he would somehow break the spell started by the entrance of the giraffe. Reality would come full circle and then he could go back to his index in peace.

He hailed a taxi. "I want to go to this pub near Moorfield's Eye Hospital," he told the driver. "I don't know its name, but it has this certain sign over the door. If you just drive around, I'm sure to recognize it."

He was rattled around a labyrinth of narrow streets near the hospital. The meter ticked away. They passed several pubs, none beneath the sign of a rose tree. Eliott began to get uneasy. The fare mounted. Finally, he paid the driver and continued the search on foot. He walked miles, doubling back on himself until the afternoon faded into the prolonged blue twilight and still no sign. Had it all been a derangement? If so, when had things last been real, when? He stumbled on, searching for the rose-tree sign, the phosphorescent geraniums along a cobbled mews, with no luck. His eyes began to water with self-pity: he must get back to that park and collect his thoughts from the grass; he had to find his giraffe.

A long time after dark, he slumped into a pub with no rose tree, determined to drink himself back into his lost park.

Van Buren found him on the steps next morning. Red-eyed, whiskered, stinking of hops, he clasped the attendant round his neck. "If tha's not solid flesh, I'll be goddamned if I know what is!" he babbled. Taking a small green bottle from his coat pocket, he squeezed two drops from it into each eye. "Keeping the li'l bastards in abeyance," he explained, winking at the perplexed attendant, who asked him didn't he think he could do with a few hours' sleep; come in at noon, perhaps?

"Are you kidding? My whole life's in there on little slips of paper. You haven't thrown them away, have you? You haven't put anything back on the shelf?"

Van Buren took him by the arm, assuring him he had not. They went inside. Van Buren delivered Eliott his books and notes intact. Eliott settled himself unsteadily into his place at F5, opened to the title page of his dissertation, and began to scream. Van Buren made his way to him calmly, as though he were merely bringing another book. He led him whimpering past the discreetly lowered eyes of other scholars and out of the circular room, which had slowly begun to spin. He stood by in the GENTS while Eliott vomited for a while, then carefully washed his face, looked in the mirror to check himself, and passed out cold.

||

May 1, 1971

Dear Mr. Eliott:

What a surprise to hear from you after all this time! Not a day has gone by that I haven't puzzled over that last morning, and I have more than once chided myself with my carelessness in allowing you to go away afterwards without eliciting some forwarding address from you. I am relieved to know that you enjoy good health and that your "wings" have passed. More on those wings in a moment. I must admit I was extremely frustrated when I received that postal card from you several years back, the one with the white giraffe and your cryptic greeting and no other address than "A detail from The

Garden of Earthly Delights, Prado Museum, Madrid." I then tried reaching you through Cook's and American Express offices in all the major European cities. Did you by any chance receive any of these letters?

You ask about the fate of your dissertation. I am curious to know more about the "agreement" you say you made about it. With whom, pray tell, did you make such an agreement? I hope you will enlighten me regarding some of these imponderables in a future letter! When several months went by and you did not return to collect it, I sent a letter to your people at the University (I got their names from your acknowledgement page, for which, by the by, I thank you for the inclusion of my own humble one) explaining the situation and asking whether, under the circumstances, they would like me to send it on to them, since the thing was so nearly finished. I am sorry to say they took their own good time in answering, and when they did it was to the effect that they were "waiting for word from Eliott." So I had to content myself with that. I took the liberty of removing your ms. to my own flat for safekeeping. As you may remember, I have always been allured by the Metaphysicals, and so it was not very long until I began leafing through your *Catalogue*, savoring each of those delightful, extravagant turns on meanings which you had explicated so thoroughly. I read through the entire ms. and when I had done with it I was impressed but nevertheless vaguely dissatisfied about something. It was as though I had been denied some particular treat of which I had been assured.

I went back and re-read the ms. carefully. And then it came to me. You had overlooked one of the most significant conceits in Metaphysical poetry. The wings, Mr. Eliott! Herbert's "Easter-Wings." In light of your final tormented days in the Reading Room, you can imagine how this discovery both excited and exasperated me. I became convinced that your "visitors" were an exemplary case of psycho-pathological prompting. It was your psyche's way of signalling to you that you'd left something out of the book. What exasperated me was the fact that you had vanished for all intents and purposes and I could not communicate to you this urgent piece of news.

I did get the feeling at times that you knew very well I was trying to reach you—especially after that frustrating postal card from Madrid. But now you have communicated and I am able to assure you that your dissertation is safe and sound, although I suppose you have heard by now of that other fellow's book which came out several years ago. Rotten luck, that; his was very disappointing indeed, compared to your compendious, painstaking treatment. We got it here at the BM.

You say that now your "wings" have departed, you suppose you ought to take up your life seriously again. Permit me to suggest that your ten years can be looked upon as serious. I have been working in a library for forty-two years, saving my pennies so that when I retire next spring I can at last have the opportunity to do what you say you ought to regret: "browse the parks of the world." All this rushing and climbing, is *that* "serious"? Really, Mr. Eliott, what for? Why *not* do a bit of browsing during your short-term lease among the stars? I am sure that when we meet again—and I do have your promise of that, don't I?—I shall find you are a much more interesting person than that frightfully intense young man who never had time to eat lunch in the park on a spring day.

Yours sincerely,
Phineas Van Buren

P.S. You say that when you sat down to your ms. that final morning that "the letters all jumbled together, swirling around like snakes on the page, it was the ultimate horror." Don't you remember that you had put drops of some kind in your eyes? I saw you do it myself. That would explain the swirling letters. I can't read for the remainder of the day when I have my annual eye examination.

During his decade of browsing, Eliott had not been an unhappy man. After he had made his deal with the *muscae*, as a rich man who has lost some of his riches promises God a sizable tithe if He will not let him lose them all, they became his excuse for the joyous search. He would not enter a library, if they would let him go on seeing. And he saw many things after he had discovered the Library of the World. Chained gently within its environs, he wandered, letting himself marvel, unable to fret, discovering anew each day the paradox that when you had nothing left to lose you began finding any number of things. The *muscae* were his inseparable traveling companions. They went everywhere with him. He played them constantly upon the deepened surface of his life, saw further worlds through them. They became inextricable from his visions. When he suddenly found his white giraffe frozen in the left volet of the Bosch triptych, the winglike *muscae* in his left eye swept conclusively down the flanks of the wondrous creature at the same moment Eliott was comprehending it. *See*, they seemed to say.

And then they left him. One morning he woke up, played his eyes drowsily back and forth across the ceiling, summoning them to wake up and help him plan his day, and realized he was alone. Nothing tempered the blankness of those pale walls. He swiveled his eyes back and forth, up and down, rotated them in circles. But the wings had flown away, leaving him alone with their implications. He was like a man who had been dropped from a great height; no, like a man left at the gates of an unknown city by his faithful traveling companions. He lay stunned and sorrowful, unable to begin the day, looking at his blank walls and searching for a link to connect him with the present. He decided to write Van Buren.

After receiving his old friend's reply, Eliott went out into the afternoon. He knocked down two drinks at a bar and walked to the library of that city. He went up the steps and, with some trepidation, entered doors that had been closed to him for ten years. Inside, he wandered for a while in the old brownish silence, working his way toward call numbers he had not forgotten. He found the book he wanted, plucked it slowly from the shelf. He sat down at a long polished table beside the window and thumbed with his old expertise to the index of titles and first lines. He made his way to the fateful page.

Easter-Wings

Lord, who createdst man in wealth and store,
Though foolishly he lost the same,
Decaying more and more,
Till he became
Most poore:
With thee
O let me rise
As larks, harmoniously,
And sing this day thy victories:
Then shall the fall further the flight in me.

My tender age in sorrow did beginne:
And still with sicknesses and shame
Thou didst so punish sinne.
That I became
Most thinne.
With thee
Let me combine
And feel this day thy victorie:
For, if I imp my wing on thine,
Affliction shall advance the flight in me.

Bending low over the wings, he wept softly. As his tears fell down on the page, the implications of the *muscae* began opening up to him like flowers, one by one; there seemed to be no end to them, their paradoxes, their analogies, their properties as controlling image. They formed the most elaborate, the most important conceit he would ever come across, the conceit of a lifetime: his.

WHY DOES A GREAT MAN LOVE?

FACTS

There are three women in his life.

The first is J. He falls in love with her in his twenties. He has done poorly at university and barely gets his degree. His poems have been declared unpromising, and there is no sign of his being great. She is seven years younger and in poor health. He is working in an isolated place and their courtship is conducted through letters. His are impatient, angry, violent. He is a hunter, he says, in uneasy pursuit of his prey. His love is a malady that has hugely infected him. How he loathes himself for flinging away his liberty on a creature whose sex has been ill-using men for thousands of years! She must make a decision now. He has been offered a tempting opportunity through an uncle's connections. He has been asked to become secretary to a great man. Ambition is an empty form and she alone can save him. He will nurse her back to health with his affections. He wants to live a simple, obscure life in the happiness of his love with J.

He becomes secretary to the great man.

He keeps his employer's accounts and ghostwrites for him. He studies the dignitaries who call daily at the great man's house. Their self-important postures. Their meaningless chitchat. Their witless puns. These are the men who govern the great world? He prefers a horse's arse, then. He spends more and more time in his patron's library. He takes furious walks by himself in the park. He finds a bright little girl, the housekeeper's daughter, and educates her. She is H., who is fourteen years younger and in poor health. He teaches her how to read and write. He teaches her what to read and what to think. She has a quick mind combined with feminine pliability. "H. thinks like a man," he says proudly. Her handwriting is an exact copy of his, which will give future historians no little trouble. He presents her with a list of her faults and she ticks them off one by one as she overcomes them.

He goes away from his patron in a fury. No more of this toadying. He will be independent or damned. His schemes fail and his patron welcomes him back. He finds little H. grown into a graceful young woman (though he tells her frequently she is "a little too fat"). She enjoys learned conversation, especially with men, yet does not speak unless it is to say the incisive thing. She refuses to discuss clothes, sex, scandal. If someone loses control or grows heated in his argument, she agrees at once and is silent. It prevents noise and saves time, she says. In spite of her poor health, she has great physical courage. One night she is alone with a servant in the house. Some thieves attempt a break-in. The servant flees. H. fetches a pistol, tiptoes in darkness to the dining-room window, and shoots one of the thieves nearly through the heart.

He becomes indispensable to his patron. He carries messages to heads of state, and speaks his mind. He publishes his essays in significant journals. People cringe, then praise his vitriolic insights. He writes poetry, still heavy with a young man's awe of the classics, but already bearing signs of the weird combination of spleen and energy that will become his trademark.

During all this time, what of J.? Their correspondence flags, but continues. Her resistance softens. His stipulations harden. Finally, she writes that she might consider marriage now. He sends back a list of his requirements for a wife. We hear no more from J.

His patron dies. But this time he is established on his own.

He buys a house in the country. He invites H. to come there. This is made respectable by the following means: along with H. goes her homely cousin, who smokes cigars and stays in the room embroidering whenever the two of them are together. While he is in the country, H. and her cousin stay in nearby lodgings. While he is in town, the two women live in his house.

Now he spends much of his year in town. He dines almost every evening at the homes of famous people. He becomes a personality. People are fascinated by this great swarthy man who doesn't give a damn about them. He lets it be known that if any woman wants to make his acquaintance she will first have to go out of her way to prove it is not "just as a man" she wants to know him, but because of his merits. And she must make all the advances. He becomes irresistible to the opposite sex.

There is a famous beauty, the toast of society. She says she would like to meet him but can't comply with his eccentric demand. It would lower the status of future ladies of the toast, she says. A truce is arranged by her fourteen-year-old cousin. He draws up an agreement between them whereby the beauty will privately make the advances to the great man, who will, in return, accept her publicly as his acquaintance and never mention her concession. The treaty is solemnized at a private dinner held at the fourteen-year-old cousin's home. His mother is a widow of some fortune who has three other children. One of these children is E. E. is twenty-one years younger than himself and in poor health. Like H., she has a quick and grasping mind, cares nothing for parties, clothes, and gossip. Unlike H., E. is lazy and temperamental. She likes the idea of ideas but hates to study. She is self-willed but not strong-willed. Soon he is dining regularly at the widow's house. He leaves a spare suit of clothes there. He takes on the education of young E. on the evenings he is not dining with famous people. She reads everything he tells her, not because she is interested in the subject, but because she is interested in him. She learns to ape his political opinions. He catches her out on this, but is pleased with her progress in general. If only she will rid herself of her "romantic ideas."

But what of H., who waits in his country home, playing cards and eating chocolates with her cigar-smoking cousin? Has he forgotten H.? Far from it. Every night, no matter how late he returns to his rooms, he writes an account of his day to H. Secure in the knowledge that she will devour the most trivial detail concerning him, he records menus, the price of the wine, dinner-table chitchat, temperature and weather conditions, his secret fear of walking home in the dark because of a notorious gang of hoodlums who have been cutting off people's noses, how he suffers melancholy, what new pills he is taking, how he is plagued by stomach disorders, how he has taken in his trousers two inches, how he suffers like Job from boils, from an itching malady, how he has resolved to walk more. Often as he writes to H., he lapses into baby talk, forming the sounds with his lips as he writes. He mails these letters in great packets and addresses them to the cigar-smoking cousin to preserve proprieties. He mails chocolates and cigars. He fusses endlessly over H.'s health. He does not always mention when he dines at the widow's house.

After a time, he leaves the town in a fit of disgust at politics, dinners, human society. He returns to H. in the country and enjoys the company he professes dearest to him in the world, always in the presence of the cousin. H. is in her thirties now. She is stout from eating the chocolates he has sent her from town. He writes her birthday poems, taking four years off her age. He writes letters to E. in town, encouraging her to read and to stop writing him so much.

E. disobeys. She deluges him with letters. Soon she

drops the ruse of politics and books and splays her female soul all over the page. Why hasn't he written her? It has been ——— days. ——— days. ——— days. A correspondent in China would have answered by now. Why did he teach her to prefer only the best, then leave her high and dry? Why can't he speak his feelings? What about all those evenings they "drank coffee" together? "I'm sure by now you have wished me religious," she writes, "so I might pay these troublesome devotions to heaven. But still you'd be the deity I'd worship."

He writes back that she should walk more, ride more, read books on history and travel. "The best maxim I know in life is drink your coffee when you can and when you can't, do without it." He suggests she might save paper and time by writing simply "——— ——— Cad" when she has to express these emotions. He fusses endlessly over E.'s health.

Her mother, the widow, dies and leaves her a small fortune. She announces her intention to follow him to the country and buy a place near his. "If you do, I won't see you," he replies.

She does and he sees her. But not enough, never enough. As soon as he leaves her, she begins pestering him to come back. "——— ——— Cad: It has been ——— days since you were here. It has been ——— days. Have you forgotten me? I was born with violent passions which have terminated in this one unexpressible passion I have for you."

"Cad assures me he esteems you above all things," he replies, "but begs that you will not make yourself or him unhappy by imaginations."

E. dies. She is thirty-five. He is not mentioned in her will. She leaves the bulk of her fortune to his public rival. The rival expresses bewildered gratitude. He has never laid eyes on the lady in his life. He uses her money for a humanitarian scheme that his rival has repeatedly opposed. She has also saved and numbered all his letters and kept copies of her own. Her executors proceed to have these letters published as she has instructed. A friend stops them. But a long poem gets into print. It is a poem written by the great man, describing their relationship beneath a thin veil of pastoral. There are several provocative lines, which say in effect: "Did we mix books and love together? The world will never know."

H., of course, sees the published poem. An ill-meaning friend says to H.: "Ah, he must have thought a lot of E. to write such fine verses." H. replies coolly that he can write finely on a broomstick if he wishes to.

H. dies five years later, at 6 P.M. on a Sunday evening. He receives the news at 8 P.M. Sunday is his night for company. He remains impassive till the last guest leaves at 11 P.M. Then he goes to his room and begins writing his famous eulogy of H. He does not attend the funeral because he is too ill. During the service, he sits up in bed and continues writing her eulogy. H. leaves all her money to a penniless hospital chaplain.

He lives on. He becomes greater, old, deaf, partially blind, and finally speechless. Some say mad as well, but others say no, it is the intolerable pain. At the last he refuses to see anyone because his incapacities enrage him. He is attended only by a nurse. His last recorded words are "I am a fool." He is buried (beside H.) under the epitaph he wrote for himself some years ago.

RUMORS

re J.:

Not many. Her letters, like H.'s, have been lost or destroyed. There are no pictures. Judging from his side of the correspondence, J.'s reluctance to marry is based on his poverty combined with her ill health. A frail person, she might also take fright at his extreme metaphors of love.

Does she die young like her successors? Does she marry a wealthy merchant and have healthy children? We don't know. Do we care? Somehow J. does not set fire to our imaginations. We feel she has little to do with the man we know.

re H.:

1. Both he and H. are illegitimate children of the man who employed him as secretary. Therefore they cannot marry.

2. H. is passionately in love with him but, having studied his character from an early age, realizes she can keep him only if she hides her passion. Only the cigar-smoking cousin knows the agonies H. suffers. Those hours, those nights, those years when he's away in town. H. to her cousin: "What is he doing now? Do you think there is some-one else? Tell me honestly, do you think he cares for me? Should I leave him? Maybe if I left him he'd realize he couldn't live without me. But how can I leave him? He isn't even here. If he doesn't love me, then whom? Here I am in his house, trusted with all his things. Who else receives his packages of night letters? In baby talk?"

3. H. reads between the lines of the night letters. "Who is this widow you are always dining with? Are they really such good company?" He writes back angrily, "As good a company as I myself." H. is silenced. She decides she must wait out her rival.

4. H. is secretly married to him. On her deathbed she begs him to consummate their union so she can rest in peace. He turns on his heel and leaves the room, never to see her again.

5. He is secretly married to H. On her deathbed he begs her to consummate their union. She says no, it is too late. He turns on his heel and leaves the room, never to see her again.

6. H. and her cigar-smoking cousin enjoy a lifelong lesbian relationship under his protection.

7. He is impotent.

re E.:

1. He falls in love with E. and wants to marry her. But he has already set up H. and her cousin in the country and hates disruptions.

2. He falls in love with E. and wants to marry her. But he is already secretly married to H.

3. He loves H. and he loves E. He cannot give up either. Since neither presses him, why should he?

4. H. is frigid, but he loves her conversation. He has sexual relations with E.

5. The many references to "drinking coffee" in the correspondence between E. and him are sexual metaphors.

6. E. finds out about H. living in his house in the country. She writes to H. and asks if they are married. H. sends back a single word: yes. E., who is tubercular anyway, dies of grief.

7. E. finds out about H. living in his house in the country. She writes H. and asks if they are married. H. passes on the letter to him without a word. He rides in a fury to E.'s, flings the letter on her table without a word, and leaves. E., who is tubercular anyway, dies of grief.

8. E.'s gardener on E. many years after her death: "She never went out and had little company. She was always melancholy except when HE came. Then she seemed happy. When she expected him, she always planted a laurel or two with her own hands. To make sure he'd come, she said. When it was fair, they sat in the bower. There were two seats and a table. It overlooked the river. There were al-

ways books and writing materials on the table between them. She often sat in the bower alone, talking to herself."

CONJECTURES

1. Look at the pattern. Each time the woman gets seven years younger. He takes on the education of H. and E. His problem is clear. A predilection for nymphets coupled with a Pygmalion complex.

2. A definitive case of arrested sexuality. Everyone knows how he was abducted by his nurse while still an infant. The violent adolescent crush on J. The baby talk in the night letters to H. The recoil from E.'s frank passionate advances. The fact is he prefers letters to personal contact.

3. He is one of those men Dr. Jung would describe as "anima-ridden." He must project his own inner-woman on the cardboard figures of J. and H. and E. His image of them is more important than their reality. J. must remain the aloof and distant woman who spurns him. H. must remain rational, platonic, devoted. E. must—what damnable trouble he has with E.! She keeps threatening to become a flesh-and-blood creature in her own right. Some say he loves her most for this failing.

4. Like all artists, he shapes and orchestrates his life to fit his art. He stunts reality in order that fantasy may grow. He writes a birthday poem to H. "at thirty-six" when she is forty. When H. is dying, he composes his series of famous prayers to comfort himself. He stays home from her funeral and writes the celebrated recollections of H. In his poem to E., he allows for the possibility of sexual love. He gives pseudonyms to J. and H. and E., and the world knows these names and forgets their own.

5. All three women exist, wait, suffer, age, and die in order that a single image may be perfected. Each woman

is a mere suggestion, a facet of his Ideal: a nine-year-old girl, forty feet high, who washes him and tends him and puts him to bed, who carries him round her garden in a box, makes him seven fine shirts, teaches him languages, becomes his "little nurse" and "loves him to excess." The three women have done their small part to bring the dream full cycle: so the nurse can once again become the nursed, the teacher taught, the great man laid to sleep on the bosom of the giant child he can't resist, yet whose entire life is consecrated to his service.

DEATH IN PUERTO VALLARTA

1. " 'Take her away, into the sun,' the doctors said."

2. "What she sought was a fresh scene, without associations, which should yet not be too out-of-the-way; and accordingly she chose . . ."

3. After three years of what she herself would describe as *admirable self-restraint,* she inquired of her lover one March evening if he intended to leave his wife. A considerate man, slightly graying at the temples, who always thought before he spoke, he thought before he spoke, running his fingers along his slightly graying temples, and at last replied in a voice not without consideration . . .

4. The beautiful west coast resort of Puerto Vallarta is now easily reached from Guadalajara. The town is pretty, situated on the Bay of Banderas with rugged, tropical mountains as a backdrop. There are beaches all along the Malecón, but most people walk south from the Jardín, cross the polluted river where the Mexican peasant women can be seen picturesquely scrubbing their family wash on the flat rocks, and proceed southward for about half a mile before turning west past quaint Mexican shops with Master Charge stickers in the window and into the PLAYA DEL SOL. . . .

5. She was a daughter who no longer wrote home.
   She was the ex-wife of a man who had remarried.

She was a reader who couldn't find anything
   good to read anymore.
She was a lover, but her lover had said . . .

6. "My wife has certain mental and moral qualities," he said, running his fingers along his slightly graying temples. "Without being called to account for them, I would have to say I still have many feelings for her. While our life together is not without strain (in many ways we could be described as incompatible), I would have to say that I do not remain with her merely out of a sense of duty."

7. The full-length mirror in your hotel bathroom is distorted. The first evening you make a joke about it. "I've left my good body at home with him while this fatwoman and I carouse beneath the whispering palms and fortify our egos with sun baths and the hot eyes of appreciative peasants," you say.

8. On the beach there is always one idyllic couple to make the average person miserable. This time there were two. The first couple she created herself. He would rather have made it with her, initiated certain overtures to show he preferred difficult women, but she explained that, appearances notwithstanding, she was a fatwoman whose heart was somewhere else and he would do better with that dark girl with the perfect thighs who smiled at everything he said. He accepted her advice and joined up with the dark girl, the two tormenting our heroine henceforward with their combined beauty. The second couple—two Argentine aristocrats in their seventies, mahogany and sleek, either face-lifted or gods—she could not restrain from watching hungrily. Those straight spines, those high faces, in their matching deck chairs. They sat with their backs to the sea. But they, too, were watching her hungrily and on the third day they invited her to their mountaintop house for an 11 P.M. dinner, after which they asked her to stay over for a *ménage à trois*. This is the story she retold

the most later when someone said, "How was your trip?" She divided her friends into two categories. The ones who said, "Oh, wouldn't that make a wonderful story," she mentally discarded.

9. You squat in front of your distorted mirror and make the fatwoman swing her breasts, tremble her haunches, and do a very obscene dance. That feels better. Now you get dressed in your glad rags and go down to the Oceano Bar to *make something happen.*

10. She took a fresh notebook in which to record her experiences but promised herself not to philosophize.

11. *"Put the blame on Mame, boys,* PUT *the blame on Mame!* I loved her in that. I adored her. The two women I absolutely and for all time adore are Rita Hayworth and Ava Gardner. I met Rita on the set once. I'll bet you'd never guess what her real name is. She's a fine person, a beautiful person. Antonio? AntOnio! *Otro ron riqui, por favor.* I see Edward tried to pick you up earlier. Our Edward is a sickie. He thinks his good looks will pay his way. Did he tell you he was a South African explorer? Last night it was an Australian writer. Lies, lies. Look at him over there with that old couple. They'll buy him dinner, just watch. He had the nerve to call me Francisco tonight. 'Hiya, Francisco,' he said. I didn't bother to answer. My name is Frank. My entire name—get this—is Francis Rodney Anthony Brewster. I always wished people had called me Tony. Do you think I drink too much? Well, 'Frankly, my dear, I don't give a damn.' I met *him* once on the set. A fine person. Not conceited at all. Of course Lombard's tragic death killed him. Killed the part of him that could love a woman. Few people understand that."

12. On the beach, which was strewn with rotting fruit, twisted straws, beer cans, and crumpled Kleenex, she kept seeing women who looked like her lover's wife. . . .

13. "She saw it all, and in a measure it was soothing. But it was all external. She didn't really care about it. She was herself, just the same, with all her anger and frustration. . . ."

14. "To tell the truth, I was kinda lonely. . . ."

15. Second night. You inspect your suntan on the fatwoman. Back is going to peel, it's irrevocable. Sides still white. Send it back to the kitchen, please, it's underdone. You rub shoulders with the fatwoman, study her intimately. How funnily she billows out from a foreshortened waist into a massive blob of hips and thighs. Just where exactly does the mirror part company with reality? Maybe you've been kidding yourself and your mirror at home is the one that's distorted. A sand flea has bit you/her unbecomingly on the right buttock just below the bikini line. (Will it heal before HE sees it again?) You got angry with the men on the beach today. Inspecting you like a piece of meat, thinking they had the right to because of the little bit extra swinging between their legs. Some were interested. A few turned away.

16. I told Frank that my Uncle William had been married to Ava Gardner's sister and that Ava sometimes still called him from London. Frank turned away, repelled by this reality, and began talking about Rita to a rich contractor from Detroit who was building a house in Puerto Vallarta. His name was Bill and he was free for dinner. Bill's wife, Gwen, was upstairs with an intestinal infection, reading *The French Lieutenant's Woman*. I wanted to tell Bill that John Fowles and I had exchanged letters and that Fowles's favorite Romantic poet was John Clare ("Free from the world I would a prisoner be . . .") but after my Ava *gaffe* could not risk another. Where else but the Oceano Bar could I sit in the evenings? An old man with a white crew cut joined us. He had worked on Hollywood sets during the silent era. "My friend came down from

L.A. today to see me," he told us sadly, "but I was taking a siesta and didn't hear her knock. She left a note saying she had flown back to L.A., she couldn't wait. Now can you understand a woman like that?" I told him she should have just walked in instead of knocking and that she would probably come back. "You are a beautiful woman," he said. "No, not beautiful," I said. Then Bill, the contractor, chimed in: "Not beautiful, let's be honest. She's *interesting.*" He smiled sexily at me for approval, showing his gold inlays. See, Baby, I level with you. I can afford to. I'm rich and I got old Gwen upstairs reading John Fowles and I'm building a hideaway house in Puerto V. near where Liz herself has built. I do not have to go around buttering up less-than-beautiful women, even at the risk of having dinner alone.

17. Night life: after dinner, which is usually taken late, the most popular gathering spot in town is the Oceano Bar. There's a good deal of table-hopping by both strangers and friends. Pretty girls from the University of Guadalajara are sometimes here on vacation, and don't think that a Mexican girl won't speak English; many of them do!

18. "*Put the blame on Mame, boys,* PUT *the blame on Mame!*"

19. "Without being called to account for them, I would have to say I still have many feelings for her."

20. A few turned away, but some were interested. "What's that you're reading? *Don Quixote,* first novel of the Western world. Mind if I sit down under the palm with you, this sun is killing me. No, I'm a fireman, actually. No, out in Brooklyn. Yeah, I remember—'66 or '67. Winter of '66—oh, yeah? Twelve killed. A terrible thing. Did you really?"

She wanted to tell him how she had gone up to Fifth Avenue on her lunch hour and how the sight of those twelve flag-draped coffins had moved her to tears. But he wanted to talk about Literature.

21. Kept seeing his wife on the beach. Certain mental and moral qualities.

22. My, that tan is coming along nicely. The sides have caught up now. Back going to peel. Can't be helped. Some things irrevocable. You take her body to the beach with you every day now, to practice how a fatwoman feels. How does she manage it? How does she convince herself she has the right to buy a floppy hat in spring or a dress made of white lace? How does she ever get up the courage to undress in front of her man? Does she sit down first, turn her back, insist on lights-out? Yet fatwomen undress before their men every night all over the world. Amazing, isn't it?

23. Too old to be a daughter
    Too romantic to be a wife
    Too sick of words to read anything but the
        chapter headings in *Don Quixote*
    A hopeless lover of slightly graying temples

24. Wary of all philosophical or metaphysical phrases that might contain her condition, she wrote in the new notebook: "11 Mar: 30 pesetas taxi, 20 ptas 2 cuba libres, 5 ptas tip."

25. a. "She rose early—as early as though she had an important appointment to keep—and was among the first on the beach, when the sun was benign and the sea lay dazzling white in its morning slumber."

    b. A scurrilous yellow film lay on top of the waves, so she did not bathe. The sun made her skin break out in a rash, so she sat braced beneath a palm. A dog or a child had peed on its rough bark.

26. "While life together is not without strain, I would have to say I do not stay out of a sense of duty."

27. I spent the evening walking up and down the esplanade where young Mexican girls metamorphosed into pregnant wives before my eyes. From then on, the disintegration was a whiz: wives to mothers to widows: nagging, sagging, telling of the beads. Went to bed while the sky was still light, after having been snubbed by Frank and Bill for kissing the old man last night. Gwen had recovered from her intestinal trouble, had ditched John Fowles for the time being, and sat stroking her drink as though it were a dangerous animal and flirting harmlessly with Frank. Gwen was a beautiful woman slightly past her prime. Her hair was a weird shade of beige.

28. ". . . impossibility of communication . . . the ineluctable struggle . . . form versus flux . . . flesh versus spirit . . . coming to terms with . . . implicit in the human situation . . . appearance and reality . . . our common anguish . . ."
    "12 Mar: 18 pesetas fried fish, two beers; 3 pesetas two cokes; 13 Mar: 13 pesetas fish, coke; chair 2 pesetas."

29. "To me you are a beautiful woman. Your coming out to dinner with me instead of Edward or Frank or Bill meant something. You have been through some great suffering, haven't you? I can see it in your face. You ought to smile more. I don't have much, but I have my pension and this little house I built for my wife a year before she died of cancer and I'm in pretty good health. I'm seventy-seven but there isn't much I can do about that, is there? To speak bluntly, I can still get it up on occasion and nothing would please me more than to attempt this feat on your behalf. Poor Frank prefers men, you know. So many sick people down here. *Night of the Iguana* ruined the innocence of this place. And now with Liz and her chartered planes full of Thanksgiving turkey and cranberry sauce, it's too much. This guacamole is shit, if you'll excuse my language, I can make better at home myself. I don't regret my life; I just wish there was more of it. Thirty-three years with the woman I loved, meeting famous

stars on the sets. You're too young to remember Buster Keaton, but we were on a first-name basis. I won and lost two fortunes at the track. Easy come, easy go. I have no regrets. I live comfortably—not extravagantly, you understand. I eat what I want and I speak the language of the people here and recently I donated a movie projector to their school. They were really tickled. I can't say I feel useless, no. Would you mind very much kissing me good night, just a friendship kiss, when we go back to the Oceano Bar?"

30. "She felt suddenly out of sorts and began to think of leaving."

31. The fatwoman got very angry at the beach on her last day. What a performance.

It began harmlessly enough. She thrashed about her towel on her enormous dimpled thighs, scattering sand indiscriminately on nearby sunbathers. After a while she sat up with her legs apart, a fist on each puffy knee, and glared up and down the beach at everybody and everything.

Suddenly, scratching sand from her mammoth cleavage, she rose from her towel where she had meekly reposed for six days. The beach shook beneath her formidable thighs, umbrellas shivered and toppled, pleasure boats overturned in the sea; the high faces of the Argentine couple hit the sand with a thud; Mexican peddlers dropped their baskets and hats and laces and began frantically crossing themselves; back at the Oceano Bar, Francisco felt the ice cubes tremble in his third *ron riqui* of the morning; fish flew out of the sea and burst in the air; the cathedral bells began pealing the Angelus prematurely; John Fowles wrenched himself out of Gwen's half-dry manicure and plunged into her hot tub; over in London, Ava awoke with a spiritual headache, vomited at once, and felt better than she had in years; and in a gray eastern city still frosted over with winter a man who had a lover and a wife stopped thoughtfully at a red light and tried in vain to recall what he had dreamed last night.

The fatwoman strode down to the surf, her little toe displacing enough salt water to drown the fishermen. She took down her straps, and every man left to look turned instantly to water. Then, peeling triumphantly out of her angry and cumbersome flesh, she began to rise slowly heavenward, lighter than a parachute.

32. "Some minutes passed before anyone hastened to the aid of the solitary young woman collapsed on her towel. They bore her to her room. Before nightfall, a shocked and respectful lover received the news of her decease."

33. "Ripe now, and brown-rosy all over with sun, and with a heart like a fallen rose, she returned to the gray city to the lover who thought before he spoke. But her sentiments had fallen like petals. The answer in her was no longer a gush of fire, but a hard white flame burning away impurities. Her back and shoulders had begun to peel."

34. "We had avocado salad, iguana, beef and rice, flan and coffee, and the bill for the two of us came to $8 for a most enjoyable evening." (Mr. and Mrs. Barry Nocks, Bronx, N.Y.)

AN
INTERMEDIATE
STOP

The vicar, just turned thirty-one, had moved quietly through his twenties engrossed in the somewhat awesome implications of his calling. In the last year of what he now referred to nostalgically as his decade of contemplation, he had stumbled upon a vision in the same natural way he'd often taken walks in the gentle mist of his countryside and come suddenly upon the form of another person and greeted him. He was astonished, then grateful. He had actually wept. Afterward he was exhausted. Days went by before he could bring himself to record it, warily and wonderingly, first for himself and then to bear witness to others. Even as he wrote, he felt the memory of it, the way the pure thing had been, slipping away. Nevertheless, he felt he must preserve what he could.

Somewhere between the final scribbled word of the original manuscript and the dismay with which he now (aboard a Dixie Airways turboprop flying above red flatlands in the southern United States) regarded the picture of himself on the religion page of *Time* magazine, his tenuous visitor had fled him altogether. The vicar was left with a much-altered life, hopping around an international circuit of lecture tours (the bishop was more than pleased) that took him further and further from the auspicious state of mind which had generated that important breakthrough.

Exhibiting for his benefit a set of flawless American teeth, the stewardess now told him to be sure and fasten his seat belt. "Bayult," she pronounced it. Seat bayult. The trembly old turboprop nosed down toward a country air-field shimmering in the heat, and the captain's disembodied voice welcomed them all to Tri-City Airport, naming the cities and towns that it served, including one called Amity where the vicar was to address a small Episcopal college for women. "Present temperature is ninety-six degrees," said the captain mischievously, as though he himself might be responsible. A groan went up across the aisle, from several businessmen traveling together, wearing transparent short-sleeved shirts and carrying jackets made of a weight-less-looking material. It was the middle of September and Lewis had brought only one suit for his three-week lecture tour: a dark flannel worsted, perfect for English Septembers.

He thanked his hostess and, still vibrating to the thrum of the rickety flight, descended shaky metal stairs into the handshake of a fat gentleman who shook his hand with prolonged zest.

"Reverend Lewis, sir, it's an honor, a real honor. I'm Baxter Stikeleather, president of Earle College. How was the weather down there in New Orleans—hotter than here, I'll bet."

"How do you do, Doctor. No, actually it seemed . . . not quite so hot."

"Aw, that's 'cause they've got the Gulf Coast sitting right there under their noses, that's why," said the other. Having thus contributed to the defense of his state's climate, he whipped out a huge white handkerchief and beat at his large and genial face, which was slick with perspiration.

They proceeded to the airport terminal, where Stike-leather pounced on Lewis's suitcase as though it contained the Grail and led the way to the parking lot. "The girls sure have looked forward to you coming, Reverend."

"Thank you." Lewis climbed into a roomy estate wagon whose doors bore in hand-lettered Gothic script *"Earle College for Women, founded 1889."* Stikeleather arranged his sphere of a belly comfortably behind the steering wheel. The vicar was going over in his mind what he'd lost just this morning in the New Orleans lecture: ("Getting further is not leaving the world. It is discarding assumptions, thus seeing for the first time what is already there. . . .") *What* was already there? What could he have meant? Once these words had connected him to an image, but that image was gone. He had continued glibly on this morning, as though he assumed everyone else knew what was already there, even if he didn't anymore. Perhaps they did know; they seemed to know. Discussing his book with people these past few weeks, he'd had the distinct feeling that they'd tapped a dimension in it that was denied to him, its author.

". . . I haven't read it yet," Stikeleather was saying, "but I sure have read a lot about it. I've got my copy, though. I'm looking forward to really immersing myself in it once the semester gets started. What a catchy title. *My Interview with God.* And from what I've heard, it was, wasn't it? Did you think up the title yourself?"

"No," Lewis said uncomfortably. "No, I shan't claim that little accomplishment."

"Oh, well," Stikeleather reassured him, "you wrote the book. That's what counts." He struck the vicar amiably between his shoulder blades and the estate wagon belched from the parking lot in a flourish of flying gravel. "Do you like music?"

"Yes, very much," replied Lewis, puzzled.

"Coming up," the president said, fiddling with knobs on the dashboard. The moving vehicle resounded at once with a sportive melody that made Stikeleather tap his foot on the carpeted floorboard. "Total Sound," he said.

"It's very nice," said Lewis. ("Matthew's familiar Chapter 6 seems at first to deal with separate subjects. It begins by talking about men who pray loudly in public rather than shut up in their own rooms, and goes on to discuss the impossibility of serving both God and Mammon. But if we look at God as Cause, or Source, and Mammon as certain outward effects, we begin to see a relation. Effects are but the reflection of something that emanates from one's own relationship with the Source. If that relationship is good— 'If thine eye be single'—the effect will be full of light; if evil, full of darkness. But any deliberate intention of an effect, casting first towards Mammon with no relevance to the Source, will destroy the possibility of producing a worthwhile one. 'Every circle has its centre/Where the truth is made and meant,' and no good effect can come from focusing on peripheries.") He'd preached that sermon once, in the quiet days before the Illumination and the wretched fame that followed from his poor attempt to deter its passing.

"I went uptown," Stikeleather said, "and bought up all the copies I could find. What I was thinking, after your talk tomorrow morning, you might autograph them. I'll give each trustee one and keep two in our library. I hope you'll write a little something in mine, as well."

"I'd be delighted," Lewis said, charmed by his host's refreshing simplicity. Pale Dr. Harkins, two weeks ago at Yale: walking Lewis down the path to the Divinity School among first fallen leaves, he said, "You seem to be the first person inside organized religion—that is, with the exception of Teilhard (naturally)—to reconcile with success the old symbols and the needs of our present ontology. I have often thought our situation today, theologically, is what the *I Ching* would call Ming I (the darkening of the light); we needed your sort of Glossary to light the way again." A Jewish boy at Columbia wedged his way under Lewis's big black umbrella and, biting his nails, hurried out with him to the taxi waiting to speed the vicar to LaGuardia for the Chicago flight. (What was his major? Something wild, eclectic, like Serbo-Croatian poetry.) He said, "But listen, Father, haven't you in an extremely subtle way, acceptable to modern intellectuals, simply reaffirmed the

Bible stories?" "I . . . I intended to *affirm*, by way of modern myths, the same truths cloaked in the ancient myths, many of which we can no longer find acceptable. I hoped to contain that Truth which remains always the same within the parallels of the old and new myths . . . if you see what I mean." "Sure, Father. God between the lines." In San Francisco, he dined one night atop the city with a Unitarian minister his own age who had published an article on the six stages of LSD. The minister found Lewis's famous Interview directly comparable to stage 3 of the Trip "during which there's a sudden meaningful convergence of conceptual ideas and especially meaningful combinations in the world are seen for the first time." Over brandy, the minister offered to assist Lewis in reaching stage 6, "uniform white light," if he would care to accompany him back to his home. But Lewis had a morning lecture at Berkeley and declined the offer.

"I declare, I feel a whole lot better now, Reverend. There is nothing more necessary, to my way of thinking, than air-conditioning in your automobile. The trustees hemmed and hawed till I finally told them point-blank: I personally cannot drive the school station wagon until it is air-conditioned. I can't go picking up people in the name of the college and be sweating all over the place."

"It's jolly nice," agreed Lewis, feeling better himself. He looked out of the closed window at a baked clay landscape. A group of prisoners whose striped uniforms were covered with reddish dust labored desultorily in the terrible heat, monitored by a man carrying a gun. He remembered the quiet rainy garden in Sussex, outside the vicarage study window—how, looking out at this scene one totally relaxed moment after many hours of thought, he had seen suddenly beyond it into a larger, bolder kingdom. He had seen . . . He tried now to see it again, focusing intently on a memory of wet green grass, a tree, the sky as it had been, soft pearl, unblemished; he pushed hard at grass, tree, sky, so hard they fell away, leaving him with his own frowning reflection upon the closed window of the air-conditioned station wagon.

". . . Unfortunate thing. My wife has the flu; she comes down with it every fall. I thought it would be risky to put you up at our house, so I asked Mrs. Grimes, our school nurse, to fix up a private room in the infirmary for you. Parents of our girls often stay there when the hotel uptown is full. I hope you aren't offended."

"Not at all," said Lewis, "It will be a change from those motels with the huge TVs and the paper seals over the lavatories."

Stikeleather whooped with appreciation over this description until Lewis began to find it rather funny and started laughing himself.

At dinner he soon became quite sure that no faculty member had actually read his book. Nevertheless, he was the undisputed focus of solicitude. Wedged between Miss Lillian Bell, who taught history and social sciences, and Miss Evangeline Lacy (American literature, English literature, and needlework), he was plied from either side with compliments, respect, and much affectionate passing back and forth of crusty fried chicken and buttermilk biscuits. He felt like a young nephew who has succeeded in the outside world and comes home to coast for a time in the undemanding company of doting maiden aunts to whom his stomach is more important than his achievements.

Miss Bell was the aggressor of the two women. Fasttalking and flirtatious, with leathery, crinkled skin and pierced ears, she played self-consciously with a tiny ceramic tomato bobbling from her earlobe. "We've all looked forward to this so much, Reverend," she said. "Most of our girls have never met an Englishman, let alone an English vicar."

"It is such a pleasure listening to your accent," crooned Miss Lacy, who had possibly been a raving beauty in her youth. Her enormous storm-gray eyes, lashed and lustrous, peered out of her old face from another era and seemed fascinated by all they saw.

"I'm going to tell you something that will surprise you, Reverend," said Lillian Bell. "Both my father and my grandfather were Episcopal ministers. You're not just saying in your book, like some are today, that God is just energy, are you?"

"Certainly not just energy," he assured her, biting into a second chicken leg and munching busily while framing his words for further explication. He was tired beyond thought. His eyes ached when he swiveled them to note that tables full of girls openly studied him. Dr. Stikeleather had gone home to make dinner for the sick wife, leaving him the only man in the dining room. He felt suddenly exhausted by explanations of something he no longer called his own. The darkening of *his* light, he felt, had reached its winter solstice. He clutched at a straw, the only thing left to him in explaining himself to this good woman: a quote from one of his reviewers. He said, "The book is, well, notes towards a new consciousness which reaches beyond known systems of theology."

Miss Bell's face closed down on him. "Are you a God-is-dead man?" she asked coldly.

"No, no!" he shouted, without meaning to. All conversation stopped. All eyes were riveted on the vicar. In a near whisper, he amended, "In my book, I try to offer a series of concepts through which persons without your fortunate religious upbringing, Miss Bell, might also have God."

"Oh, of course," said she, relieved. "I've been saying the same thing myself for years. It's our duty to share with the less fortunate. Will you have another buttermilk biscuit, Reverend?"

After dinner there was, it seemed, a coffee hour to be held in his honor. "You'll have a chance to meet our girls," said Miss Lacy, "some of them from the finest families in the state. Marguerite Earle is in her second year here."

"The Earle of the college's name?" he inquired politely. A tiny throb had set up a regular rhythm just behind his left temple.

"Dabney Littleton Earle was Marguerite's great-great-great-grandfather," explained Miss Lacy. "He was a wealthy planter and built this place as his home in the late seventeen-hundreds. During the War Between the States, it was given over as a hospital for our wounded. After the war was over, unfortunately, it fell into the hands of the Freedman's Bureau, who used it for their headquarters." Here she sighed sadly and her friend Miss Bell shook her earrings furiously at the outrage. "But in 1889, the Episcopal diocese bought the property and established the college. As a matter of fact, I went here myself, but that was an awfully long time ago."

The coffee hour was in the drawing room. He stood, with a whopping great headache now, backed against a faded brocade curtain, facing a semicircle of avid ladies; holding his cup and saucer close against his chest like a tiny shield, he accepted their admiration. President Stikeleather entered suddenly. En route to Lewis, he plunged briefly into a cluster of girls long enough to pluck from it the flower of them all. Steering this elegant creature by her elbow, he cruised beaming toward the vicar.

"Reverend Lewis, may I present Miss Marguerite Earle, president of the Earle Student Body," he announced, his voice breaking with pride.

"How do you do?" said Lewis, marveling at the sheer aesthetic value of her. The flaunted English complexion paled beside this girl's pellucid sheen in which morning colors dominated. He counted five such colors in her face: honey, rose, gold, pearl, and Mediterranean blue.

She took Lewis's hand in her cool one and looked up at him with deference. "I have really looked forward to this," she said. "All of us have. Won't you sit down? Let me get you another cup of coffee."

At this gentleness within such beauty, Lewis felt close

to tears. Gratefully, he let himself be led to a beige settee. Stikeleather, overflowing with pleasure, stepped over to compensate the semicircle of ladies abandoned by the vicar.

Marguerite returned with his coffee and sat down. "I think it would be wonderful to live in England. Especially the English countryside. When I graduate, if I ever do, and take my trip abroad, I'm going straight to England. I love those people in Jane Austen. So relaxed and witty and tactful with one another. You know something funny, Reverend Lewis? I felt more at home reading her than I sometimes feel in real surroundings."

"I can understand that," he said. "Yours is rather a Jane Austen style. I'm a fan of hers, myself. *Emma* has always been my favorite, however, and you know one can't honestly say she was always tactful. The thing with Miss Bates, for instance, was—Have I said something to upset you?"

"Oh, dear, I've only read *Pride and Prejudice*. We had it in Miss Lacy's class last spring. You must think I'm an idiot." The girl flushed, laced her long fingers together in confusion, and looked perfectly charming.

"Not to worry," he said. "All the better, to have *Emma* ahead of you. You can go back into that world you love without waiting to graduate. But look—a favor for me: remember when you come to Reverend—Reverend—oh, blast, what is his name. You know, Miss Earle, I have forgotten everything but my own name these past few weeks. Well, anyway, when you come to that pompous reverend somebody in *Emma*, don't believe all vicars are like him."

"Oh, whenever I think of an English vicar, I certainly won't think of *him*," she said. She wore some delicate woodsy scent that opened up long-neglected channels in his dry bachelor existence. "Will you tell us about the country homes tomorrow, and the English nobility?"

"Well, certainly if there's time. I mean—if there's time. I've been invited to give my, you know, lecture on the b-book." He paused, amazed. He had not stuttered since his Oxford days, when he'd never quite mastered the knack of smooth conversation with lovely women.

"Oh, I hope there'll be time," she said. "The girls have loads of questions. Where exactly do you live?"

"In a s-small village in Sussex, near the Downs—"

"I declare I hate to disturb you-all, looking so relaxed." Stikeleather stood before the settee. "But there are some who haven't met you yet, Reverend. May I borrow him for just a minute, Marguerite? I want you to meet Miss Julia Bonham, who teaches modern dance, Reverend." He led Lewis away, toward a fulsome lady awaiting them beside the silver service.

Having finally achieved his bed in the infirmary, he couldn't sleep. He fingered the choice of bedside reading left for him by Mrs. Grimes. There was a mint-green *Treasury of Religious Verse,* brand new, with the price $8.95 written in pencil just inside the cover; a choice of Bibles (RSV or King James); and back issues of an inspirational pamphlet called *Forward: Day by Day.* There was a paperback book of very easy crossword puzzles, most of which had been worked in pencil, then erased. Book thoughts led inevitably to consideration of his own 124-page effort, out there in the world, an object in its own right now, separate even from the thing that had inspired it, which was gone. What was that vile vicar's name in the Emma book? Pelham? Stockton? The wife with the brother-in-law in Bristol with his everlasting barouche-landau . . . When you began forgetting the villains of literature, you were definitely losing your grip.

He tried different positions: board-straight, scissors-legs, fetal. He clanked around the hospital bed like a lorry full of scrap metal. His bones strummed with phantom vibrations from the turboprop and under the bottom sheet was a waterproof pad that caused his feet to slide. "What a catchy title; did you think it up yourself?" ("What were you thinking of calling it, Mr. Lewis?" over a pint of bitter at the publisher's lunch. "Oh, I don't know. It's difficult to call it anything. It was what it was, simply: a very fleeting glimpse of God on His own terms, quite apart from all my previous notions of Him. I've said all I was able to say about this, er, glimpse, in my book. Why not just *View from a Sussex Vicarage*, something of the sort?" "Ah, come, Mr. Lewis, let us put our heads together over another pint and see if we can't come up with something more provocative. After all, 'Feed my Lambs' has become today a matter of first winning their appetites, has it not?") 'Every circle has its centre/Where the truth is made and meant,' and no good effects will come from focusing upon peripheries. "We needed your sort of Glossary to light the way again." Going out to LaGuardia in the speeding taxi, through sheets of rain, he saw the most appalling cemetery, miles and miles of dingy graves, chock-a-block. . . . "Sure, Father, God between the lines." "When You're Out of Schlitz, You're Out of Beer," he was warned again and again on the turnpike. Blessed are the pure in heart, for they shall see . . . uniform white light? And then darkness, darkness, darkness, plenty of it. What was that damn vicar's name? Parkins, Sheldon; force it. Can a fleeting vision be seized by the tail, made to perform again and again to circus music? That perfume she was wearing . . . The Blessed Henry Suso, after seeing God, was tormented by a deep depression that lasted ten years. . . . The scent reminded one of spicy green woods, hidden fresh-water springs; he knew so little of women's lore, how they created their effects, yet he was not even old, thirty-one. Was this to be his dry and barren decade, his Dark Night of the Soul? (Mr. Knightley was thirty-seven when he proposed to Emma Woodhouse.) He had been so immersed in his commitment: representative of Christ on earth. Vicar, vicarius: God's deputy. No light matter. He had trod overcarefully, unsure of his right to be there at all. Had his most unsound days, then, been his most profound? Parnham, Parker, Pelton, Felpham, Farnhart, Rockwell, Brockton? Hell. Was there to be no Second Coming? He slept, then, dreamed he and Stikeleather sat under a tree in the vicarage garden, discussing how much it would cost to air-condition the vicarage. Marguerite and her friends, wearing flowing afternoon dresses to their ankles, played a lively game of croquet. Marguerite smashed a red ball CRASH! through his dusty study window, and he was alarmed, but then Stikeleather began laughing, his large belly jiggling up and down, and Lewis, infected, began to laugh, as well, until tears came into his eyes.

At breakfast, there were more of the buttermilk biscuits, which one soaked in a spicy ham gravy called "red-eye." Anxious about giving a lecture that had dried up on him in New Orleans, he ate too many. He signed Miss Bell's copy of *My Interview with God* feeling an impostor.

When he mounted the speaker's platform in the little chapel, everyone applauded him. Eight biscuits soaked in red-eye clumped stubbornly together and refused to digest. He shuffled his pile of note cards, dog-eared from fourteen other lectures, and cleared his throat. He addressed Dr. Stikeleather, who was perspiring lightly in seersucker in the front row, and called every faculty member by name (there were only six). This caused another flurry of delighted clapping. He wished he might repeat the stunt with the girls, but there were too many of them; "charming young ladies" would have to suffice.

"Well, now," he began, flushing, and looking down at the first 4 x 6 note card. One more time, he must give this lecture. He thought of the VC-10 that would depart tonight, with him aboard, for London.

The first note card read:

a. Unitive life, df. state of transcendent
   vitality (Underhill)
b. Luke 14:10
c. things *seen*

He failed utterly in seeing how these puzzling frag-
ments had ever arranged themselves into an effortless,
meaningful opening. Yet here he was; here they were.
What, in his totally depleted hour, could he tell them? His
feet, it seemed, touched down on the abyss; the light that
had been darkening steadily for a year and a half now
switched off. And they were waiting, with upturned faces.
What to say?

Then he saw Marguerite Earle, his croquet girl, sitting
by the window, her bright hair aflame like a burning bush
from the morning sun, and he remembered. His Amity
muse, a veritable earthly vision, shone before him in her
raiments of color with the promise of a rainbow and gave
him his topic. Hands folded neatly on her lap, she smiled
at him, waiting to hear.

He squared his note cards with a final clack, turned
them face down on the rostrum, and said, "The reason I
am here with you this morning is because nearly two years
ago I was sitting calmly in my vicarage study, looking out
on a peaceful rainy afternoon, and, being more or less at
one with myself, was admitted—very temporarily—to the
presence of God. Afterwards I thought I should preserve
the experience by, ah, minting it, in printed words, rather
like—well, your Treasury Department distributing the late
President Kennedy on silver half-dollars. Only they never
for a moment, I am sure, fooled themselves into thinking
they were giving away with that coin the essence of the
man. It was only a tribute, don't you see, in the same way
that my book can only be a tribute to a very special happening. St. Thomas Aquinas once said, long after he'd
completed his ponderous *Summa*, 'There are some things
that simply cannot be uttered,' after which he serenely

folded his hands over his great stomach and spent his last days elevated, they say, in rapturous prayer. Can you not see it, that great portly body floating like a thistle by the Grace of God?"

(There was a short hush during which his audience teetered between respect for a dead saint and amusement at the spectacle of a floating fat one. . . . Then Stikeleather broke the tie by laughing heartily and they all followed suit.)

"Well, then," Lewis said, a bit breathless, standing naked before them now, a man like any other, no vision standing between them, "rather than try and give you a third-hand rendition of a faded illumination, or to go over material which is there for better or for worse in a little green-and-white volume which my publishers call *My Interview with God*, I'd like to return your hospitality to me by taking you briefly into my own world. What shall I show you first? Shall we start with where I live, my vicarage in Sussex, which is five hundred years old?"

Their enthusiastic answer rang out. Marguerite Earle began clapping and they joined her. So he took them first into his study, lined with over four thousand books, many belonging to past vicars dead several hundred years, and warmed even in summer by a fireplace. He led them up narrow circular stairs to his *pièce de résistance*, the loft under the eaves where, in the sixteen-forties, it was rumored that a Royalist vicar had once hidden Charles II from his murderous pursuers. They adored this. He took them to his garden, blushing when he said, "Large enough f-for, um, a game of croquet." In summer, he told them, the Queen's orange-braceleted swans swim upriver and come waddling boldly in the garden at teatime. . . .

He took them on a Cook's tour of London; then, for the benefit of Marguerite, who loved the countryside, he returned them to Sussex Downs for a ramble. It was while lingering there, relaxed and at one with his happy group, in this dreamy country air that he remembered his old friend Mr. Elton, petty vicar of Highbury. Elton, Elton, Elton, of course! He lightened, began the upward trip from his abyss, as though St. Thomas the old dog himself had loaned him a bit of divine buoyancy. Eight buttermilk biscuits melted like hosts in his stomach. Elton! Spouse of Augusta Hawkins for the sum of ten thousand. Hypocrite, flatterer, pompous ass. Lewis had never been so glad to see anyone in his life. His universe expanded as the dark began to fade. He chuckled aloud in the midst of his guided tour. Agreeably, in a body, Earle College chuckled, too, for they were with him.

A SORROWFUL
WOMAN

One winter evening she looked at them: the husband durable, receptive, gentle; the child a tender golden three. The sight of them made her so sad and sick she did not want to see them ever again.

She told the husband these thoughts. He was attuned to her; he understood such things. He said he understood. What would she like him to do? "If you could put the boy to bed and read him the story about the monkey who ate too many bananas, I would be grateful." "Of course," he said. "Why, that's a pleasure." And he sent her off to bed.

The next night it happened again. Putting the warm dishes away in the cupboard, she turned and saw the child's gray eyes approving her movements. In the next room was the man, his chin sunk in the open collar of his favorite wool shirt. He was dozing after her good supper. The shirt was the gray of the child's trusting gaze. She began yelping without tears, retching in between. The man woke in alarm and carried her in his arms to bed. The boy followed them up the stairs, saying, "It's all right, Mommy," but this made her scream. "Mommy is sick," the father said, "go and wait for me in your room."

The husband undressed her, abandoning her only long enough to root beneath the eiderdown for her flannel gown. She stood naked except for her bra, which hung by one strap down the side of her body; she had not the impetus to shrug it off. "If only there were instant sleep," she said, hiccuping, and the husband bundled her into the gown and went out and came back with a sleeping draught guaranteed swift. She was to drink a little glass of cognac followed by a big glass of dark liquid and afterward there was just time to say, "Thank you and could you get him a clean pair of pajamas out of the laundry, it came back today."

The next day was Sunday and the husband brought her breakfast in bed and let her sleep until it grew dark again. He took the child for a walk, and when they returned, red-cheeked and boisterous, the father made supper. She heard them laughing in the kitchen. He brought her up a tray of buttered toast, celery sticks, and black bean soup. "I am the luckiest woman," she said, crying real tears. "Nonsense," he said. "You need a rest from us," and went to prepare the sleeping draught, find the child's pajamas, select the story for the night.

She got up on Monday and moved about the house till noon. The boy, delighted to have her back, pretended he was a vicious tiger and followed her from room to room, growling and scratching. Whenever she came close, he would growl and scratch at her. One of his sharp little claws ripped her flesh, just above the wrist, and together they paused to watch a thin red line materialize on the inside of her pale arm and spill over in little beads. "Go away," she said. She got herself upstairs and locked the door. She called the husband's office and said, "I've locked myself away from him. I'm afraid." The husband told her in his richest voice to lie down, take it easy, and he was already on the phone to call one of the baby-sitters they often employed. Shortly after, she heard the girl let herself in, heard the girl coaxing the frightened child to come and play.

After supper several nights later, she hit the child. She had known she was going to do it when the father would see. "I'm sorry," she said, collapsing on the floor. The weeping child had run to hide. "What has happened to me? I'm not myself anymore." The man picked her tenderly from the floor and looked at her with much concern.

"Would it help if we got, you know, a girl in? We could fix the room downstairs. I want you to feel freer," he said, understanding these things. "We have the money for a girl. I want you to think about it."

And now the sleeping draught was a nightly thing; she did not have to ask. He went down to the kitchen to mix it; he set it nightly beside her bed. The little glass and the big one, amber and deep rich brown, the flannel gown and the eiderdown.

The man put out the word and found the perfect girl. She was young, dynamic, and not pretty. "Don't bother with the room, I'll fix it up myself." Laughing, she employed her thousand energies. She painted the room white, fed the child lunch, read edifying books, raced the boy to the mailbox, hung her own watercolors on the fresh-painted walls, made spinach soufflé, cleaned a spot from the mother's coat, made them all laugh, danced in stocking feet to music in the white room after reading the child to sleep. She knitted dresses for herself and played chess with the husband. She washed and set the mother's soft ash-blond hair and gave her neck rubs, offered to.

The woman now spent her winter afternoons in the big bedroom. She made a fire in the hearth and put on slacks and an old sweater she had loved at school, and sat in the big chair and stared out the window at snow-ridden branches, or went away into long novels about other people moving through other winters.

The girl brought the child in twice a day, once in the late afternoon when he would tell of his day, all of it tumbling out quickly because there was not much time, and before he went to bed. Often now, the man took his wife to dinner. He made a courtship ceremony of it, inviting her beforehand so she could get used to the idea. They dressed and were beautiful together again and went out into the frosty night. Over candlelight he would say, "I think you are better, you know." "Perhaps I am," she would murmur. "You look . . . like a cloistered queen," he said once, his voice breaking curiously.

One afternoon the girl brought the child into the bedroom. "We've been out playing in the park. He found something he wants to give you, a surprise." The little boy approached her, smiling mysteriously. He placed his cupped hands in hers and left a live dry thing that spat brown juice in her palm and leapt away. She screamed and wrung her hands to be rid of the brown juice. "Oh, it was only a grasshopper," said the girl. Nimbly she crept to the edge of a curtain, did a quick knee bend, and reclaimed the creature, led the boy competently from the room.

"The girl upsets me," said the woman to her husband. He sat frowning on the side of the bed he had not entered for so long. "I'm sorry, but there it is." The husband stroked his creased brow and said he was sorry, too. He really did not know what they would do without that treasure of a girl. "Why don't you stay here with me in bed," the woman said.

Next morning she fired the girl, who cried and said, "I loved the little boy, what will become of him now?" But the mother turned away her face and the girl took down the watercolors from the walls, sheathed the records she had danced to, and went away.

"I don't know what we'll do. It's all my fault, I know. I'm such a burden, I know that."

"Let me think. I'll think of something." (Still understanding these things.)

"I know you will. You always do," she said.

With great care he rearranged his life. He got up hours early, did the shopping, cooked the breakfast, took the boy to nursery school. "We will manage," he said, "until you're better, however long that is." He did his work, collected the boy from the school, came home and made the supper, washed the dishes, got the child to bed. He managed everything. One evening, just as she was on the verge of swallowing her draught, there was a timid knock on her door. The little boy came in wearing his pajamas. "Daddy has fallen asleep on my bed and I can't get in. There's not room."

Very sedately she left her bed and went to the child's room. Things were much changed. Books were rearranged, toys. He'd done some new drawings. She came as a visitor to her son's room, wakened the father, and helped him to bed. "Ah, he shouldn't have bothered you," said the man, leaning on his wife. "I've told him not to." He dropped into his own bed and fell asleep with a moan. Meticulously she undressed him. She folded and hung his clothes. She covered his body with the bedclothes. She flicked off the light that shone in his face.

The next day she moved her things into the girl's white room. She put her hairbrush on the dresser; she put a note pad and pen beside the bed. She stocked the little room with cigarettes, books, bread, and cheese. She didn't need much.

At first the husband was dismayed. But he was receptive to her needs. He understood these things. "Perhaps the best thing is for you to follow it through," he said. "I want to be big enough to contain whatever you must do."

All day long she stayed in the white room. She was a young queen, a virgin in a tower; she was the previous inhabitant, the girl with all the energies. She tried these personalities on like costumes, then discarded them. The room had a new view of streets she'd never seen that way before. The sun hit the room in late afternoon, and she took to brushing her hair in the sun. One day she decided to write a poem. "Perhaps a sonnet." She took up her pen and pad and began working from words that had lately lain in her mind. She had choices for the sonnet, ABAB or ABBA for a start. She pondered these possibilities until she tottered into a larger choice: she did not have to write a sonnet. Her poem could be six, eight, ten, thirteen lines, it could be any number of lines, and it did not even have to rhyme.

She put down the pen on top of the pad.

In the evenings, very briefly, she saw the two of them. They knocked on her door, a big knock and a little, and she would call "Come in," and the husband would smile though he looked a bit tired, yet somehow this tiredness suited him. He would put her sleeping draught on the bedside table and say, "The boy and I have done all right today," and the child would kiss her. One night she tasted for the first time the power of his baby spit.

"I don't think I can see him anymore," she whispered sadly to the man. And the husband turned away, but recovered admirably and said, "Of course, I see."

So the husband came alone. "I have explained to the boy," he said. "And we are doing fine. We are managing." He squeezed his wife's pale arm and put the two glasses on her table. After he had gone, she sat looking at the arm.

"I'm afraid it's come to that," she said next time. "Just push the notes under the door; I'll read them. And don't forget to leave the draught outside."

The man sat for a long time with his head in his hands. Then he rose and went away from her. She heard him in the kitchen where he mixed the draught in batches now to last a week at a time, storing it in a corner of the cupboard. She heard him come back, leave the big glass and the little one outside on the floor.

Outside her window, the snow was melting from the branches, there were more people on the streets. She brushed her hair a lot and seldom read anymore. She sat in her window and brushed her hair for hours, and saw a boy fall off his new bicycle again and again, a dog chasing a squirrel, an old woman peek slyly over her shoulder and then extract a parcel from a garbage can.

In the evening she read the notes they slipped under her door. The child could not write, so he drew and sometimes painted his. The notes were painstaking at first, the man and boy offering the final strength of their day to her. But sometimes, when they seemed to have had a bad day, there were only hurried scrawls.

One night, when the husband's note had been extremely short, loving but short, and there had been nothing from the boy, she stole out of her room as she often did to get more supplies, but crept upstairs instead and stood outside their doors, listening to the regular breathing of the man and boy asleep. She hurried back to her room and drank the draught.

She woke earlier now. It was spring, there were birds. She listened for sounds of the man and the boy eating breakfast; she listened for the roar of the motor when they drove away. One beautiful noon, she went out to look at her kitchen in the daylight. Things were changed. He had bought some new dishtowels. Had the old ones worn out? The canisters seemed closer to the sink. She inspected the cupboard and saw new things among the old. She got out flour, yeast, salt, milk (he bought a different brand of butter), and baked a loaf of bread and left it cooling on the table.

The force of the two joyful notes slipped under her door that evening pressed her into the corner of the little room; she had hardly space to breathe. As soon as possible, she drank the draught.

Now the days were too short. She was always busy. She woke with the first bird. Worked till the sun set. No time for hair-brushing. Her fingers raced the hours.

Finally, in the nick of time, it was finished one late afternoon. Her veins pumped and her forehead sparkled. She went to the kitchen cupboard, took what was hers, closed herself into the little white room, and brushed her hair for a while.

The man and boy came home and found: five loaves of warm bread, a roast stuffed turkey, a glazed ham, three pies of different fillings, eight molds of the boy's favorite custard, two weeks' supply of fresh-laundered sheets and shirts and towels, two hand-knitted sweaters (both of the same gray color), a sheath of marvelous watercolor beasts accompanied by mad and fanciful stories nobody could ever make up again, and a tablet full of love sonnets addressed to the man. The house was redolent of renewal and spring. The man ran to the little room, could not contain himself to knock, flung back the door.

"Look, Mommy is sleeping," said the boy. "She's tired from doing all our things again." He dawdled in a stream of the last sun for that day and watched his father tenderly roll back her eyelids, lay his ear softly to her breast, test the delicate bones of her wrist. The father put down his face into her fresh-washed hair.

"Can we eat the turkey for supper?" the boy asked.

LAYOVER

Here I am again at the airport. My destinations connect here and I am beginning to know the place as intimately as the feel of my own skin.

My flights in and out are much the same. Takeoffs and landings are predictable and painless. Flying time is unmemorable. Going up and coming down bring no exhilaration. Some time ago I stopped stimulating myself with the hope of a hijacker and frightening myself with the possibility of a crash. It is all smooth flying in the skies they have christened "friendly" in the same tone they name "turbulence" and even "mechanical failure."

There is neither danger nor ecstasy in these skies. We are fed into the great machines through narrow tubes with red-carpeted ramps and fed out at the other end, spared all changes in the weather. We are processed through our journeys to emerge as bland and untransformed as the instant domes of pale desserts set securely into our plastic dinner trays.

Everything outside the airport changes, but in here it remains the same. I have begun to nourish my disgust for it the way some people become self-satisfied in unhappy homes. Compared with its patient everpresence, its built-in insistence upon my repeated returns, my destinations seem sadly transient, pointless. They are always bound to end. Like those foolish jaunty clouds that can't hold their shape for a minute that I often observe through two layers of treated glass from my window seat. Why fly at all? Why not stay in the airport and imagine the destinations and save all this useless going up and down, the anticipation that never fulfills itself on arrival, the discomfort of withdrawal afterward?

.   .   .

Today I missed my connection on purpose. It was one of those quick layovers they are so proud of, an efficient herding from one red-carpeted tube to another, with not an extra minute to look around or think.

I am in the LADIES, bolted into a cubicle. I have hung my purse on the hook where it says "Do Not Hang Purse Here," and I am thinking of the potential shapes and shades of furtive hands that might reach over and snatch away all my money, my credit cards, my ticket, my identification before I have time to pull up my pants. I look down at my own hand, pale and restless, and imagine it capable of quick crime.

Nobody is going to steal my purse. I'll explore. Is there anywhere I have not yet been in the airport? If I go into the main terminal, where I have killed so much time fingering souvenirs that come apart in my hands and leafing through paperbacks that promise everything, I will have to be X-rayed on my return to make sure I have acquired nothing deadly on my person or in my purse.

I go to a standup cocktail bar "within limits" instead. The man next to me orders something called a Red Snapper. I order one, too. We avoid looking at each other as we stand side by side, drinking our identical drinks. Our ice cubes hit the sides of our glasses at the same time. I know that if I drain my Red Snapper at the same moment he drains his, he will ask, "Can I buy you another?"

I hurry down to my ice cubes and leave the bar.

At the convergence of the E Gate and the F Gate, there is a door marked "Observation Tower." A new sign has been Scotch-taped below. "Closed Till Further Notice." Boundaries shrinking even here, as our mistrust for one another grows. I try the door and it opens. I slip in and go up the cement stairs and suddenly I feel better. At the top there is a turnstile that says "25¢." I put a quarter in but it won't turn. There is not enough room for me to climb under, unless I became a small child again, and I am not limber enough or suitably dressed for straddling it like a country fence.

Outside I can hear the great planes going out and coming in, taxiing up and down on the earth, making a kind of music. If only I could have seen the whole pattern!

Halfway back down the stairs there is a red door with "Private: Members Only" written in pretentious gold "Gothic" letters. For a moment I hesitate. Then, shouldering my purse, I walk in.

It is a lounge, also furnished in reds and golds. Thick red carpet. Low lights. There is a bar, around which a dozen or so men stand or sit or lean. They look exactly as affluent businessmen between destinations are supposed to look.

I walk across the red carpet to the bar. "May I have a Red Snapper, please?" I ask, though no one is tending bar.

Like Rotarians just before a banquet, they bow their heads as a group and give thanks. Then a member goes behind the bar and fills my order.

I accept the drink. Another member steps forward. He says gently but officially, "May I see your ticket?"

As I have done so many times before, I hand it over automatically.

He scans it, seems pleased, and says: "Do you have any preference as to seating? Where would you be most comfortable?" He looks around the dark room glowing with easy reds, and directs my eyes to choose.

I selected a couch, large, deep, and red. It looks like leather, but I can tell from the smell when I sit down that it is only imitation. The members gather around me and allow me to finish my drink.

One of them takes the empty glass from my hand. "Would you like to lie down now?"

"I have no protection," I explain.

"Oh, it is perfectly safe in this room," another one

assures me, and his friend beside chimes in earnestly: "No one will ever know outside this room."

They begin to sing a round. They clasp one another about the shoulders and blend their voices, barbershop-quartet-style. The words are: "I WANT YOU TO BE THE MOTHER OF MY CHILD."

Their phrases ("This time it will be different . . . bigger and better product . . . undo all our harm . . . a dependable representative who will unclutter our congested skies and make the world a safer place to live in . . .") are as stock as their performances, but there are enough of them to give me time to comprehend. It *does* all happen in this room. Under the right conditions, birth, like flight, becomes instant. Nevertheless, one clings to old traditions, and as they pass through me, I try to select some small individual detail about each of them to match up with the characteristics of my child. Their separate destinies throb through corridors mysterious even to me as each contributes his parenthood. I relax as I begin to accept, and every time another member enters I feel a hitherto unexperienced satisfaction. I contemplate myself as Indispensable Center, the Point X of their ambitious conspiracy, and though my belly remains flat, I feel myself stretching, lengthening, expanding until I burst into a receptacle ample enough to harbor infinite pleasure.

I am not allowed to see the child. A member swaddles it in a red napkin. Several of the others follow him out of the room in a sort of processional. They are weeping with emotion.

"See?" says a remaining one. "It didn't hurt a bit, did it?"

"Think of the contribution you have made," another reminds me.

"You didn't have such a bad time, either, honey," says a third. "How about a little rerun?"

"Yes," I say.

When I grew too big for the couch, I was moved to the carpet. I have lost count of the members I have accommodated. So many pass through me, glance at their splendidly accurate watches, and depart. But always the door opens and new members come.

How can I explain what has happened to me? Each time a new one enters, I grow that much larger. It seems very simple to me; having done my part, I can lie here forever with plenty of time to think and enjoy.

Outside somewhere is the child: my poor, pleasureless representative making repetitive journeys through a weary world. May it move cunningly, at least, accumulating wisdom for its own survival. Did they really expect it to change anything?

Sometimes, during the rare lull, I imagine myself suddenly rising to my feet and deciding to continue my own journey.

(Where was I going that last time?)

I look around for something big enough to cover my nakedness, strip the imitation velvet draperies from the window (which proves to look out on nothing), and somehow manage to make myself decent. I descend the remaining stairs, bowing low to keep from smashing my skull against the ceiling. I find my gate.

"I'm sorry, Ma'am," the ticket agent says. "I can't let you go through."

"Why not?" I ask. I can hardly contain my laughter. He is so small, a toy official. I could squash him between my thumb and finger. Doesn't he know I am only imagining him?

"Because," he says, craning his neck to meet my eyes, but keeping his own studiously blank, as if I looked no different from the average passenger, "you haven't got your ticket."

"Oh, yes, here it is." My giant fingers fumble through that tiny purse again.

"Ma'am, that ticket has expired."

"Why don't you say what you mean?" I say. "That I am too big. That I would endanger the lives of the other passengers."

"I didn't say that," he says defensively, looking away.

Too big, yes, and I grow bigger with each new entry. I burst the bounds of this room, I flow down the stairs and through the corridors, cracking cement. I must have room for my extremities, which are constantly expanding. They hurry to build new extensions for me, while I lie throbbing at the center, my head raised, my eyes flirting the dark skies to bring new arrivals homing into me.

Inside I feel them moving about, the monotony of their tiny heartbeats, their little projects, their selfishnesses, their microscopic hopes and frauds. They have become indistinguishable from one another. The thrusts I used to enjoy have become mere tickles and I spend all my time assailing the fertile skies.

I want them all.

THE WOMAN
WHO KEPT
HER POET

They were married in a strictly private ceremony (". . . he for the second time, she for the first," said the newsmagazines) with only her baffled parents as witnesses. A photographer snapped a close-up of the couple as they entered the waiting car. In this photo, the disparity of their ages could be seen, but the disparity of their sizes could not.

He had walked out on his old life for her, shed forty years with another woman, a former great beauty, a titled beauty, to go with her, this big girl still in her teens, whom he had known exactly thirteen days when he made his decision. His grown sons, established in respectable lives, pronounced him an old fool and predicted that this autumnal frolic with a baby giant would cost him his art. The truth was, he had written nothing in a year. His "old" wife behaved like the aristocrat she was. She refused to speak to reporters. She told her husband he must do what he must do; he always had, anyway; she had no wish to cling to a dead form for the sake of the past. She refused his offers of settlements. "Marriage is not a life-insurance policy," she said. Her sons thought this was a noble gesture. They were well off; they could provide her with everything.

The new couple went abroad, to an old resort, high in the mountains. They were anonymous there. If anyone stared (which nobody did), it would not have been because of who he was but because of how they looked together. They were a memorable pair. Mountains, he said, were the emblem of his spirit. He explained to his young bride—who listened a great deal more than she spoke—that the whole purpose of his life had been to find the right images to complete his art. He announced that as soon as they had rested for several days, grown used to the amenities of this grand, feudal old establishment, they were going to climb a certain mountain together. He pointed it out to her from their bedroom window. It was called Stone Man's Prospect.

She did not say no, but she made up her mind to postpone this climb as long as possible. She was so afraid he would overexert himself and die. She wound her great young limbs about him and kept him in bed for late breakfasts. She confessed to him, her words coming haltingly, what a lazy climber she would make, how clumsy she had been at school sports. She worried about him constantly in her heart; she was terrified of losing him. Her love for this man was so great she could not contain all of it, big as she was, and it overflowed into fears. He would be taken from her, this miracle of a man who adored her so. If she had "stolen" him from another woman, would not Death steal him from her? She couldn't bear it. She loved him so much, this man who now belonged so completely to her, and she felt it her sacred duty to protect him. That was her vocation, so simple! And her parents had been so worried she would find nothing to do. She would learn all the ways to keep him safe. For his sake she could learn anything: perhaps even to talk, to "be articulate," as her parents had so wanted her to be. Try and say what you feel, darling, they said. Learn to capture in words what you know and feel. The power of words is magic. The right word can accomplish anything.

She lay holding his frail, precise body in her arms, protecting him from the boundless night, and in that chamber high in the mountains her large eyes adjusted to the dark until they accommodated the swarms of visions of all the ways he could be taken from her. Each time she saw a new one, her heart broke. How could there be so many ways for a human being, the one she loved most in the world, to be destroyed!

Out of her great love was born an idea: perhaps her parents were right about words being magic. The three people she loved were in love with words. Perhaps she should give them a try. She would lie here in the darkness, holding his sleeping form, cradling his live body in her arms, and she would think out in words every possible way he might be taken from her; she would embrace them, too; she would let her heart be broken by each one of them in turn, and in this way she would weave a magic cordon about him and keep him forever.

So each night while he slept, she held him close to her and took into her own heart his deaths, one by one. If she could absorb them first, completely, they would never reach him.

Slowly in that dark, while her husband slept, she became articulate with her heart. She lay curled around him, taking his deaths, at the same time listening to his heartbeat. He was still there. He was still there. He was still there. His heart beat slower than hers. Was that good or bad? She was sorry that their hearts were not on the same side as they lay face-to-face. She would gladly have had hers cut out and removed to the other side, so that in this deep blue hour when he rested within her trust, they would become mirror images and her young, powerful heart might caress and stimulate his with new energies. She felt (still struggling with her native incoherency, so inadequate compared to the ranging sureness of her heart) that in a love like theirs there ought to be a way to share everything you had. Machines could do it, machines had achieved it with the help of people, why could not people do it for themselves? A transfusion of loving, vital energies. Two machines could run off the same current. Easily. There must be a way for him to "run" off her, should the day ever come when he was used up.

While he slept, she sniffed him tentatively, as an animal sniffs its mate. She loved the smell of him, his physical, earthy smell. She did not think he himself was aware of how nice his own smell was. She had noticed it that first evening, on the bicycles, when they had gone off together that first time on that expensive little island, so far away from this mountain, where she had been staying with her parents and he with his wife, his "old" wife. In a way, she had fallen in love with him through this smell. Unlike his poems, which were formal, cool, pure little gems of intellectual control, which sank like stones into your consciousness and refused to be dislodged or disintegrated into anything other than themselves, his smell was warm, pungent, and perishable. It was sweet and vulnerable. It changed constantly, by the hour, according to what he was doing. After lovemaking, it was rampant and strong, so that if she shut her eyes she might believe she lay next to a beast. At night when he slept, breathing deeply, it subsided into a gentle but constant reminder of his mortality. She sometimes thought this might be the way his body, newly dead, might smell. Dead!

"Let's not climb the mountain today," she begged.

"All right. Not today. Today will be our day to wander around our 'estate.' But your time runs out tomorrow, little girl. Tomorrow we are going to the mountain."

They explored the curious old resort. She had never seen anything like it. It belonged to another era, when people came for long stays and did things leisurely, in the grand manner. They admired its gardens, formal and beautiful, tended by a silent wrinkled old man who might have been Time himself. They examined the rather baroque old statuary about the grounds, gods and goddesses stretching their lusty arms, lifting their wings, frolicking magnanimously in the musical waters of small ponds, as if the everyday world were populated by none other than gods and goddesses like themselves.

They walked slowly, hollowly, through the high-ceilinged rooms, which echoed with vastness, with time's secrets, and they touched the furniture, the old, odd furniture, wondering at the usefulness of some of the pieces. Were there some activities that had ceased to exist in the lives of people? Yes, testified some of these mysterious, clumsy shapes. Yes.

Suddenly the poet gave a cry. He led her to an enormous chair. It was formidable in size, it might have been made for a giant. Its wooden canopy was chained to the ceiling, as if otherwise it might come crashing down on a guest. Carved around this canopy and on the arms and legs of the chair seemed to be the entire story of a civilization. The poet took his new wife reverently by the arms and pushed her toward this chair.

"Sit down," he whispered. "I want to see how you look in it."

She obeyed. She fit it perfectly. At last, a chair big enough for her. She sighed and smiled down at her husband. How she loved him at this moment. The poet smiled back. He was silent.

She was the daughter of the critic T——— and his wife, the novelist M———, who had won a fair reputation with her deft social comedies. These two were small, slim, delicately made, articulate human beings. They gave meaning to their lives through the superbly chosen word. Their one child stunned them. She was the one thing in their lives that evaded definition. Perhaps that is the reason they did not take a chance on further offspring. By her second year, it was clear to them that she was as unlike them as a member of their species could be. By her eleventh year, she towered over them. They had long since given up on music lessons, riding lessons, dancing lessons, encouraging her to write little verse dramas as did the children of their articulate friends. They kept to their separate, well-appointed studios, on separate floors and opposite ends of the house, between which she ranged and roamed, not seeming to mind her solitude, yet grateful when either of her parents noticed her or stopped to pet her, as they might stop to pet a beloved Great Dane. They thanked God that she passed from one grade to the next in her school and never got lower than a C in any subject. (The C in English rankled a bit.) When she graduated from high school, they asked her delicately, tentatively, what she might like to "do"; she did not have to go to college, but if she did want to go, they would do their best in finding the right one for her gentle abilities. She said she *had* thought of medicine, but she supposed her average wasn't good enough. Veterinary medicine, perhaps? The couple exchanged a look, both thinking simultaneously of the unremarkable average. Then the father had an idea that relieved all three: why not take a vacation? They all needed it: a late-spring vacation, a month under the sun on the smart little island of ————, easy to reach yet remote when you got there. They could all three relax and consider the best future for their daughter.

So they went to the island. Man and wife took along their portfolios. Each had worked so long and hard in words that they would have been bereft with all that sand and sun and water and no words to fill up the space. They sat with gin-and-tonics and their papers spread out on a white table under an umbrella, watching their "daughter"—after eighteen years, the word, applied to this special creature, still struck them as odd—standing quite unself-consciously by the water's edge, wearing the one-piece bathing suit her mother had picked out for her. Her mother had excellent taste. The suit was green, a lovely, gentle green, natural as leaves. It draped about the girl's body in soft folds, making her unobtrusive—that is, in the way a tall, massive oak is unobtrusive when clothed in spring green.

"She's certainly not *fat*," ventured the wife.

"Oh, no, indeed. That's *all too solid flesh*."

"Her eyes are extremely eloquent."

"Yes. She doesn't *need* to say much."

The pair lapsed into an apologetic mutual silence, caressing their cool gins, having once more exhausted their combined vocabularies in trying to come to terms with this girl. There was a pain in the heart of each, though neither of these wordsmiths could have said what it was. It had to do with some division in themselves that tore at them cruelly. For, secretly, each loved the shy, great creature to excess. They could not keep from watching her, from touching her with their hands, though each touched her freely only when the other was not around to see. When each was alone with her, her size seemed normal. She was just right, perfect, what a *real* daughter should be. It was only in the critical, diminishing eyes of others that she became excessive, embarrassing, too much.

The man was the first to sigh and look away. His restless, critical eye scanned the beach. "My God," he said.

"What?"

"I would swear that is ———— down there." He pointed discreetly with fingers that had started to tremble to a proud couple, already deeply tanned, who sat like stately mummies in matching striped deck chairs. ———— was the very person the critic was writing a book about at the moment.

The wife scrutinized the couple for a few moments behind her prescription sunglasses. "I think it is. I remember seeing her photograph in *Vogue*. It will take a lot more than sixty years to erode all *that* beauty and breeding."

"Oh, God," repeated the husband. His fine, narrow fingers fluttered to the pages of the typed manuscript on the table. Instinctively they touched words on the page, like a blind man inspecting a face, as if they would have the final say-so as to whether or not the great inscrutable ———— was really down there in his chair.

The wife continued to watch the couple. After a while she said, a curious wonderment in her voice, "He seems to be staring at our daughter."

At dinner, their speculation was confirmed. It was ———— and his wife. They walked past the critic's table to their own, in the corner by a window with geraniums, over-looking the sea. The wife was gauntly, blondly beautiful, like an ageless Viking saint (thought the novelist, pleased with her description). She carried her years as she carried the cane with which she walked: with a grave asceticism that was almost arrogance. She looked neither to the left nor the right. Her eyes were a light, burned-out blue. They seemed to see nothing, to be but a formality in her face. The great poet slowed his pace slightly as he passed their table. He was inches from the critic; he was near enough to touch, every line in that famous face so close!

He nodded at their daughter and passed on.

Immediately after dinner, the critic went up to his room and went straight to bed. He could not do anything more that day, he was so agitated. He apologized to his daughter. Earlier he had promised they would all take a walk after dinner while it was still light, explore the is-land, and she had been so excited. Now she knelt by his bed and nuzzled him with her hot cheek and said she hoped he felt better. She said she would go out by herself for a while.

The wife gave him a tranquilizer and sat on the edge of the bed. The closest times in their marriage seemed to be when one shored up the other at some particularly rocky point in his professional life. The wife had also looked for-ward to the walk; she had come here already sketching out a possible novel about a couple who come to an island, ostensibly to decide on the future of their child but really to replenish their own creative sources, which were going dry. She had looked forward to the naturalistic touches they would discover on the walk, the interesting native faces and flora. But they could walk tomorrow; her partner needed her now. He had done the same for her, given her a tranquilizer and sat on the edge of her bed when she was languishing over reviews that had not yet appeared, or smarting over those that had.

"The first thing to remember," he said, "is that they are on holiday. People on a holiday are entitled to their privacy, no matter who they are."

"Yes," she said, "but if something should present itself naturally, well, that will be another story."

"He never answered a single letter of mine." Thinking of all the drafts, the dozens and dozens of drafts of those unanswered letters.

"I know. But now both of you are here on the same island," she said. "One day you and he might be climbing over the same rock and you'll sit down together by the sea, and talk. On the other hand, some morning, quite unexpectedly, somebody or other might snap a picture of you together. . . ."

He groaned.

"You will just have to keep yourself open," she said, thinking, A novel where a middle-aged couple, both writers, go to an island. Meanwhile, on this island is a famous, an internationally famous, poet, who symbolizes the ability to make use of all the great and dangerous metaphors this couple cannot quite rise to. . . . An interaction with this great poet revives the couple . . . he gives them the courage to go on.

Shortly before midnight their daughter came in to say good night. They had completely forgotten about her.

She said she had gone for a bicycle ride round the island. The hotel had bicycles for its guests. "A very nice man went with me," she said. "You know what, Daddy? He is the man you are writing your book on."

"What!" cried the father.

The mother, formidably calm, asked, "What did you talk about?"

"We didn't talk much. He seemed sad. He seemed tired. His wife has arthritis in her back. That is why they are here. That must be very painful."

"Sweetheart," said the father, trying to control his trembling hands (he gave up and hid them under the covers), "come and sit here with me on the bed. Do you mean to say you have been with this man since you left this room? That's . . . why, that's four hours!"

"It went so quickly," said the girl, sitting down on the edge of his bed. It sank.

"We know how you are reluctant to describe things," said the mother. "But do you think, just this once—it would mean a great deal to your father—you could try and reconstruct everything that happened, everything that was said between you and . . ." She could not quite bring herself to use the great name.

"Well, I was just pedaling off . . ."

"Yes?"

"And he came out of the hotel and said, 'Where did you get that bicycle? May I go with you?'"

"Just like that: *May I go with you?*" The father sank down in his pillows, thinking of all the unanswered letters.

"So I showed him where they were and he got one and . . . the seat of his was too high and he had trouble pedaling, so he suggested we trade, since his bicycle was bigger than mine and I was so much larger than he was. . . ."

The mother shut her eyes. Her mother's pride constricted her heart.

"And then what did you do? What did you say?" pressed the father.

"We just rode around the island." And the girl raised her great soft eyes and there was a sorrowful, shamed look in them both parents had seen many times before. She was saying with her eyes: I am failing you again. I cannot bring my experience to you in words. If the wife had not been there, the father would have pulled his wonderful girl down beside him and calmed his trembling fingers in her hair and scratched her head. If the husband had not been there, the mother would have reached her arms as best she could around her daughter in an old-fashioned mother's embrace and told her she was lovely, lovely, just as she was, with her hot cheeks and her poignant dark eyes.

But, as it was, both demanded at once: "You 'just rode' for four hours?"

"You didn't *say* anything?"

"He kissed me. . . ." the girl said.

"What? Where?"

The daughter touched her own mouth with wonderment. "Here."

"No," said the mother, "I meant where. On the hotel grounds? Some secluded part of the island?"

"It was when we brought the bicycles back and locked them up," said the girl.

"Did anyone see you?" the father wanted to know.

"I don't know. I was looking at him."

The critic and his wife exchanged a look.

"Did he say anything about seeing you again?" asked the mother.

The girl thought. "No. He said they would be here two more weeks . . . only he said 'fortnight.' "

"Two more weeks, two more *weeks*," chanted the critic. His eyes had gone slightly crazed.

"He did say—" the girl began.

"Said what? What did he say?"

"He said he dreamed about me last night. He dreamed I was standing with my back to him, just as I was today on the beach, only it was not at the beach."

"But we only came today," said the mother. "How could he have seen you in a dream last night?"

·   ·   ·

So they climbed the mountain. She had imagined it would be steeper, more difficult and tiring, from the way he had described it. The climb cost her hardly a single short breath. But she lagged behind and complained and sank down with a loud sigh beneath a pine tree whenever she counted one too many a bead of sweat on that dear forehead. "Wait!" she would say. "Let's stop for a minute." And he would fuss over her. "A big girl, a big young healthy girl like you? Already tired? Shame. An old man like me can do it." But he sat as long as she made him. He took out his big handkerchief and mopped his face till the handkerchief was soaked. Under each resting tree he would kiss her. Today the taste of his sweat was so distinct in her mouth she knew it would stay with her always.

At last the top. It was not as she had expected from his descriptions. It was flat and rather dry and had no trees. But he was ecstatic. He paced around, giddy, a little mad. His memorable face with its many cracked surfaces gleamed like a child's. She hurried toward him to kiss that face, but he put out his hands and held her off.

"Not yet," he said hoarsely, "not yet."

Then he made her take off her knapsack and all her clothes, even her hiking shoes and high socks, and stand naked with her back to him in one certain spot.

"There. No, over to the right a little. Just there. Don't move," he said.

"But why?" She was afraid and hurt. She did not like hearing his voice and not being able to see him and touch him.

But presently it was over and he took her in his arms. They sat down together on the dry grass and he explained very carefully how everything in his life had led up to this moment, how, from almost the first moment of his consciousness, he had known what he wanted of his art. "Everything in life is mutable, destructible, subject to age and change and pain and death. This body of mine, this body you say you love so much, this aging, smelly old body

. . . perishable, vulnerable! All of it! Subject to any accident, germ, any fluke of chance, any idiot random circum-
stance that comes along. Pah!" His eyes narrowed with a
kind of hatred.

Then a holy look, which excluded even her, came into
these eyes as he said, "My work, my final completed work,
the body of my work, will be a form freed from all of this.
No accidents can befall it, no mutability ever distort it. I
have one more poem to write. It will be the last poem in my
collected works. You are my last poem."

Then it started to rain. She was glad. It meant they had
to leave that awful, barren top and run a little way down
the mountain and shelter under a tree. They ate their lunch,
a marvelous lunch packed by the hotel, and drank good
strong red wine from their canteens. He ate well and
praised the food in simple terms, repeating himself. Just
like any hungry man having his lunch. He seemed to have
forgotten his mountaintop speech, and she was glad. He
had gone away from her then. It was as if his body had
faded away and left her with only that cold, spiritual voice,
like an angel's, denying life, denying all the things she
loved most about him.

After lunch the sun reappeared. They made love under
the tree. At first he was strangely reluctant, then let go and
ravished her in a way he never had before: like a young
man—no, a young animal. His need for her was insatiable.
There was a peak to it that she knew came once in a lifetime, if ever, to lovers. In this moment, she understood
without words why her extraordinary dimensions—which
often gave pain to those smaller ones who loved her—had
been necessary. She had to be *this big*, not a centimeter
smaller, to contain this one man's great desire for her.

Afterward he said, "I had not planned on this." He sank
his head on her breast and fell asleep.

That night, back in their room, he did not come to bed.
He sat up all night writing his poem, his last poem. She
lay in the shadows, propped up on pillows, her great dark

eyes never leaving him as he sat over the table, penning page after page with hardly a line crossed out, that famous, ragged profile turned toward her love.

At dawn he finished. He showed it to her. She scanned the lines slowly, wanting to understand every word. It was about their mountain climb, everything! As it had happened. The poem knew that she had feigned her tiredness to preserve the poet for "the last, faltering step into eternity." The poem read with a preplanned sureness, almost as if he had mapped out everything before they had ever climbed the mountain. It was called "The Stone Man Surveys His Work." The last line she did not understand. It seemed to equate her with death. How could that be: she who was determined to preserve his life at all costs?

There was no mention of the rain or the lovemaking afterward. She was sad.

Autumn. Time to leave the old resort in the faraway mountains, where everything was done for the lovers. Time to go home. But in his hurry to shed his old, worn-out life like a husk, the poet had shed his house as well.

Where were the newlyweds to spend the winter?

The critic and his wife wrote to them. No problem! Come home, said the critic, to our own summer house on the Cape. He was having it winterized for them, every inch, everything was being seen to. He had even had their daughter's special bed moved from their place in the city to the master bedroom on the Cape. The poet and his young wife would have the critic's own bedroom, of course.

The night before the awaited couple was due, the critic left his wife downstairs with her drink. She was exhausted. She had postponed her novel to refinish furniture, hang curtains, take down old pictures that had seemed good enough for them but might not be for *him*. The critic, too, was exhasted, but never had he felt so happy, so full of accomplishment. He walked around the master bedroom, excited, taking quick, nervous sips of his own drink. He was seeing the room through the eyes of the poet. Everything was in readiness. The comfortable, shabby old sofa in its tasteful new slipcover of bright, casual, splashy country flowers (chosen by his wife). The elegant antique desk they had paid too much for last week in order to have it here, ensconced in its corner by the fireplace, as though it had been there for generations. ——— himself would sit at that desk, the winter sea roaring in his poet's ear, warmed by the critic's own logs, writing his immortal poems!

It was too much. The critic's legs gave way under him and he lay down on the bed, his daughter's huge bed. He remembered how evasive, how embarrassed he had been when he had given the order for this bed several years ago. Suddenly he was ashamed. He blessed his child. He shyly pulled down the new bedspread and kissed the pillow where she would lay her head.

For the first time in his life, he felt he understood the purpose of everything.

After the couple had been back a month, the critic and his wife decided it would be appropriate to call on them. They drove over from the mainland in late afternoon. It was a beautiful, waning October afternoon. They had waited because they did not want to arrive while the poet might still be "working."

When they arrived, they saw a shabby old man in work clothes kneeling down on the flagstone walk. He had a little pan of wet cement on one side of him and was replacing a stone. His hands glistened grayly with wet cement.

"I knew we forgot something. That bloody walk," said the critic. "Well, I'm glad ——— has hired somebody. Of course, he is an orderly person."

But the old man in the work clothes turned out to be ——— himself. He was very friendly, very glad to see them. He looked much older in these awful clothes, but he seemed content.

"You must have had a good day," said the critic, crafts-man to craftsman, as they went inside.

The poet said yes, it had been a lovely day.

"Did you . . ."—the critic hesitated, a little abashed at their new relationship, which permitted such familiarity—"write . . . ah . . . a new poem, perhaps?"

"Oh, I have finished my work," replied the other calmly. "It is all revision now. Getting it set, getting it right." He looked back with humorous eyes at the replaced flagstone drying in its cement, as if to say, We just can't keep our hands off those metaphors. "I've arranged everything with my publisher; yes, it's all dull, laborious revision now. Getting it set the way it will stay."

"I don't suppose . . ." ventured the critic (when he had accepted this reversal as he had had to accept the poet's rather demeaning appearance in these inelegant clothes). "That is . . . might I be of any help?"

"Yes," the other replied at once: to all those dozens and dozens of drafts of the unanswered letters. "You could save me a great deal of work and a great deal of time. Thank you."

Their daughter came out of the kitchen and enveloped them in her arms. How large she was! They had forgotten just how large. Now she was larger than ever. She was pregnant.

In her sixth month, it was December, she awoke in the middle of the night. She had been having a strange, vivid dream but could not remember what it had been about. Outside, the wind was blowing very hard and the waves were lashing . . . lashing. Her husband was in her arms. She sniffed him. The smell was the gentle one he often had in deep sleep. She felt his heartbeat. It seemed lower down. On her stomach. Then she realized that the heart-beat was not coming from outside but inside. It was the child. Suddenly a portion of the dream came back: someone, something, just a voice, had been warning her, rousing her languorous mind to wake up, wake up and articulate some particular thing.

She listened for her husband's heartbeat.

Then she knew what it was. The thing she was supposed to articulate with her waking mind. It was the one way she had neglected to imagine that he could be taken from her.

He could die in her arms.

INDULGENCES

*"Give me the child until he is seven;
after that, you may have him."*
　　　　　—St. Ignatius of Loyola.

Jack Cooley
Andy Harkins
André ———
Rick Yelvington
Sven (Vespa)
"Malibu" Miller
Phil Starnes
"X" (train to Montreal)
Conrad Ten Eyck
Joost ———
Dr. Corchran

She sat at her desk by the window, in the fading light of a gloomy November day, writing their names—or the parts she could remember—down a yellow legal pad. At first she had been chronological; it came easy. Yet the first part of the list had been painful, because parts of her earlier vulnerability still clung to those first names. ("Ah, how impressionable I was!" "The tears I cried over him would fill a small reservoir." "What did I ever see in him?" "How happy I was when he told me, 'You seem so uninvolved,' for that was how I wanted him to see me.")

But then the list grew longer and took on a rather sinister quality. The names were only names. They connected her with nothing but . . . anecdotes. So she abandoned chronology and went by free association. Or, sometimes, like Don Giovanni, took them country by country. Was she a female Don Juan, then? She had been to more countries than he had.

The name of one might recall to her his physical opposite: the tall dark remind her of the small light, etc. Or a name might lead to its counterpart in another language. The eminent judge with a Dutch name recalled the young tour guide in Amsterdam who had given her a disease. Or she recalled a missed period that had dogged her afterward, a conveyance upon which one had ridden into her life—and out again. Yet she had touched and been touched by them all. She had chosen them. They had been her "lovers," whatever that word now stood for. "X": an IBM executive, met on the train; too cautious to tell his name. He got off at Poughkeepsie, kissed his wife and children, then followed her to Montreal in his private plane. But what had she felt for "X"? What had he felt for her? They had been, both of them, extraordinarily pleased about their anonymous little adventure. For, of course, she had given a false name, too. After the grubby Dutchman (she remembered most clearly, for some reason, a child's small brown shoe in his messy apartment—his young wife and child had left him), she had flown to London when the rash appeared. The nice Dr. Corchran, at St. Thomas. So suave. "Not to worry," he said, trying to help her control her humiliation. "All the debs have it this season." His name made the list, too, but he had been careful to protect himself.

She had the feeling Don Juan had enjoyed his "conquests" more.

An hour ago, she and a man had a "lovers' quarrel," here in this very room. "Why do you insist on being so elusive about your past?" he said. "I know you've had other lovers. So have I. I talk about my past freely enough. Why must you withhold yours, unless you're ashamed of it."

"Why should I be ashamed? It's just that it means nothing. My 'past' has nothing to do with me, with the person I am now."

"Everything has a meaning," he said. "Every life has a pattern. If you care about someone, you're naturally interested in their patterns. What is it? Surely you aren't afraid I won't 'respect' you if you tell me you've had ten or fifteen lovers."

The figure is nearer to sixty or seventy, she thought. She said: "There are men who coax a woman into telling these things to titillate themselves. Or to use it against her later."

"When are you going to stop confusing me with 'men'? I'm a person who happens to love you," he said.

She had stood facing him. They were both exactly the same height. She remembered the exotic joy she'd gotten from creating him. The day she knelt down at his feet and ran a tape measure from his ankle to his thigh and then turned to her assistant and said: "Our Banquo here has deceptively long legs. I think we should capitalize on the legs, give them a silvery-metallic quality, let them rustle when he walks, in true ghost-style. When he comes back from the dead, let his face be covered, but the stockings be the same. The stockings will be his trademark."

And then the inevitable jokes together when they became "lovers." Wrapping the ghostly legs around her in bed. "Do I scare you?" he asked. "A little," she said. She was still able to superimpose the freshness of their situation upon the real man, an actor now out of work. But when he wasn't acting, his energies dammed up and he turned nasty. He picked quarrels. He pried into her life. She knew what he was up to; she did it herself. When the drama wore off old scenes, you created "scenes" to entice it back.

So, an hour ago, she had screamed at him, "You won't be satisfied till I make you a *list*! Shall I put little stars by the ones who satisfied me the most? What else would you like to know?"

"I'd like to know," he said, drawing himself up to pronounce the sacred sentence she knew was coming, "whether you have it in you to love."

"I don't know. I need to think about it. Maybe I will make the list."

"I'm tired," he said suddenly. "Let's go and eat something."

"No, I'd rather do my list," she said, with a touch of malice.

"Suit yourself, then. Shall I come back later in the evening?"

"Suit yourself."

"I'll check back about seven. See how you're coming with it. Or do you think," with his own little twist, "you'll need more time?"

"I'll have to see how it goes. I wouldn't want to leave anybody out."

Exit ghost, she thought.

Her apartment was high up in a thick-walled old building overlooking the Hudson. Her bathroom had been made over from a butler's pantry, and she took long baths in generous amounts of scented oil, surrounded by wainscoting. She denied herself nothing. She liked to soap her breasts with French soap and sometimes took a bottle of cream sherry and a wineglass, and lay in water hot as she could stand it, sipping the sweet, nutty taste, and rereading praise of herself.

> The true magic of Adriana Trachey's ("Pelagia") designs lies in their unerring revelation of *the latent*. Her costumes zero in on the meaning behind the word, the private obsession of the public figure. A "Pelagia Design" transcends the conventional aspect of "role" and manages to undress the soul. Thus it goes beyond the usual costumer's achievement of merely gilding the persona.

Framed round the pale yellow walls of her living room (fast growing dark on this sunless November day) hung some of her favorite designs: her Edinburgh Lear in his reversible robe of burlap and fake ermine; her Tyrone Guthrie Antigone in leather; her St. Joan, naked except for the invisible body stocking and the delicately striated wire cuirass and the silver-coated goggles to cover her eyes in battle.

"You can't love," they said. "There's a leak in you somewhere. No man will ever be able to fill you up. You'll go from man to man. Remember, nobody will ever love you as much as I did."

And, the final poisonous thrust, when they had given up on her: "You are going to end up alone."

How long had she taken that word at full value? "I love you." Going back to the beginning of her list, she recalled herself using the word, holding it back until the last possible moment, terrified any prematurity might lessen her value. Then the glorious feverish capitulation. ("I *love* you." "Oh, I love you, too.") The relief when you found it was a two-way thing! Then the period when you indulged yourself in the word at the slightest stimulus: Oh I love you I love you I love you I love you I love you I love you. Once, as a small girl, she had said the word "pig" aloud, over and over again, until it lost all meaning.

Then came the period when they began to say, "You are so cool, so detached. Somehow, I can't imagine you loving anyone." And she quivered like a huntress behind a tree, watching her prey, her arrow of "coolness" taut in her bow.

The list grew longer. At what point had it become a thing in itself, leading its own life, separated from what she thought of as her "real" life, which, more and more, in the last few years, was her work?

"Everything has a meaning," her last lover had said. "Everything has a pattern."

But lives could be festooned, could they not, with paper streamers of extraneous matter.

But if her lovers were extraneous, why did she go on committing herself to new ones? Many of the men on this list would have been inconceivable on a shorter list, the modest list of "ten or fifteen" he'd had in mind for her. But scattered about on a longer one, they looked merely colorful, like interesting accidents or errors. Was that it? Was she trying to cover up her earlier bad judgments and losses with a "pattern" of randomness? Which names, if you erased them from this list, would make a difference to her life, the way she had developed? Would make her a different Adriana Trachey on this particular November afternoon?

Several she had "loved" in the days before she began to put love in quotation marks; several had obsessed her; one or two had turned away, rejecting her.

But only one, perhaps, had made her some of what she was. And his name, of course, was not on the list. Though maybe it should have been.

Her uncle had raised her. He had informed her tastes. Exacting of himself, he was forbearing, even amused, by the shortcomings of others. He had the constant appearance of trying to conceal from them that they were fools. He was a busy tax lawyer and worked late into the evenings in his warm library filled with books of law and the lives of saints. His hobby was hagiography and he had once labored for a whole year over an essay about St. Clement, which he submitted to *Analecta Bollandiana.* It was sent back with a respectful letter. They had found his theories fascinating, but were unable to publish it because of certain apocryphal elements. If he would care to revise . . . But of course he would not. He put the letter and the essay away, with his quiet, bemused smile.

There was always a fire in his library at night. His wife, who seldom smiled, lit it each evening and swept away the ashes the next morning, but at night she went into her bedroom, the coldest room in the house, covered her legs with an Army blanket, and mended or crocheted. The uncle, it was said, had been about to become a priest when he met and fell desperately in love with this beautiful woman. Her aunt a beautiful woman? The pinched face and the cold voice that was constantly saying "No"? And the child could not imagine this stern, forbearing uncle "desperately in love" with anyone.

With her, he was stern, exacting—and tender. "I have work to do, sweetheart," he'd announce every evening. "I hope you do, too." The little girl went with her uncle into the cozy library and spun out her homework, copying everything over a second time "for neatness." After that, she was allowed the freedom of his shelves of saints and martyrs. He had several rare block books, from Germany and Holland. She got crayons and paper and copied the crude look-alike woodcuts of smiling martyrs being beheaded by executioners, also smiling. The neck—or other parts of the body—so recently severed, or hacked to pieces, were so strangely dry and clean. She added great quantities of blood. She gave the pictures to her uncle, who raised his eyebrows and smiled. "You are a realistic little soul, aren't you, Adriana? Better not show these to your aunt. She prefers things sapless."

She progressed from these primitive tortures to the more sophisticated variations. Not all martyrs were surprised by the ax, she found when she learned to read better. They often went in search of it, or inflicted it on themselves. In her uncle's little volumes of de Voragine, she found (and illustrated) the rebellious Christina of Tyre, who threw her father's false gods out the window, and threw pieces of her flesh in his face as fast as he could tear them from her body by hooks; when a pagan judge cut out her tongue, she flung it back and blinded him in the eye. It took arrows to still her heart, so zealous for suffering it was. And she drew St. Lawrence, roasting on his pyre and calling out merrily, "Turn me over! I'm done on this side!" And Elizabeth of Hungary, who liked to put on rags at night, after her husband was safely asleep, and leave the castle and go down into the streets and hug lepers and beggars to her breast. Adriana offered the fruits of her work to her uncle, two bright spots of color on her cheeks from the warm fire. He filed each picture away in an old volume of Blackstone. It was their secret.

For his birthday, she did a "comic strip" of the life of St. Pelagia. How the life of this saint fascinated her! Adriana was drawn to the elegance of this young woman, who was first in everything in the town of Antioch: shapeliness, finery, riches. She was even drawn to her drawbacks; she loved the sound of their names as well: "*Vain and variable of courage, and not chaste in body.*" It was a joy to costume such a heroine; it was a challenge to illustrate the dramatic chronicle of her life and present it to the person she wanted most in the world to please. But when she came to the last "picture" in the life of Pelagia, she could not illustrate it.

"The last scene's not finished," she told him after he had professed himself delighted, *delighted*, with her gift. "You are nine years old, and you still know what most of us have forgotten," he said. "You know you can do anything you set out to do. I want you always to remember that, Adriana. And now come and sit here on my lap and tell me what it was about the last scene which gave you trouble. The one where the nuns are laying out the body. It looks finished to me."

She was a little too big for his lap, but glad he did not seem to think so. Sitting there, she explained, "What . . . the nuns saw. The thing that made them realize St. Pelagia was . . . one of them. I'm not sure . . . I don't know how it would look."

Her uncle got a very funny look on his face. One she had never seen before, and she was an avid student of her uncle's face. She was in the habit of measuring the increase of his esteem for her there.

At last he said, "You are certainly one for the truth,

Adriana. If you're sure you want it, I suppose I could show you what—what I can see—what I have seen—better than you. Do you want that?"

He was trembling slightly, the way he did sometimes when he was trying to control his temper after her aunt had done something stupid.

"Yes, I want it," she said in a small voice, feeling this was the answer he wanted. She was a little scared.

He kept her on his lap while he drew. He held her tightly by the waist with his left hand and drew with his right. He pressed the crayon down so hard once that it broke in two. He used red and pink and purple and brown —and, at last, black. He breathed like a man exhausted, climbing up to the top of a hill. She was aware of tensions and tremors in him that she could not explain. At last he finished climbing the hill. He put down the black crayon with its blasted tip. He was perspiring and distraught. "There you have it, Adriana. The reason it is so hard to draw . . . the reason you could not draw it . . . is because you could not see it as the contradiction it is. It is"—and he smoothed her hair compulsively with his hand, a strange baptismal gesture that seemed to cleanse her of all implications—"it is both the gate of heaven and the mouth of hell."

Outside her window it grew dark. A tugboat, inching along behind a barge, suddenly turned on its lights. This reminded her of another name, and she switched on her desk lamp and wrote:

Christian Rasmussen

Rasmussen was the Captain of a freighter. She (and he) was bound from Hoboken to Oslo. Her aunt had just died. She had not a single relation left in the world. She had finished art school but had not yet found the art that suited her best. Thus she was miserable, bent on marrying one minute and dissipating herself the next. She had tried and

failed to abnegate herself with a man who would have
saved her from the uncertainty of a real vocation. And now
she was running away to "enjoy herself," determined to
fling caution to the winds and become as cheerful and
wanton as her aunt had become in that strange meta-
morphosis of her widowhood. She decided to fall in love
with the Captain—why not? This hulking giant of a man
who had to stoop to enter cabins, who smoked pipes of a
pungent, foreign odor, whose shy English went up and
down in an attractive singsong. At meals he wore summer
whites and gold bars; charmed everyone with his lore of
tonnage and storms. She saw him standing on the bridge,
in khakhi shorts and sandals, calling orders in a man's language, the language of the sea, through a megaphone. She
heard his men refer to him as "the Master." Well, he would
be her master, too, on this summer sea journey. But to her
the Captain was distant and respectful. When anyone told
an off-color story at the table, he frowned nervously her way.
He invited the other passengers, in small groups, for drinks
in his cabin: the port engineer and his wife; a young scholar
from Ann Arbor; two widows traveling together; a loud,
raucous middle-aged California couple . . . but not her.
She dawdled over her lunches on the days he sat at her
table. She slowly consumed salmon, spiced herring, smoked
eel in jellied eggs, salami, liver paste, meatballs, and hot
potato salad. "You like our Norwegian food, I think," he
said, smiling. She told him, looking him boldly in the eye,
"I think I have fallen in love with everything Norwegian."
But still no invitation. Until, sketching in despair on deck
one day, she saw him approach. Could he see? His face
brightened when she told him she was an artist. "You mean
to say, that is your profession? Your only profession?" And
that night she was invited to his cabin for beer and
schnapps. He had an extra-long bunk bed to accommodate
his unusual height—but he could not accommodate her
that night. "I'm sorry," he said, looking down forlornly at
his sad member. "I think what is causing it is for almost

a whole week I believed you to be a nun. Our purser told me you were a nun. You signed yourself that on the passenger list." "I wrote *none* after occupation," she said. "Because I have no job." "Ah," he said, "but in our language, *nonne* means Bride of Christ, do not touch." Then they had laughed. She snuggled her face against those mammoth thighs. "You are master of this ship, steer her anywhere you want," she said. "Oh, oh," he moaned afterward, "how I am sorry that we wasted all our good time!"

His wife came aboard for the Captain's dinner in port. A serious blond woman, a little too heavy, who spoke no English and obviously adored her husband. Adriana sat next to the wife and drank Spanish sherry, two white wines, the first of whose name meant "Reach for Heaven," the Captain told everyone, just grazing her with his humorous eyes. Then she drank two red wines, one bitter and one sweet, and consumed lobster, duck, and a flaming ice cream. And afterward "the Captain's own brandy." The scholar from Ann Arbor, who was doing his thesis on the friendship between George Crabbe and Sir Walter Scott, got drunk and stuck a lobster leg behind his ear. She seduced him that night in her cabin, imagining the Captain and his wife above them. At three in the morning, she woke, utterly disgusted with herself. It seemed she must get him out of her sight at all costs, so she made up a lie about how she was religious and always said early-morning prayers. He was sullen, but he left. The sun was already shining in the Land of the Midnight Sun. "With the Captain I could have been happy," she said to herself, weeping and swallowing gulps of clean air through her open porthole. She knew she was putting on an act for herself, but went on for a while anyway. The ghost of her uncle watched beside her. "You signed me in on this voyage, didn't you, you bastard," she said to him.

She spent three months in Europe before her money ran out. It was the easiest thing in the world, she discovered, to have lovers. By the end of the summer, she had stopped keeping track.

Her uncle had died slowly, sparing himself no pain. But he said, "Adriana, I want you to go on with your school life. I want you to be a normal teen-ager and have fun." As always, she obeyed. She went out with the captain of the football team and wore his monogram sweater, which came below her knees. They danced glued together from cheek to thigh. They planned to be married. She ate supper at his house several evenings a week. How different from her own! His mother made her own pasta and wore swinging hoops in her pierced ears and belted out "Domani" as she washed the dishes. His father drove a bakery truck and smelled like fresh bread, and pounded his fist on the table to make his point. At the table, the family talked openly about Adriana's marriage to Tony; they accepted it as perfectly normal that she had not yet told her aunt and uncle. "All that suffering over there!" said Mrs. Rosa. She gave Adriana little gifts: a pair of shortie pajamas; a little painting of a kitten and a puppy, which her sister in New Jersey had done; a large bottle of Tigress cologne. After the meal, Adriana and Tony would go up to his room, filled with sporting trophies and her own photographs. They would lie on his bed and tempt each other's chastity. "My wife, my wife," Tony would say, and she imagined herself metamorphosed into this utterly new thing, a "wife." Sometimes Tony would stroke her until she truly forgot who she was; she melted away and was nothing.

Then she would walk home, quite herself again, hugging her coat close, hurrying past the lighted windows of neighbors. And she would spend the remainder of the evening reading to her uncle from the lives of the saints, of repentant hearts and startling conversions, and the eager search for a pain large enough to settle the old debt. Her uncle's face grew sterner and holier as it lost flesh. One evening he said, "I want you to take all those pictures we drew out of Blackstone's—it is the volume on the nature of crimes and their punishment—and after your aunt is asleep I want you to burn all of them." At first she had forgotten what pictures he meant.

Soon after, he sent for the local priest, a man he despised. She could not remember her uncle ever setting foot in church. He made her sit holding his thin, cold hand while he confessed to this stranger about how they had "drawn pictures" in the library. The folds of the priest's white lace sleeve brushed her—the moth-touch of death on her hand—as he anointed her uncle with the oils.

She did not marry Tony. Had she ever believed she would? Even when she melted away in raptures, imagining herself a "wife"?

Her aunt became gay and abandoned in her widowhood. Her personality seemed to have done a complete about-face. When Adriana came home on holidays from college, there were clues everywhere that her Aunt had a lover. One night she and her aunt went out to a bar. "Tell me, Adriana, have you had a lover yet?" asked her aunt, her freshly tinted head cocked brightly to one side. "Oh, don't worry, dear, *I'm* not going to censure you. He made me out an ogress, I know that, but I've earned my indulgences. I had a nice lover long ago, Adriana. I feel you should know this. He would never let me tell you. I betrayed him because I fell in love with this man—a handsome young Army officer—and this man and I had sex together. Yes, sex! This man used to lick me all over; he said I tasted like honeysuckle. And then your uncle found out and the young officer killed himself. Yes, it was quite a tragedy. His young wife left him, she was so upset when your uncle told her. She skidded off the road and was killed. A broken neck. And her husband killed himself. He hung himself in the attic of his house. His dear brother had to go and cut his body down. His dear brother, Adriana, was your saintly uncle, and that young couple was your mother and father you were told died together in a car crash. I have not been well lately, and if, God forbid, there is an afterlife, I don't want this on my conscience."

Jacques Ferian

The one who had all those tiny mirrors in his bathroom. Everywhere you looked, from floor to ceiling, a small mirror. "But you can't see all of yourself in any of them," she said to him. "I don't try," he had replied.

She finished the list at a quarter to seven. Under the glow of her green-shaded lamp, she counted them up. If she'd left any out, it was a fault of memory. It couldn't count technically as a sin of omission.

Over a period of fourteen years, it came to five and two-sevenths lovers per year. Not too shocking by contemporary standards. Out of curiosity, she figured up the total of the average housewife. Three times a week, fourteen years, would come to 2,184 times. Beside this figure, Adriana's output seemed quite modest. How much did it really matter whether it was the same man or a different man each time?

The last name on her list was the person who would shortly receive it. She scrawled a short note:

I drink to the general joy o' the whole table,
And to our dear friend Banquo, whom we miss.

Enclosing the list, she left the envelope stuck in the door.

She went to a double-feature film and then checked into the Plaza Hotel. "My water heater's gone on the blink," she told the desk clerk, curious about her lack of luggage. "And I must have my bath." Her face shone out at him, boyishly candid, above the upturned collar of her autumn-haze mink, which matched her eyes.

Early next morning, she walked over to a little restaurant she knew on Broadway, sat down at the counter, and ordered a huge breakfast. She ate eagerly, with gusto.

A man sat down beside her. He ordered coffee and a Danish. He wore a soiled raincoat and had dark circles beneath his eyes. He had crisp reddish hair, rather long. She bent demurely over her hash browns to let him assess her. Then they exchanged a very brief look of mutual understanding. He had the trickster's twinkle in his weary, intelligent eyes. In many ways, this was the moment she always loved best.

"Just visiting in town, are you? What do you think of our fair city? Got anyone to show you around? I'm the barman over at the Tara. Not a bad place. Good jazz. Do you like jazz? You ought to come round. Maybe tonight. Any week-night after ten. So your rich friend's on a cruise, eh? That's not very nice of her, to go away and leave you alone. Where is her place? Not far from here?"

"I was always the black sheep of our family, back in Omaha," she told him as they walked convivially down the street, toward the river. Her hands thrust deep in her pockets, a bemused smile on her upturned face. She liked the tall ones. "My younger sister is married to a nice doctor in London, and my older sister is a nun, but I guess I have always liked adventure."

"What kind of a name is Pelagia?" he asked her as they rode up in the elevator. His fingers traced the shape of her face lightly.

"It's an old family name. The first Pelagia was a beautiful young woman from Antioch—"

"I'd rather know more about the beautiful young woman from Omaha," he said.

"She had lots of lovers." They had reached her floor. She pressed up against him and touched the tip of her tongue to his cold stubbly cheek. "She was known for the splendor of her attire and for her lewdness of mind and body."

"And her love of adventure?"

She unlocked her door. The envelope was gone. She led him into the lovely room, filled with morning sun. The well-kept plants and bright fabrics and the elegantly framed costumes made their impression on him. "My friend is so talented," she said. "She is a successful costume designer."

"I don't go to many plays. But it must be nice to live in a place like this. Does your friend have a bedroom? I want to hear more about this Pelagia."

"Well, one day Pelagia was walking through the city in her latest clothes . . ." She began to remove her own clothes, a fixed dreamy look in her eye. "And followed by many young men and women, all of whom were her lovers. When suddenly she met the Holy Veronus, Bishop of Heliopolis. When he saw her, do you know what he did?"

"Not this."

"No, though perhaps he wanted to. No, he beat his brow and wept. He felt that God had sent him a sign in the sight of this elegantly dressed woman with her lovers. 'Look,' he said, 'how studiously this woman has clothed herself to give pleasure to her earthly lovers, while I—Veronus—have given so little care to pleasing my Heavenly Spouse."

"Weird guy. Oh, what nice sheets your friend has. We mustn't spoil them."

"We won't. If we do, there's a good Chinese laundry right around the corner. Don't you like my story?"

"I like you better. . . ."

"Oh, but," and she laughed and tickled him, "I am my story. Funny, I've just seen it."

"Well, let's hear it, then. But don't make it too long, huh?"

"So Pelagia was impressed by this Holy Veronus. She sent word to him she wanted to be converted and could she see him alone. He sent word back that if she was serious, she would have to bring a chaperone."

"Dumb guy."

"She went to him—with the chaperone—and Veronus baptized her, and she cast herself at his feet and denounced herself as a quagmire of wickedness and so on. Then she went home and settled her affairs with the devil, spent a couple of nights with him for old times' sake, and after that she dressed as a monk and spent the rest of her days as a holy man in a monastery."

"Very interesting story. You're quite a girl, Pelagia."

"No, wait. There's a bit more. She passed herself off so well as a holy man that in time she was made superior at a nearby convent of nuns. But then one of the nuns got pregnant and 'Brother Pelagius' was blamed. The nuns imprisoned him in a cave till he died. When they came to lay out his corpse, they discovered—tell me the honest truth, now: does this look like the gate of heaven to you or the mouth of hell?"

"Neither," he said. "But you talk too damn much, Pelagia. I'm sorry, I can't."

He began to dress again at once. He sat on the edge of the bed, sullenly drawing on a sock. "What kind of a freak are you, anyway? Christ, I'm tired. If I wasn't so tired, I'd kill you. Girls get murdered every day for less than you've done, Pelagia, or whatever the hell your name is."

"I'm sorry—" She, too, began to dress. The whole thing seemed suddenly very shabby.

"Well," he said, putting on his raincoat, "so long, you mixed-up girl. Take my advice and don't try your game on just any stranger. I happened to be harmless, but the next one might not be."

She sat at her desk by the window. The morning was clear and beautiful. The pure winter sun glittered in little spangles on the river. Everything so clean and lovely: no one would guess the filth beneath its spangled sheen. She made rapid, feathery sketches on a watercolor pad, and her mouth actually watered at the thought of the colored washes she would stroke on, later today. As she worked, she began to feel less awful about this morning. The sketches were for a new play, *Eve's Girls*, about a house of prostitution in the year 2000. For a week, she had been unsuccessful in coming up with anything. Having exhausted the shock of nudity on St. Joan of Arc, what was left in her repertoire for prostitutes? But, lying briefly beside the strange red-haired man, she had begun to see a design.

The phone rang. Banquo. "I've got to see you," he said. "Darling, this incredible list. You're mistaken if you think I wanted this . . . all these names and numbers. Darling, let's stop hurting each other. Let me come and see you now. . . ."

"I can't," she said. "I'm working. And also, there's someone here. He's asleep."

A long silence.

"You bloody whore," he said, and hung up.

She unplugged the telephone and went back to her desk. She sketched lawn sleeves, caftans, talmas; experimented with high-necked vestal gowns; drew feminine versions of cassocks, surplices, albes, and soutanes. Was that what came next, then: the costume of chastity? It seemed so, the way the rhythms of her pencil swung back, creating a counter current, balancing with paradox this new need in her soul.

From outside her window came three thrilling blasts. She looked down at the sparkling river and saw—like her own portent—a large ship putting out to sea, flags flying, the cheeky tugs nudging the great white stern. Adriana felt the fervor and excitement of the ship's crew, the throb of mission in the great engines. She knew the captain was standing on the bridge, calling out orders to shake off the casual entanglements and the market dust of shore, to trim ballast down to a scary minimum, to train eyes, heart, hands on the lonely prospect.

The economy of the human soul amazed her. Why, her own childish hand had pounced upon and blocked out, in early drawings, the pattern she would follow, and she had the rest of her lifetime to make the individual alterations and apply the personal shades of meaning. "You can do anything you set out to do," her uncle had said. Regardless of whatever else he showed her, he had also taught her that.

NOTES FOR A STORY

Working Title: CHILDHOOD FRIENDS

A woman, CATHERINE, visiting her childhood friend, NORA. The two have been friends since second grade. Now both are in their mid-thirties. Time of the visit: Thanksgiving, 1973. Place: Woodstock, N.Y. CATHERINE, at this time, is going through a lonely and humiliating phase of her life. NORA, on the other hand, is having her first uneasy bout with security and success.

1 / TWO WOMEN

The story might open with Nora walking through the house in Woodstock, going over their friendship, her own life, life in general, etc., while she waits for Catherine's arrival. Catherine telephoned last night to say she had gotten as far as New York and was spending the night with some Yoga people. These past few years, Catherine seems to be running more and more with people on the fringe. Nora, walking through the house—the first real house she has ever lived in—is now remembering how, from early girlhood, both she and Catherine wanted to be writers. They discussed their destiny seriously, as though nothing could possibly interfere. Nora would go over to Catherine's big red house with the four white columns, and the two girls would lie around in Catherine's splendid bedroom with the door closed, writing stories, while downstairs Catherine's mother wept over some burnt cookies (she was going through the change early) and Catherine's father, a successful surgeon, listened to operas when he was home. Nora would say, "Let's start with the sad whistle of the train today," and both girls would check the clock and write furiously for ten minutes. Nora's heart was in her throat. What if she didn't finish in time? "Time," calls Catherine. Then Nora would read aloud what she had written, and Catherine would read what she had written. From downstairs came the sounds of *Aïda* or *Boris Godunov,* until Nora knew long passages by heart. Nora's stories usually featured a solitary person, a Romantic Outcast. He wandered outside in cold weather, gazing through the lighted windows of big houses, or stood near the tracks and watched the train hurtle by with its low sad whistle. Catherine's stories were social comedies. The train whistle, however sad, was outside the train, while inside, in dining cars or Pullman, the amusing dynamics between human beings went on. She had an ear for dialogue and a knack for getting inside people of all ages.

When Catherine came over to Nora's apartment, Nora always tried to make the room she shared with her mother look as though it were hers alone. Scattered animals around, her books, etc. Hung up things with Scotch tape on the walls. There: an ordinary girl's room. Nora made cookies or brownies. Her mother worked all day. At Nora's, they once took the working title "The Magic Lipstick." They agreed their stories should both be about a girl who goes to a dance and has a terrible time until she goes to cry in the Ladies Room, where she meets a beautiful older woman, who says, "Here, try some of my lipstick," and the girl goes back to the dance and is the center of attention. In Nora's story, told from the viewpoint of the young girl, the girl's unhappiness seems to be a permanent state of mind. Therefore the lipstick was truly magic. Anything less than the supernatural would have failed to undo such misery. Catherine told her story from the older woman's point of view. She did lend the girl her lipstick, and they talked. It turns out the reason the girl is unhappy is that she's with a beastly date. The older woman, a chaperone, introduces the girl to her own son, a charming young man, who insists on dancing with her the rest of the evening.

"Catherine has always been so mature," says Catherine's mother in a telephone conversation to Nora's mother. The two women speak dutifully of their daughters, unable to discuss anything else. They move in such different worlds. "No, Catherine was born a young woman," her mother goes on, speaking in a slightly nasal voice, which her daughter inherits. "It's my guess she will marry very young." "How nice," replies Nora's mother, awkward in these conversations because she can never forget that this woman lives in Forest Park and *volunteers* her services to the Community Chest, whereas she herself is the only paid employee. She types the letters, balances the books, runs errands, and makes tea and coffee for these rich women who like to play at working, rushing in and out to show off their new clothes to one another. "Nora is still very much a child," she allows herself to admit ruefully.

Nora, walking around the rooms of the big house in Woodstock, waiting for her friend Catherine to arrive on this sunny Thanksgiving Day, indulges herself in a moment of amazed self-congratulation. "And yet," she says aloud to the warm yellow walls of the room, "and yet, I MADE IT AND SHE DIDN'T."

At about this point, Catherine should drive up in the Volkswagen with her young man. He is extremely handsome but rather ethereal. Pale red hair, translucent skin, not an ounce of fat. Clear green spiritual eyes. He sits down in the best chair and graciously accepts coffee. He looks round the sun-filled room and says in a gentle drawl, "There are special vibrations in this house." He is going on to Oneonta, to a Yoga residence there, to fast and meditate over the Thanksgiving weekend. He will drive Catherine's car. Then on Sunday, he will pick Catherine up and they'll drive south again. He is one of Catherine's students at a small Quaker college in Pennsylvania. As soon as he leaves, Catherine bursts into sobs. "I'm cracking up," she says. "I'm being torn apart by the disorganized Byrons in my life and the Astral people. The Byrons sleep with me and run; the Astrals, when they're not flying around in space every night, lecture me on how I should abandon my fleshly lusts."

Nora sits facing her weeping friend and thinks how, for years, she has had the following recurrent nightmare. In this nightmare, Nora is leafing through a *Mademoiselle* magazine, and her heart stops. There is a story by Catherine. That is the whole dream. Nora began having this dream her last year in college, when Catherine was already married and living in Gibraltar with her naval-officer husband, when writing was probably the last thing on her mind. Nora continued to have the dream after she herself had published many stories in national magazines, and several novels. In reality Catherine has published nothing. She is a professor now and sometimes writes songs, which she sings to her students. She doesn't even want to be a writer anymore. In the dream, Nora has published nothing. The reason it is a nightmare is because of the way she feels while having it: a sick, heavy certainty that she will never be acknowledged. She still has the nightmare from time to time. Often, when she is stuck in a novel or a story, she works the following magic on herself. She pretends that somewhere in the country a person like Catherine is sitting in a room racing her to finish the same story, or that person's version of it. This usually gets her going again. If it doesn't, she "steals" the other person's story: she pretends she is her competitor and writes it from the competitor's point of view.

Have the two women talk a while longer. Have Catherine relate, *in detail*, some of her cataclysmic experiences with lovers. (Catherine has a weakness for younger men; Nora likes the older ones.) Catherine frequently refers to her "constant horniness." Nora disapproves of the term and is a little put off by the thought of this floating lust, or whatever it is. Over the years, Catherine has told some fascinating tales about her adventures. For instance, the time when she was divorced from her Navy husband and getting her Ph.D. at Columbia and living in the Village. Her father, concerned for her welfare, used to send his friends regularly to check on her whenever they were in town. He sent a colleague, a distinguished obstetrician, to look in on her. The obstetrician took her to dinner; then they went back to the Village and she gave him some pot and they went to bed. As a result of the evening, she had one of the first legal abortions in the state of New York. Her father thought he was paying for a set of the Oxford English Dictionary. And the time when an old lover dropped by and they went to bed for old times' sake, and then he asked if he and his new love could use Catherine's apartment when she was away for a weekend. So Catherine went to great trouble cleaning her apartment, stocking it with good food and drink—flowers, too—and while she was putting clean sheets on the bed for them, she *got turned on*. Also the time when she was sleeping with one of her students, a staunch young Quaker, who always got out of bed afterward and asked God to forgive him.

Nora has written several stories based on Catherine's experiences, trying to get inside Catherine and see how such a life would feel. Or she takes Catherine's stories and uses them as anecdotes, scattered about in her novels as conversations overheard in restaurants, etc.

After Catherine has told Nora her latest problems about the young men who are driving her mad, Nora tells Catherine of an experience she had recently. She has been dying to tell it ever since she knew Catherine was coming. What happened was this: alone in this house, she has discovered a rather dangerous little trick. If she catches herself at a certain point just before she falls asleep, she can get out of her body and wander around the house and meet emanations of herself in the various rooms. These emanations are sometimes the unlikeliest ones imaginable and often she scares herself. For instance, last week she made herself "float" down to the basement, where sat a dikey woman in a WAC uniform who signed her up for a husband. Nora turned slowly to face this husband, having no idea what she would have to face. It was a tiny, shrunken child, neither girl nor boy. "Oh, God!" cries Catherine. "Another Astral friend." She weeps again. Then she becomes very helpful and offers theories about arrested sexuality, possible doubts about one's femininity, fear of loving a man, etc. It is so good to have Catherine here.

"She has known me longer and more intimately than any other person, outside of my family," Nora told her lover, the man with whom she lives, just before he drove away this morning. He said he was sorry he wouldn't be there when Catherine came, but he'd look forward to meeting her tomorrow. Nora's lover, a respected playwright, left his wife and daughter for her. But there are a few tendrils clinging to him from that old life, and he has to go to Boston to have Thanksgiving dinner with them. His daughter, home from college, refuses to visit him in Woodstock. Nora was a little hurt that he chose to desert her for a family occasion, but is also relieved to have Catherine all to herself for a day. "You'll love Catherine," she told her lover (who, to her continued disbelief, seems to have eyes for no one but herself). "In many ways, Catherine and I are the same. We're two sides of a coin. I could have been Catherine, if things had been different; Catherine could have been me, if things had been different."

That night, sleeping badly in the guest room of his wife's house, Nora's lover dreams he is making love to both Nora and Catherine. "Both women were really aspects of you," he is later to tell Nora, after the calamity. To excuse himself? To feel less guilty? "In a way," he will tell Nora, "you set the whole thing up."

Physical description of Nora.

Physical description of Catherine.

After lunch the two women put on walking shoes and go for a hike. As they cut through the fields, Nora is thinking about the way her friend has become a compulsive eater. At lunch: the way she couldn't stop helping herself to more salad, the way she kept picking bits of leftover food from Nora's plate, just reaching across the table, perfectly unaware of herself, and breaking off pieces of cold broccoli and pushing them hurriedly into her mouth. The way she kept sloshing wine into her glass. Compulsive drinking, too. Could it be that she was like that about sex, as well? Is she really about to have a breakdown?

"I am beginning to feel like my old self again," says Catherine. They linger beside the shell of an old stone cottage in the middle of the field. The roof has fallen in, but the stone walls are still firm. Already Catherine has collected (compulsively?) an armload of things: strange dead grasses, dried pods with some cottony stuff bursting out, stiff cornstalks, a few pine cones. Now she exclaims over some loose rocks near the abandoned cottage. She tells Nora that these rocks are probably "special," and they'd better take some home. "I already have plenty of rocks," replies Nora. "Ah," cries her friend mysteriously, "but maybe you need some of these!"

Could it be that Catherine really is cracking up?

On the way back, Nora feels suddenly expansive. The world converges around her in a moment of rightness. She has this house. She has this man. She has this interesting old friend. She has her work. God! It happened, after all. She is no longer lurking on the outskirts watching the trains hurtle by; she is on the train, going somewhere definite, warm and safe and moving. She puts her arm around Catherine, rather amazed at how solid and broad her shoulders are, and says, "I'm so glad you came. We have to stick together. It's people like us who have to make it safe for others like us: *people who go too far.*' Catherine hugs her. Nora has the sense of having said just the right thing. Catherine is at this moment seeing herself as "a person who goes too far." She tells Nora this. She says, "What I'm trying to do, ideally, is preserve the fine edge of my madness without destroying myself." For some reason, Nora suddenly feels jealous. Then Catherine says, "I have a confession to make. When I walked into that house this morning and saw that old fireplace, and the books, and the two chairs facing each other—everywhere you looked, things set up for two—I was horribly jealous. But now I don't feel jealous. I feel truly happy. Now I feel I can ask you about your man and not be jealous. What is he like? I can't wait to meet him. How are the two of you together?"

Brief monologue by Nora re "her man." Jake? Edwin? Sebastian? Benjamin? Name should somehow suggest his temperament: volatile but generous; arrogant, sometimes even insulting to friends and equals; indulgent and careful with strangers and inferiors; a few irrationalities left in his character, but on the whole a completed adult; edgy temper; way of fathering things: the way he is always the first to discover the plants need watering; the way he always greets the cat in the morning, benevolently inquiring if he had a good night. As Nora describes ———, the reader should get a sense of the unsaid as well. Like many unsure people, Nora is slightly uneasy about her relationship with ———. Is there something slightly wrong with him to have chosen her, to have upset his life to such a heroic degree simply to live with her? She tells Catherine about the fights they have, exaggerating a little. "You can imagine it. A playwright and a writer. He admits it, too: how a second self stands beside him, directing: 'Now what this scene needs here is an Accusation . . . or a Martyrish Aside.' And I know I have to say the next evil thing that's shaping itself in my head, no matter what happens. I'm already possessed by the words, you see."

"He sounds wonderful," says Catherine. "Your Rudy is clearly one of us."

Get them through rest of day. Quick short scenes, maybe only a paragraph each. Catherine makes quite a pretty arrangement with her dried things for Nora's mantle-piece. She suggests they smoke some dope she brought with her. Nora declines, saying, as always on such occasions, that she doesn't want to "mess up her mind." The rapport between the two cools. Both are embarrassed by it. Catherine sits stroking the cat, who has climbed into her lap. "This is a very special cat," she says in that mystical knowing way her Yoga friend proclaimed the vibrations in this house to be special. Catherine tells how the Yoga boy-friend is trying to persuade her to give up sex. Last night in New York, they all sat cross-legged around a chair and prayed to a pair of bedroom slippers belonging to the Maharishi, she tells Nora. Then the two women have a really good discussion, which Nora can't wait to get down in her journal for fear of forgetting the vital points. Nora is weary. This always happens when she is around anyone, except Rudy, for very long. She feels the urge getting stronger and stronger in herself to get off alone and assess the experience she has just had, so that she can contain it, digest it. Otherwise she will either lose it or be over-whelmed by it. "Would you mind if I went up to my room and took a short nap?" she asks Catherine, who says no. Catherine takes the proofs of Nora's latest novel to the guest room across the hall.

Nora scribbles rapid-fire in her journal.

(. . . But the main thing we agreed on was that it's most important to have new experiences, to let in-tuition dictate rather than pattern. Patterns = hab-its. She really needed to come here. Is being torn in half by the disorganized "Byronic" impulses and the "Astral" desire for some organizing principle that would redeem her. She feels no style has yet superseded the Romantic, and yet we're dying for something more. The next "movement" may be "an inner movement within each person." Says the last guys to have said anything pertinent to where we are were Blake, Lawrence, Freud, and Jung. I asked why hadn't anyone gone further. She laughed weirdly. "Because they're scared, maybe," she said. She said it *is clear* to her that within the next ten years everything will change: "Our private passions, our way of viewing our intellectual activities, our concept of 'men and women,' everything." "Britain is already gone," she said. "Now our country is going. Soon we'll be controlled by nations whose histories we don't even understand." I said, "So are you running out to read the histories of these nations?" She said in that irritating new "mystical-mysterious" voice of hers: "No. I think things are going to be resolved less on a practical level than on an intuitive one.")

From the guest room come regular eruptions from Catherine as she reads Nora's proofs. She snorts. She chuckles. She murmurs, "Hmm?"

Nora wriggles nervously beneath her silk comforter. She can't stop herself from calling out, "What?" "What are you laughing at?" "What did you just read?"

Catherine calls back, "Did that really happen that way?" Or, "I never realized you felt so bad about that." Or, "Devil! You stole my story about how Gregg recorded hate-messages to me on my tape recorder."

"Are you angry?" calls Nora timidly. Then Catherine begins giggling so frequently that she can't stand it. She goes to her friend. Who is lying under the patchwork quilt, puffing happily on a handmade cigarette. Nora sniffs the air. "Ah, that's why my book seems so amusing," she says.

Supper. Catherine's compulsive eating. Two bottles of wine. Catherine has brought her guitar and sits cross-legged on the floor and sings a new song she's written about how she wants to be buried beneath an old apple tree, her legs spread slightly apart, to receive her last lover, the earth. Her body sways. Nora suddenly hears the exact nasal intonation of Catherine's mother. She remembers all those cookies. The *Aïda*. The *Boris Godunov*. All of it.

Cut to the next morning, Friday. Phone rings. Nora afraid it's *him*, saying his wife has to have an emergency operation, his daughter has killed herself and he can't come back.

It's Catherine's young man in Oneonta. Her VW broke down completely. A local dealer says either put a new $600 engine in or might as well junk it. Dealer offers a flat $200 for the "junk." Catherine begins weeping, but speaks kindly to the young man, says it's not his fault, etc., she's sorry his retreat is being ruined, etc. They agree to talk later, when Catherine can think properly.

Nora says, "Why don't you call your father and ask him what to do?"

"Are you crazy?" asks Catherine. She weeps some more, then tells Nora how she and that VW went all the way to California and back. She tells about a wild young man in Santa Barbara; a woman hitchhiker in a red cape; a brass bed in a haunted house in a thunderstorm.

The two women wash their hair. Nora borrows Catherine's herbal shampoo. It makes her feel good to use other people's things. As if some of their aura rubs off on her.

II / THE TWO WOMEN AND THE MAN

Rudy arrives. He's pale and emotional. Had to stop en route for a drink. Saw a horrible thing. Hunters had a huge deer strapped on the back of a Land-Rover. Right in front of him. The dead buck worked itself out of the ropes and splattered to the highway. Rudy swerved, narrowly avoided overturning his car. The animal was a mess.

Physical description of Rudy.

Rudy and Catherine talk. Nora is so nervous she can't

listen properly. Will Rudy like her friend? Will Catherine like Rudy?

Rudy steals up behind Nora in the kitchen and kisses her neck. "It seems I've been gone weeks!" he says. Tells her, "Your friend is very nice. But I thought you said you two were alike. Not at all. Does she have Scandinavian background?" Nora is making veal Marsala, asparagus with mock Hollandaise, and a salad. The three of them dine by candlelight. Much wine consumed. Catherine has brought several bottles of Pouilly-Fuissé and apologizes for not being a real connoisseur of wines. "But this is excellent," Rudy says, toasting their guest. It is clear that Catherine finds Rudy attractive.

After dinner everything speeds up, gets blurry. More wine. Catherine shyly brings out an old-fashioned lozenge box with violets on it. She produces a small ceramic pipe, into which she carefully packs some dried herblike stuff from the lozenge box. "You're probably like Nora," she says to Rudy, "and don't want to mess up your mind. But it relaxes me." She lights the pipe and sucks deeply. "I've never tried it," says Rudy pensively, watching Catherine close her eyes and exhale, a trancelike sheen on her face. "But then, until I met Nora, I went around avoiding new experiences." Catherine smiles understandingly, keeping her eyes closed.

Both Rudy and Nora try the pipe. He shrugs. "I don't feel anything."

"Me neither," says Nora.

She and Catherine are dancing together. They sing songs from Girl Scout camp. "Just plant a little watermelon on my grave, let the juice trickle through . . ." "White coral bells upon a slender stalk . . ." "My name is Jan Jansen, I come from Wisconsin . . ."

Rudy says, "Do you have Scandinavian blood?" "No, Dutch," says Catherine.

They all get down on the floor and do Catherine's Yoga exercises. They twist their spines, put their legs behind their heads, squat with their heads between their elbows. "I feel the blood in my eyes," says Rudy. "Perhaps that's enough for now."

Rudy has an arm around both women. "One dark and one fair," he says, delightedly looking from one to the other.

The lights are off. They are lying on a fur blanket in front of the blazing fire. Nora is writhing about in someone's embrace. Someone kisses her very softly on the mouth. Rudy is talking to Catherine in a teasing voice. Catherine laughs. Her breasts are somehow bare. She is taking down her tights when Rudy explains in a cordial voice that it's only proper that he be with Nora first. Catherine says, "Of course." Nora closes her eyes. Someone is expertly removing her jeans, then her panties. Now they are rubbing her. She puts her hands over her eyes and says, "No, you two go first. I don't mind, I don't mind. . . ."

Rudy and Nora in their bedroom. "It's all right, it's all right," he is saying. "Nothing happened. Thank God. What brought me to my senses was seeing you lying there, those poor little bare legs, with your fingers over your eyes, and that sad little voice saying, 'I don't mind, I don't mind, I don't mind. . . .'"

Nora thinks he ought to go down and comfort Catherine. "Her life lately has been one long stream of rejections." So Rudy goes down. He comes back and says, "She's fine. We sat and talked. I rubbed her back. She was fully dressed. She said she wants to stay down with the fire for a while and read the proofs of your book."

Later, Rudy was to say: "It was a bit much. First two women wanted me, then neither of them would have me. It was she who took off your jeans and your panties, you know."

III / THE COUPLE AND THE WOMAN

First thing next morning, Saturday, Nora makes herself go to Catherine and say, "I'm sorry about last night." She expects Catherine to be cool, stand-offish, but Catherine puts her arm around Nora and says warmly, "Don't worry! You two just weren't ready yet." Once Nora and Catherine were captains of rival teams at the grammar school. They agreed to split their prize, whichever team won. Nora's did. The prize was a white yo-yo with a purple stone in it. Nora can still see the young Catherine, blond hair streaming from the open window of her father's Lincoln, as she calls cheerfully to Nora, who is walking home alone with her prize, "It's okay! Everyone knows you can't split a yo-yo!" The sleek black car gathers speed and disappears through the gates of the school.

What to do about Catherine's VW? Should Rudy drive them to Oneonta so Catherine can at least say goodbye to her car? He looks tired this morning, but seems willing. Catherine is the one who must be looked after today, he and Nora have agreed. They look up Oneonta on the map. Too far for a sentimental journey. Should she take the $200 or put in a new engine? Nora says, "Please, *please* call your father." Catherine: "Look, I haven't been struggling free of all that for years to call him now." But Nora wears her down. While Catherine speaks long distance to her father, Nora sits beaming, her eyes bright. She can just picture him—older now, of course—the everlasting pipe clenched in the prominent jaw, so pleased that his daughter still consults him. "What are you so happy about?" Rudy asks, smiling with puzzlement.

Catherine telephones young man in Oneonta. Says junk the car. She'll take bus and meet him in New York tomorrow and they'll rent car to drive back to school. "My father's giving me one of his," Nora hears her say with a sigh. "He always hated my having VWs and was rather pleased about the whole thing."

Catherine's last evening. Whispered consultation between Nora and Rudy. *No smoking tonight.* Calm, civilized evening. Good food, modest amount of wine, send her away with good memories. Rudy builds a nice fire. Cath-

erine, wearing long quilted skirt, lies on the floor. She is
trying to finish Nora's new book. Nora is particularly anxious for her opinion and gets annoyed when Rudy keeps
interrupting her with questions. "What do you think of
Nora's book?" he asks. "It must be interesting for you, set
in the place where you both grew up." Catherine says, "I
think she'll get attention for this book. Yes, it is fun for
me to see how these things looked from her side."

"They looked different from your side?" Nora asks,
pouring herself more wine.

The two friends get into an involved discussion of their
youth, the town, the way Catherine saw things, the way
Catherine thought Nora saw things, etc. What must come
out here is Nora's realization that her *best and oldest
friend* never knew that she, Nora, suffered. The more
Catherine tells her how "I always thought you were a con-
genitally private person," the more loudly Nora protests,
"No, no . . . that was a front." They forget the time. They
forget where they are. Their voices become high, like
little girls. It is as though they are back in Catherine's
bedroom, revealing their true selves at last. Have Nora
become conscious of how much she withheld in those days.
Even in those stories they wrote, how she had been careful to conceal, behind the persona of that sexless Solitary
who stood aloofly apart, her envy and her longing to have
Catherine's easier way of being in the world, calling sport-
ingly from her father's car, "Can't split a yo-yo!" How
lightly she had ridden away from her losses! Had winning
meant little to her as well? Is this why she was able to
lend her apartment to other lovers, and let young men drive
away her cars and lose them, and pass it off with cheerful
gallantry when, in front of a fire, a potential lover suddenly
desists for the sake of someone else? Is this why she found
it unnecessary to become a writer: she just didn't have
that many scores to settle? "I had no idea you felt that
way," Catherine keeps repeating. Nora, feeling that she
can at last be herself, that her accomplishment allows her,

says: "If you knew how I wanted to make my début with you!" "How odd!" cries Catherine. "I remember how caustic you were about it. The day we met downtown and you wouldn't come with me to fit my dress. I cried the rest of that day. I considered not going through with it. You convinced me the whole thing was so shallow." More such revelations on both sides.

Suddenly they smell burnt hamburger. Nora rushes to the kitchen. "But what are you doing?" she says to Rudy, who stands rather petulantly over the frying pan, the flame on too high. Her good copper-bottom pan, too. "We're having steak for supper!" she cries. He says he can't wait all night to eat, etc.; it's already ten o'clock. Nora realizes he resents them for leaving him out for so long. He takes his burnt hamburger to the table and begins eating it. She flies into a rage and tells him he has ruined Catherine's last night. The two begin shouting at each other. Catherine rushes in and tries to make peace. She takes the steaks out and begins to season them. "Come on, you two!" Nora goes upstairs in a fury, calling back she wants no dinner. She bolts herself into the bedroom and for some reason (the wine, perhaps?) goes into the closet and sits on the floor. She hears them come after her. "Nora, please," Catherine calls, rather amused, through the door, "let's all make up and have dinner." "I'm not mad anymore," calls Rudy. Nora hugs her knees in the closet. Hears them consult in lowered voices. "Better let it be," says Rudy. "No, it's childish," says Catherine. "Nora?" she calls, "Nora, listen: if you don't come out right now, Rudy and I are going to screw right in front of this door." Rudy says, "No, no, that's not the tactic to take, Catherine. You go on down." Then he calls through the door, "Nora? We all drank too much. Please. Come down and let's have our steak and go to bed. I'm very tired."

The three at dining-room table. Somehow, dinner has gotten made by someone. They are having an animated discussion about risk-taking vs. security. Catherine, very drunk, is declaiming about the necessity of taking chances in order to "stay alive." She is treating her hosts rather like small children who have quarreled and been foolish and now must submit to a lecture on the responsibilities of life. She tells them that artists especially must court the unseemly, look violence and change in the face, or their art will become hermetic and dead. "I abhor violence," says Nora suddenly. "I don't want it in my life or in my art. The security I've had here in this house has allowed my work to blossom." Rudy is moved. Puts his hand over Nora's. "There is too much worship of violence for its own sake," he says gently to Catherine. "As for change, that, too, can become overvalued. We are too much a nation of fads as it is." Nora is thinking of his fury over a certain sentence in the *Times* about his last play. Catherine reaches across the table, picks green beans first from Rudy's plate, then from Nora's. She seems unaware she is doing this. She hums under her breath. When she has picked everything off their plates, she shakes salt into her hand and eats it from her fingers. Rudy pours the last of the wine from that bottle. His face looks drained. He excuses himself and says he'll turn in early, if the women will forgive him.

Catherine and Nora washing and drying the dishes. Catherine, very agitated, pursues the subject of violence and change and risk. Nora gives short, noncommittal answers, wanting to go to bed herself. Catherine says, "The trouble with you, Nora, is that you are not a person who goes too far, like you said on the walk. You are only a voyeur of people who go too far. You like to hear about my risks, but you curl up like a hothouse lily if anyone asks you to share them."

"If you mean about last night," says Nora, "I just don't go in for group sex." She rewipes a wineglass that Catherine has dried carelessly. "What's wrong with *sharing*?" asks Catherine. "He loves you. There's enough love there. It wouldn't have depleted his store of love for you. He loved the idea of our friendship, too. And there is love between you and me, whether you'll admit it or not. Last night could have been beautiful if you had let it. It wouldn't have diminished you *or* your precious art."

"It would have been demeaning," Nora replies curtly.

"Demean?" Catherine says in a strange, hushed voice. "Demean? What is demean?" She shakes her head from side to side. Her eyes look glazed, like a zombie's. "Demean is just a word in the dictionary," Catherine says. "I'm more important than the damn dictionary."

Here it must be made clear that Nora sees that her friend has gone out of control and that the best thing to do would be agree with her. ("Of *course* you are more important than the dictionary, Catherine.") But, at the same time, she is looking at this raving, glassy-eyed woman, her chin thrust aggressively into Nora's face. Just like a prize-fighter, Nora is thinking, a strident aggressive person. How could I ever have thought her beautiful? At the same time, certain irresistible words are forming themselves into a sentence in her head. Exactly as they do in her fights with Rudy, the fights she was telling Catherine about yesterday. The words are "The dictionary is all we have," and she, of course, must say them. With a wicked calm.

A few seconds later, she has fled outside, into the freezing night. She is crouched behind a pile of rocks, her cat shivering beside her, as they listen to the smashing of glassware, the splintering of wood, dishes being thrown against the walls. And a woman's voice shrieking, over and over: "The *dic*tionary! The *dic*-tionary! Oh, my God, the goddamned dictionary! I'll tear this fucking house apart, you fucking coward bitch!" Then hurried footsteps on the stairs. The deep, angry voice of a man: "Stop that. Stop that. Come to your senses or I'll have to hit you."

"Hit me! KILL me!" comes the banshee shriek.

Give atmosphere of utter silence. No sounds from the house. The close, clear stars, winking impersonally from the cold sky. The calm impersonality of the Solitary, alone in the night with a black cat, gazing toward the lighted windows of a big house . . .

Later he is to say: "The strength of that girl was phenomenal. I had to use the full force of my body to hold her down. That is when my dressing gown came open. That is when I saw there was nothing . . . nothing. She was lying under me with her skirt around her waist, and I hadn't the least urge . . . not the least." He repeats this afterward many times. It seems important to him. Once he adds: "I was relieved to find that out about myself. I have often been afraid . . . certain people are aroused by sadistic opportunities . . . but, no, I hadn't the least urge. At that moment she wasn't even a woman to me. And I think she knew it, and because of this I was able to calm her. We would have talked awhile and all gone to sleep, if you hadn't come in and started everything over."

When Nora returns to the house, she is obsessed with only one thing: tidying up the mess. The cat refuses to come in with her. Nora single-mindedly edits out the sound of their voices coming from the living room. She sweeps broken glass into one pile . . . broken dishes into another. She must put her house in order. That is the only task in the world she cares about.

Rudy calls from the living room, rather apologetically: "Er, Nora, could you come in here for a moment? Catherine would like it if we all talked for a few moments. Please. You can sweep later." Nora goes to the living room, still carrying her broom. The two of them are sitting cross-legged on the floor, near to the fire, which has died. Catherine is explaining, in the singsongy-preachy tone she used on them at dinner, that all she wants from life is for people to share. She is willing to share everything: if the rest of the world was the same, there would be no war, no poverty, no loneliness. Her body is swaying. She has another glass of wine now, and as she sways with it some of it slops over the edge of the glass and onto the carpet, just missing Nora's proofs. "Yes, yes," Rudy is saying, humoring her like a child or a dangerous inmate. "Nora," he says, "do come and sit here with Catherine and me. That's all she wants. For us all to be friends. Then we can go to bed."

Nora stands looking down at them. She leans on her broom.

"Please, come sit with us in a circle," says Catherine. This time, her wine makes a tiny splatter at the edge of Nora's proofs. Nora swoops down and rescues them. Holding them tightly in one arm, balancing on her broom, she feels the fatal fully formed sentence rising in her throat. "I refuse to sit down on the floor, in a *circle*, with a god-damn middle-aged hippie who has wrecked my home," she says.

How are fights, real physical fights, described in fiction? Movies much better medium to get action across, the slow angelic flight of a body through the air, the clean crack of bone against bone. In the less sophisticated plays, Rudy says, a wooden clapper is still used to stimulate a fist hitting a jaw. Are fights to the finish different in quality when they are between women instead of men?

"THE SLOW ANGELIC FLIGHT OF A BODY THROUGH THE AIR." Nora is mesmerized by these words. For months after, she has only to think them softly and the entire scene comes back. How, effortlessly, as in a dream, her own slender arm reached out and gracefully wound Catherine's long light hair in a secure coil round her own wrist. The simple snapping action of that wrist, with a strength in the arm that must have lain unused for years, like so many of her other hidden powers, which were now, in this atmosphere of security, revealing themselves for the first time. How had she done it? The miracle of Catherine, not a slender woman, floating light as a thistle in that momentary arc of night air. For, somehow, they were all outside. Rudy, in his green silk dressing gown and the old pair of bedroom slippers. He calls something to them urgently, but neither

can hear him. Catherine in the long quilted skirt and torn blouse . . . the skirt swirled gracefully
<blockquote>billowed elegantly?
wafted gently?</blockquote>
in its own trajectory as Catherine's head floated down, toward the rock.

("I already have plenty of rocks," replies Nora. "Ah, but maybe you need some of these!" cries her friend mysteriously.)

Two women. Two women and a man. A couple and a woman. Three civilized people. An intellectual and two artists. A professor of English at a small Quaker college. A respected playwright who, according to a *Times* critic, "still labors, albeit brilliantly at times, under the medieval assumption that morality can be legislated by the dramatist." A not unknown novelist who writes mostly about the Person of Sensitivity who, by his sensibilities and stubborn sense of self, manages to transcend the miseries and deprivations of childhood.

IV / THE WOMEN

Nora's journal.

Tues., Nov. 27—On Sunday morning, at app. 2:30 A.M., the troopers and the ambulance left. Rudy left yesterday for New Haven. Long Wharf may do *Thieves' Honor* next spring. On Sunday we stayed in bed all day, with the door locked and the shades down, trying to assimilate It in order that It might not swallow us. We made tea for each other. I got up after dark and vacuumed up the rest of the glass. We put the broken chair in the garage. We had already flushed the pot down the toilet. We kept finding dried blood everywhere, a drop even on the lampshade. (?) Rudy dreamed we were in a Land-Rover and her carcass was tied to the back—just like that deer's—and it kept falling off, onto the road. I nursed my arm, fearing gangrene. How long will her teeth marks be on my left arm? A perfect bite. She had the best orthodontist in town. I keep remembering (with something fearfully akin to pleasure) how I grabbed her so effortlessly by her own hair and whipped her to the ground. It will be a long time before I forget the sight of her face as she sat astride me, the ashtray lifted over her head. The last words she said to me as she left with the troopers were "And, Nora, I hope you keep your precious sensitivity." A very shocking thing happened. At one point Rudy broke down and sobbed like a baby. I have never seen a man cry. Catherine brought back the entire experience with his sister. When she came to live with him after she got out of the asylum. How she attacked him with a knife and he couldn't handle it and called the asylum people to come and get her. Just as he called the town rescue squad when we got too much for him the other night. He sobbed and sobbed. He still blames himself for his sister's suicide in the asylum. We lay around scaring each other about how much worse it could have been.

N: "If her head had hit the rock . . ."

R: "Her head was nowhere near the rock."

R: "If I hadn't had the quick instinct to put that little tin of marijuana in my pocket when I did. I just walked past the trooper, my heart in my throat, and slipped it casually into my dressing gown. . . ."

N: "We would have made headlines in the *Enquirer* . . ."

R: "PLAYWRIGHT'S WOODSTOCK HAREM: SEX, SIN, POT . . ."

N: "The one thing I'll never be able to forget from this whole thing is how easy it would be to kill someone . . . that light, carefree sensation . . . the

/ joyful disposal of an encumbrance. I know now that I am a person capable of killing."

R: "Oh, come. You're being too hard on yourself, as usual. Well, one thing for sure. She had her way. She made us look violence in the face."

Wed., Nov. 28—She just phoned. We talked for an hour on her money; then I called her back and we talked for another hour on mine. She said she "blanked" from just after the time she came up to plead with me to open the door before dinner till the time she and the woman from the rescue squad were kneeling together on the floor and the woman was asking her if she'd ever been in a mental hospital before. Said she snapped to her senses. "I imagined myself calling the chairman at my college, telling him I was in a mental hospital and couldn't meet my classes on Monday. . . ." Said she also called to apologize if she had destroyed anything. Said when she discovered bruises all over her body and cuts on her hands and feet she wondered if she had been violent with anyone. Her theory: that we had all three, somewhere in ourselves, made a pact to have a witches' sabbath. She said what had made her so angry with me was my assurance that I could have my safe, well-ordered life *and* my interesting demons in the basement. She hates for people like me not to come up from underground and be counted. The troopers took her to a hunters' lodge in Saugerties and then to the bus station next morning. They told the man at the desk there'd been a drunken party at some playwright's house and we all went mad. One of the troopers was interested in her. "If I had given him the least sign, I could have made him come back later, but I thought I'd done enough for one night." Said she hoped we could be friends again. Said she didn't entirely discount what I'd said about conserving your energies for the things you wanted to do most, since she had been bringing catastrophes on herself with some regularity lately. Said she might see a psychiatrist. Said Sunday in New York she just sat around the yogis' apartment and meditated on her lack of spiritual progress. "There was an analyst in the same room; he'd been through a Jungian analysis himself, but it was Sunday and he was playing with his kid and I didn't want to dump that on him." All the way back to the Quaker college, she said, the young man had played a tape deck of his horoscope in the rented car.

We both agreed to write up accounts of what happened that night and exchange them.

> The pattern: the united couple disrupted by outside force. In most Gothic fiction, the innocent comes to the house of the dark forces. In this case, the dark force (disguised as the fair heroine) will come to the house of the innocents.
>
> Dilemma: can the couple who have fought so hard for their work and love feel justified in sacrificing the dark force without murdering a part of themselves?
>
> How could they have assimilated her?
>
> Explanation: breakup of the conscious status quo by influx of new energies from the unconscious.

I told her how we had been so upset by it that we had spent most of the day holding on to each other. She began to cry softly and said, "I had nobody to hold on to."

V / THE COUPLE

It is the following spring. Rudy and Nora walk in the fields. She can't get started on anything new. He is in the middle of a play based on the life of his sister. They pass the ruined stone cottage. Someone is rebuilding it from the inside. It has a new shingled roof. A perfect situation for some artist with limited means and a large need for privacy. Nora says, "I tried again today to write about the Catherine Thing (their name for it now), but it didn't get anywhere. I couldn't decide on a beginning or an end. I do wish she had kept her promise and sent her side of it, but she said she got busy with school and then she fell in love with the new religion professor."

"Oh, yes, how is that going?" asks Rudy.

"It's not, unfortunately. He's had to fight against homosexual tendencies for years and he says because of her rampant aggressiveness she's almost pushed him over the edge. His psychiatrist told him not to see her anymore. He's very nasty to her at school and one day she got so paranoid about it she stayed home. She says she still loves him. She loves the potential shape of all he was meant to be."

They walk awhile, without speaking. Describe fields, springtime, nature, etc. Nora says: "I couldn't decide how the story should end. First I thought, Let her head hit the rock. But then I thought, No, that way she would win: she would have brought violence into my art as well as my life. Also, violent endings are so easy. They spare the characters the necessity of coming to terms with all the disturbing loose ends. Also, I had already killed Catherine once in a story I wrote when we were sixteen. I had her and her boyfriend go over the edge of a mountain in his car. It was a sad story. It was told from the friend's point of view. I called it 'Friends and Lovers.' The boy's name was Derwent. I had dated him first, but he fell in love with Catherine and they went steady all during high school. It was because of him that she rushed through college, did four years in three, so that they could get married. In the end, she married someone else, however."

Rudy says, "Your friend is certainly a mixed-up girl."

The following November, Rudy and Nora go to great trouble to find a Thanksgiving card for Catherine. They finally choose a Dutch interior with a bowl of fruit on the table by a window. Rudy writes in the card, "We hope someday you will come and see us again." "We really mean it," adds Nora. And they did mean it.

On the days when she is alone in the house, Nora shampoos her hair in the herbal shampoo Catherine used. She puts on a black leotard just like Catherine's and does the Yoga exercises from a book recommended by Catherine. These rituals have a magic calming power on her soul, which is still troubled by having found love and success after all.

Jerry Bauer

About the Author

GAIL GODWIN was born in Alabama, grew up in Asheville, North Carolina, and received her doctorate in English from the University of Iowa. She has taught at Vassar College and Columbia University and has received a Guggenheim Fellowship and the 1981 Award in Literature from the National Academy and Institute of Arts and Letters. Her short stories, essays, and articles have appeared in numerous magazines and newspapers and her highly praised books include *The Good Husband* and *Violet Clay*. She currently lives in Woodstock, New York.